D1616269

THE LITTLE TRILOGY

THE
LITTLE
TRILOGY

Henryk Sienkiewicz

Translated by
Miroslaw Lipinski

HIPPOCRENE BOOKS
New York

For information, address:
HIPPOCRENE BOOKS, INC.
171 Madison Avenue
New York, NY 10016

Library of Congress Cataloging-in-Publication Data
Sienkiewicz, Henryk, 1846-1916
    [Short stories. English. Selections]
The little trilogy / Henryk Sienkiewicz; translated by
Miroslaw Lipinski.
        p.   cm.
    Contents: The old servant—Hania—Selim Mirza.
    ISBN 0-7818-0293-8
    1. Sienkiewicz, Henryk, 1846-1916--Translations into
English. I. Lipinski, Miroslaw. II. Title.
PG7158.S4A25
891.8'536--dc20   95-8297
                                                      CIP

Printed in the United States of America

THE LITTLE TRILOGY

INTRODUCTION

When, in 1875, Henryk Sienkiewicz began writing "The Old Servant," the first part of what was to be known later as "the little trilogy," he was twenty-nine and in the midst of scribing feuilletons and distinguished stories of local color. In this respect, "The Old Servant" did not differ from the rest of his fiction, except in advancing his name as a talented young man of letters and someone who could paint with a few words a vivid, warm portrait of a human being. "Hania," the novella follow-up to that story, made even more of a mark and increased his literary fame.

Because it presents an accurate picture of the life of a 19th century Polish manor, "Hania" is, perhaps, more significant today than it was during the author's time. The attitudes and habits of an age no longer even a distant memory are given life here, and if some of the poses of another century seem dated, surely the spirit that underlies them is not, even if it is held in check nowadays by cynicism and psychiatric prescriptions.

"Hania" is also noteworthy for being partly autobiographical. As Sienkiewicz admitted to his American translator, Jeremiah Curtin, the character of Henryk was based on himself, and we can freely presume that Sienkiewicz was, at the very least, describing his adolescent soul, even if certain events of the story were fabricated.

The success of "Hania" did not prepare the Polish populace for what was to come. No one could yet suspect that this young man was destined to be regarded as Poland's greatest author, in terms of sales, popular affection and international acclaim. But then, in 1876, Sienkiewicz made an important journey to the United States, and his stay in California invigorated and expanded an already striking artistic vision. It was amid the panoramic beauty of the West that Sienkiewicz partook of the energy and heartiness of a young, vibrant country and made them his own; it was here that he found inspiration for several priceless "Western tales," jewels of pathos and humor, and it was here that he finished the last story of *The Little Trilogy*—"Selim Mirza."

"Selim Mirza" was a tale that Sienkiewicz had trouble writing. He had wanted the action to take place in his native land and concern the Polish Insurrection of 1863, but political censorship in a partitioned Poland would have made this effort futile. To his regret, he had to move the action to a foreign country and dramatically alter the motivations of his characters. Furthermore, he complained that he did not know anything of the terrain he was writing about. For Sienkiewicz, a meticulous researcher who liked to see with his own eyes the physical backdrop of any story he would pen, this was another regret. Yet if "Selim Mirza" did not turn out to be a coda involving the quest for nationhood, if it did not quite accurately portray the landscape and its inhabitants, it did, in an odd way, speak quietly to one of the tragedies of Polish history—the Polish exile. More importantly, "Selim Mirza," besides being a splendid adventure tale, is the first clear indicator of the author's fondness for things military. As such it is the spiritual seed that would give birth, seven years later, to *With Fire and Sword,* the first book of Sienkiewicz's larger *Trilogy.*

In fact, most of the aspects that make the larger *Trilogy* memorable—flesh and blood personalities, impassioned souls, heroism, humor, lively battles, tantalizing pictures of pastoral beauty—are present in *The Little Trilogy,* an honorable and important entry in the canon of this writing genius, a masterpiece in miniature.

I dedicate this translation to another masterpiece, rapidly growing out of miniature status—Christopher, my son.

Miroslaw Lipinski

THE OLD SERVANT

Aside from old stewards, overseers and foresters, there is another type of individual who is rapidly disappearing from the face of the earth—the old servant. During my childhood my parents were served by one of these dinosaurs whose bones, from time to time, will be dug out of the strata of forgetfulness by researchers in old cemeteries. His name was Nicholas Suchowolski. He was a noble from Dry Wola, a village he mentioned often in his stories. He came to my father from my grandfather, whose orderly he was during the Napoleonic Wars. He did not remember exactly when he began his service with my grandfather. Whenever he was asked, he would take some snuff and answer:

"I still had no hair on my face, and the colonel, may God bless his soul, was still a lad."

He fulfilled various duties in my parents' house. He was a butler and a man-servant. As the overseer, he went to the harvest fields in the summer and to the threshing area in the winter. He kept the keys to the vodka room, the cellar and the granary. He wound the clocks. But, above all, he grumbled.

I do not remember him other than grumbling. He grumbled at my father, at my mother. Even though I liked him, I feared him as if he were lightning. In the kitchen he kicked up a row with the cooks; the butler's people he pulled by the ear around the house. Nothing satisfied him. When he got a little drunk, which happened once a week, everyone avoided him—not because he permitted himself words with his master or mistress, but because whenever he latched onto someone, he followed that person about all day, nagging and grumbling without stop. During dinner, he would stand behind my father's chair, and though he did not serve, he watched the man who did and made his life a living hell with a special passion.

"Pay attention to what you're doing," he would mutter; "pay attention to what you're doing, or I'll pay attention to you! Look at him! He cannot serve quickly but keeps dragging his legs like an old cow. Just look at him! He doesn't hear the master calling him. Change the lady's dish. Why are you gaping like that? Well? Look at him! Take a good look at him!"

He always interfered in the conversation at table and was always opposed to everything. My father would frequently turn to him during dinner and say:

"Nicholas, after dinner tell Matthew to harness the horses." And he would mention some destination he had in mind.

And Nicholas:

"Go for drive? Why not? Sure! That's what horses are for. Let the horses break their legs on such a road. But if you have to go for a visit, then you have to go. Of course, your lordships are free to do what you want. Do I forbid it? No, I don't. Why not go for a visit! The accounts can wait; the threshing can wait. The visit is more important."

"It's unbearable with this Nicholas!" my impatient father would cry out at times.

And Nicholas, once again:

"Did I say I wasn't stupid? I know I am stupid. The

steward has gone to Niewodow to court the priest's housekeeper, so why should you not go for a visit? Is this visit worse than going to a priest's housekeeper? What's allowed a servant is allowed the master of the house."

And on and on it went in a circle. Nothing could stop the old grumbler.

We—that is, my brother and I—feared him almost more than our tutor, Father Ludwik, and for certain more than either of our parents. Yet he was more polite with our sisters. He would address them as "young ladies," though they were younger than us, but he addressed us without ceremony. Nevertheless, he had a special fascination for me: he always carried firing caps in his pocket. Many a time, after my lessons, I would walk timidly into the pantry, smile as nicely as I could, be as friendly as possible, and say in a meek voice:

"Nicholas! Good day, Nicholas. Will Nicholas be cleaning weapons today?"

"What does Henryk want here? I'm going to put on a dish-cloth, and that's that!"

And then, mocking me, he would say:

"'Nicholas! Nicholas! Nicholas is nice when it comes to caps, and if he's not, then let the wolves eat him.' It would be better for you to study. You'll never get smart from firing a pistol."

"I've already finished my lessons," I would answer, half in tears.

"He's finished his lessons. Ha! he's finished them. He's studying, studying, but his head is as empty as a barrel. I won't give you any caps, and that's that." Saying this, he would already be searching around in his pockets. "One day a cap will go off in his eye, and Nicholas will get it. Who's to blame? Nicholas. Who let him shoot? Nicholas."

Grumbling like this, he would go to my father's room, take down the pistols and blow the dust off them, assert-

ing a hundred times more that no good will come of this;
then he would light a candle, put a cap in a pistol and
let me aim. Even then I would frequently have a heavy
cross to bear.

"Look at how he holds the pistol!" he would say. "Like
a barber holds scissors! How can you expect to ever put
out a candle? Perhaps like an old man in church! You
should become a priest, recite '*Ave Marias*' and forget
about being a soldier."

He taught us the military art he had learned. Often
after dinner my brother and I would practise marching
under his watchful eye, and we would be joined by
Father Ludwik, who marched in a rather amusing manner.

Nicholas would look at him from the corner of his
eye, and though he feared and respected him more than
anyone, he would not be able restrain himself, and finally would say:

"Eh, your reverence marches exactly like an old cow!"

Because I was the eldest son, I was under his command more frequently than anyone else, and so I suffered the most. Yet when I was sent away to school,
Nicholas cried as if the greatest tragedy had occurred.
My parents told me that after my departure he became
even more of a grumbler, and for two weeks he tormented them. "They took the child and carried him
off," he would repeat. "And if he dies! O God, O God!
What does he need school for? Is he not the heir? Will
he be studying Latin? Do they want to turn him into a
Solomon? What kind of nonsense is this! The child has
left, he's left, and you, old man, putter about and look
around for something you have lost. Hang it all!"

I remember the day when I came home for the first
time for the holidays. Everyone was still asleep. It was
just starting to dawn. The morning was cold and snowy.
The squeaking of the well-sweep and the barking of the

dogs interrupted the silence. The shutters of the house were closed; only the windows in the kitchen were gleaming with a bright light, giving a rosy color to the snow nearby. I had come home sad, worried and afraid because the first grades I had received were not particularly good. This happened because I had not yet become accustomed to school routine and discipline. So I feared my father, and I feared the stern, silent look on the face of Father Ludwik, who had conducted me from Warsaw. There was no comfort from any side, until I saw the door of the kitchen open, and old Nicholas, his nose red from the cold, comes wading through the snow holding a tray with two pots of steaming cream.

When he saw me, he cried out: "Ah, my dearest, precious young master!" And putting the tray down quickly—and turning both pots over in the process—he grabbed me about the neck and overwhelmed me with hugs and kisses. From that time on, he always called me "young master."

But for two full weeks he would not forgive me that cream: "Here I am quietly carrying some cream," he repeated, "and then he arrives. He picked the proper time..." — etc.

My father wanted—and promised—to give me a thrashing for the two poor marks in calligraphy and German that I had brought with me, but on the one hand my tears and my promises, and on the other hand the intervention of my sweet mother and the fuss that Nicholas created stood in the way. Nicholas did not know what kind of creature calligraphy was, but he did not want to hear a word about any punishment for German.

"Is he a Lutheran or some Kraut?" he said. "Perhaps the colonel knew German? Perhaps"—here he turned to my father—"you know German? Well? When we met the Germans at—what was it?—at Lipski, and the devil knows where else, we didn't speak to them in German; they just immediately showed us their backs and that was that!"

Old Nicholas had one more characteristic. He rarely talked about his past, but when he was in a particularly good mood and he would talk, then he lied through his teeth. He did not do this in bad faith; one fact probably got mixed with another in his head, and everything grew to fantastic proportions. Whenever he heard about the military exploits that occurred during his youth, he would apply them to himself and to my grandfather, the colonel, firmly believing in the truth of what he said.

Sometimes in the barn, overseeing the peasants while they threshed wheat, he would begin talking, and then the peasants would drop their work and, leaning on their flails, listen with open mouths to his stories. Soon he would notice this and cry out:

"Why have you fixed your mouths on me like cannons, well?"

And once again: Whoosh! Whoosh! Whoosh! For some time the swinging of the flails could be heard. The old man would be silent for a while. And then:

"My son writes me that he has become a general under the Queen of Palmira. It's good for him there, his pay is high, but they have terrible frosts in that country..." — etc.

Incidentally, he did not have success with his children. He did have a son, but his son was a great scoundrel who, when he reached adulthood, did God knows what, and finally went out into the world, disappearing without a trace. His daughter, apparently a great beauty in her time, flirted with every official who found himself in the village, and finally died after giving the world a daughter. That daughter's name was Hania. She was my age, a beautiful but frail girl. I remember that we would often play soldier together. Hania was just the drummer, yet the nettle of our enemies. She was good and gentle like an angel. A terrible fate awaited her, but those are memories which have no place here.

Anyway, let me return to the old man's stories. I myself heard in the barn how the uhlans' horses capered at Mariampol, and how eighteen thousand of them stampeded through the gates of Warsaw. Oh, how many people were trampled! What a day of judgment it was before the horses were caught! Another time he told the following—not in the barn, however, but to all of us in the house:

"Did I fight well? Of course! I remember once there was war with the Austrians. I was standing in the ranks—in the ranks, I say—and the commander-in-chief rides up to me and says, as if wanting to give me a message from the Austrians, from the opposite side: 'Eh, Suchowolski, I know you! If we'd caught you, the war would've been over!'"

"Didn't he say anything about the colonel?" my father asked.

"Of course! Didn't I just say that he said this to me and the colonel?"

Father Ludwik lost his patience:

"Nicholas, you tell lies as if you're getting paid for each one."

The old man frowned and would have snapped something out, but he feared and respected the priest, so he kept silent. Yet after a while, wanting to somehow straighten out the affair, he continued:

"Father Sieklucki, our chaplain, told me the same thing. Once, when I got a bayonet thrust in my twentieth rib—I meant to say fifth rib—I was in a bad state. Ha! I thought, now I will die. So I confessed all my sins to Father Sieklucki, and Father Sieklucki listened, listened, and finally said: 'Dear God, Nicholas, you've told me every lie you know!' And I answered: 'That may be; I don't remember any more.'"

"You got better? They cured you?"

"Of course, I got better! But how could they cure me? I cured myself. I mixed two charges of powder in a quart of vodka. I drank it at night before going to sleep and woke up in the morning the very picture of health!"

I would have gladly heard more of these stories and put them down here, but Father Ludwik, I do not know why, forbade Nicholas "to turn my head completely." Poor Father Ludwik. As a priest and a quite villager, he did not know that, firstly, every youth whom a storm casts out of his peaceful family nest into the wide world will have his head turned and not just once; and secondly, that it is not old servants and their stories but someone else who turns their heads.

Anyway, Nicholas's influence on us could not have been harmful; to the contrary, the old man watched over us and our conduct very diligently. He was a conscientious man in the fullest sense of the word. From his military days one fine characteristic remained with him: he carried out every order implicitly. One winter, wolves were giving us bad trouble. They even became so bold as to enter the village at night—at first a few at a time and then in packs. My father, a born hunter, wanted to arrange a hunt. He wanted a neighbor of ours, Lord Ustrzycki, a known hunter of wolves, to take charge of the hunt, and to that end he wrote him a letter, and called Nicholas, saying:

"One of my tenants is going to town. Go with him, Nicholas, and get out at Ustrzycki Hall and give the lord this letter. It is necessary that I get an answer, so don't come back without one."

Nicholas took the letter and went off with the tenant. That evening the tenant returned. Nicholas was not with him. My father assumed that he was spending the night at Ustrzycki Hall and would return the following morning with Lord Ustrzycki. Meanwhile one day passes—no Nicholas; another day goes by—again, no Nicholas; a third day goes by—no Nicholas. In the house there is lamentation. My father, fearing that wolves attacked him on his return, sends out people to look for him. They search; nowhere is there even a sign of him. They are sent to the Ustrzycki estate. At the manor they are told that he had been there and, not finding the master of the house at home, had inquired where he had gone. Then he borrowed four rubles from the man-servant and went off God knows where. The next day the messengers returned from other villages with the news that they had found nothing. At that point we had already begun to mourn for him, when on the sixth day, in the evening, while my father was making dispositions in the chancery, he heard beyond the door the wiping of feet and someone hawking and grumbling in a low voice. He knew immediately who it was.

It was indeed Nicholas—chilled, thinned, tired, with icicles hanging from his moustache—almost unrecognizable.

"Nicholas, dear God! What have you been doing all this time?"

"What have I been doing, what have I been doing," muttered Nicholas. "What was I to do? I didn't find Lord Ustrzycki at home, so I went to Bzina. At Bzina they told me that it just so happened, damn it, that Lord Ustrzycki had gone to Karolowki. So I went after him. But he left Karolowki also. What? Isn't he allowed to go where it pleases him? Isn't he a lord? Besides, he doesn't travel on foot. Very well, I said. From Karolowki I went to the city, for they said, that the lord was there. What business had he there? Is he the mayor? He went to the governor's place. Should I have returned at that point? I went to the governor's and gave Lord Ustrzycki the letter."

"Well, did he give you an answer?"

"Yes and no. He gave it, but he laughed so loudly at me that I could see the back of his teeth. 'Your lord,' he said, 'asks me to go to the hunt on Thursday, but you are giving me this letter on Sunday. The hunt is already over.' And he laughed some more. Well, here is the letter. Why shouldn't he have laughed? Because—"

"What did you eat during this time?"

"What of it if I haven't eaten anything since yesterday? Do I suffer from hunger here? Am I denied food here? I haven't eaten, but I will eat...."

Since that time no one gave Nicholas unqualified commands, and any time he was sent somewhere, he was always told what he had to do in case he did not find a particular person at home.

Several months later Nicholas went to a fair at a nearby town to buy some horses, for he was quite knowledgeable about them. In the evening the steward came to say that Nicholas had returned with the horses, but that he had come back beaten and was ashamed to appear before us. My father went to see him at once.

"What is the matter with you, Nicholas?"

"I had a fight," he muttered out.

"Be ashamed of yourself, old man. Are you going to brawl in the marketplace? Have you no sense? You're old, but a fool! Know this, that I would throw out anyone else for something like this. Be ashamed of yourself! You must have been drunk. Instead of setting a good example for my people, you are going to spoil them."

My father was really angry, and when he was angry, he did not joke around. But what was strange was that Nicholas, who usually in such cases did not forget the tongue in his mouth, was silent this time. He became obstinate. In vain others asked him what had happened. He muttered to one and the other and did not reveal anything.

They had beaten him pretty badly. The following day he became so sick that the doctor had to be sent for. The doctor finally explained all that had happened. A week ago my father had quarrelled with his overseer, who ran away the following day. This person made his way to a certain Mister Zoll, a German and a great enemy of my father, and entered into his service. At the fair were Zoll, our former overseer, and Zoll's servants, who had driven fattened cattle to the fair to be sold. Zoll saw Nicholas first. He came up to his wagon and started to talk against my father. Nicholas called him a fish out of water, and when Zoll added a new insult against my father, Nicholas hit him with the handle of his whip. Then the overseer, together with Zoll's servants, jumped him and beat him until he bled.

When my father heard this story, tears came to his eyes. He could not forgive himself for berating Nicholas, who had been silent about the entire affair on purpose. When Nicholas recovered his health, my father went to reproach him. At first the old man did not want to admit to anything, and as was his want, he grumbled, but later he opened up, and the both of them cried like two long-lost friends. My father challenged Zoll to a duel for the affair, which the German remembered long afterward.

Had it not been for the doctor, however, Nicholas's sacrifice would never have come to light.

Nicholas had hated this doctor for a long time. It was like this: I had a young aunt, my father's sister, who lived nearby. I loved her dearly, for she was as good as she was beautiful, and it did not surprise me that everyone loved her, including the doctor, a young, intelligent man who was highly respected in the region. At first Nicholas liked the doctor and even said that he was a clever fellow who knew how to ride a horse. But when the doctor began to turn up in our house with obvious intentions toward Aunt Marynia, Nicholas's feelings toward him changed dramatically. He began to be polite but cold toward him, as if he were a stranger. Previously he had, on occasion, grumbled even at him. When he sometimes stayed with us too long, Nicholas, helping him with his coat, would mutter: "What's the purpose of wandering about in the night? It makes no sense. Has anyone ever seen anything like this?" Now he stopped to grumble, but was silent instead, as if made of stone. The good doctor soon understood what this was all about, and though he smiled kindly at the old man as he had before, his heart must have been saddened.

Luckily for the young Esculapius, Aunt Marynia cherished feelings for him that were directly opposite those of Nicholas. One beautiful evening, when the moon was lighting up the parlor most wonderfully, when the smell of jasmines was wafting in through the open windows, and Aunt Marynia was singing at the piano: "*Io questa notte sogno,*" Doctor Stanislaw approached her and asked in a tremulous voice if she knew that he could not live without her. My aunt, of course, expressed her doubts in this matter, after which came mutual entreaties, calling the moon to witness, and things of a similar sort that are always done at such a time.

Unfortunately Nicholas came in at that moment to call them to tea. When he saw what was happening, he rushed immediately to my father, and because my father was not at home, for he was walking around the farm buildings, he went to my mother, who with her usual gentle smile asked him not to interfere in the matter.

The confused Nicholas was silent and seethed inside for the rest of the evening. When my father, before retiring, went to the chancery to write a few letters, Nicholas followed him and, standing by the door, began to hem and haw loudly and shuffle his feet.

"What do you want, Nicholas?" asked my father.

"Eh . . . Well . . . I wanted to ask you if it is true that our young lady is, eh . . . getting . . . is she going to get married?"

"Yes, it's true. Why?"

"But it can't be that the young lady is going to marry that—barber."

"What barber? Have you gone crazy? Must you always put your nose into everything?"

"But this young lady is our young lady. Is she not the daughter of the colonel? The colonel would never have permitted this. Isn't the young lady worthy of an heir and a lord of lords? But the doctor, with your permission, who is he? The young lady will be a laughing stock."

"The doctor is an intelligent man."

"He is and he isn't. I've seen my share of doctors! They went about the camps and hovered around the army staff, but when it came to something like a battle, they were gone. The colonel called them 'lanceters.' When a person is healthy, they will not touch him, but when he is lying half-dead, they go at him with a lancet. It's nothing to cut up someone who can't defend himself because he can't hold anything in his hand. But try to cut him when he is healthy and has a weapon in his hand! Oh, my! It's a great thing to go over people's bones with a knife! Nothing good will come out of this! The colonel, if he heard of this, would turn over in his grave. What kind of soldier is a doctor! What kind of heir! This cannot be! The young lady will not marry him. This isn't how it should be. Who is he to aspire to the young lady?"

Unfortunately for Nicholas, the doctor not only did aspire to the young lady, but he even got her. The wedding took place half a year later, and the colonel's daughter, covered with the tears of relatives and the servants of the house, and particularly the tears of Nicholas, went away to share life with the doctor.

Nicholas could not bear her a grudge for long, for he loved her, but he would not forgive the doctor. He almost never directly mentioned his name, and in general tried to avoid talking about him. Incidentally, Aunt Marynia was most happy with Doctor Stanislaw. After a year God gave them a beautiful baby boy, after another year a girl, and so on in turn, as if prescribed. Nicholas loved these children as if they were his own; he took them around all over the place, caressed them, kissed them; but I noticed not just once that there smouldered in his heart a bitterness at the misalliance of Aunt Marynia. One Christmas Eve supper, when we were sitting down to eat, we suddenly heard the distant noise of a carriage riding along the frozen ground. We always expected a large number of relatives, so my father said:

"Nicholas, see who is coming."

Nicholas went out and soon returned, his face beaming with joy.

"The young lady is coming!" he cried out from the doorway.

"What young lady?" asked my father, though he already knew whom Nicholas meant.

"The young lady!"

"What young lady?"

"Our young lady," replied the old man.

And you should have seen that young lady as she entered the room with her three children. Some young lady! The old man intentionally never called her anything else.

But finally his antipathy toward Doctor Stanislaw ended. Hania came down with a serious attack of typhoid fever. Those days were also a distressing time for me because Hania was my age and my only playmate; therefore, I loved her as if she were my sister. Doctor Stanislaw hardly left her room for three days. The old man, who loved Hania with his whole heart, walked around during the time of her illness as if in a state of shock. He did not eat, he did not sleep; he just sat at the door of her room, because no one was permitted to go in except my mother, and he silently endured the hard, iron pain which tore at his breast. His was a soul hardened to the toils of the body as well as to the blows of adversity, and yet it almost broke under the weight of despair at the bed of one little girl. Until, after many days of mortal fear, Doctor Stanislaw quietly opened the door of the ill girl's room and, with a face beaming with happiness, whispered one little phrase to the gathering waiting in the next room: "The fever is broken." The old man could not contain himself, and throwing himself at his feet, he bellowed like a bull and repeated between his sobs: "My benefactor! My benefactor!"

Hania soon recovered completely, and the doctor, of course, became the apple of the old man's eye.

"A clever fellow," he would repeat, stroking his walrus moustache. "A clever fellow. He sits on a horse well, and if it had not been from him, Hania—oh, I don't even want to think about it. Knock on wood!"

But a year or so later his own health began to fail him. His straight, strong figure began to bend. He became quite senile and stopped to grumble and lie. Finally, when he reached almost ninety, he became completely child-like. All he did was make snares for birds, and he kept a large number of them in his room, particularly coaltits. Several days before his death he did not recognize anyone; but on the very day that he died the expiring lamp of his mind lit up once again with a bright light. My parents at that time were abroad for my mother's health. One evening I was sitting with my younger brother Kazio in front of the fireplace. With us was Father Ludwik, who had also grown quiet old. A winter gale was beating at the windows. Father Ludwik was praying; my brother and I were preparing weapons

for a hunt that would take place the following day on the
newly fallen snow. All of sudden, we were informed that
Nicholas was dying. Father Ludwik went immediately to
the house chapel to get the Sacrament; I ran as fast as I
could to the old man. He was lying on the bed, very pale,
yellow and nearly cold, but quiet and conscious. His
bald head, ornamented with two scars from sword-cuts
he had received during his military days, was beautiful
at that moment. The head of an old soldier and a good
fellow. The light of a holy candle threw a funereal gleam
on the walls of the room. The old man pressed a crucifix
to his chest with one hand, while his other hand was held
and covered with kisses by Hania, who was pale as a lily.
Father Ludwik came in and confession began. Afterward
the dying man asked to see me.

"My master is not here nor my beloved mistress," he
whispered, "so it is difficult for me to die. But you are
here, my precious young master, my squire.... Take care
of this orphan.... God will reward you. Do not get
angry.... If I have committed some offence ... forgive me.
I was bad-tempered but faithful...."

Suddenly, roused anew, he cried out quickly in a loud
voice, as if his breath were leaving him:

"Young master!—Squire!—my orphan!—God, into
Your—hands—"

"I commend the soul of this valiant soldier, faithful
servant and righteous person!" Father Ludwik finished
solemnly.

The old man was no longer alive.

We knelt, and the priest began to read aloud the
prayers for the dead.

Since that time many years have passed. Luxuriant
heathers have grown over the tomb of the good servant.
Sad times have come. A storm swept away the blessed
and quiet hearth of my little village. Today, Father Lud-

wik is in the grave, as is Aunt Marynia. I earn my bitter daily bread with my pen. And Hania—

Tears are coming to my eyes!

HANIA

I

When on his death bed old Nicholas left Hania in my care, I was sixteen years old, while she was just a few months younger and likewise just barely emerging out of childhood.

I had to lead her out of her grandfather's room almost by force, and both of us went to the family chapel. The doors were open. Two candles were burning before an old Byzantine picture of the Virgin Mary, their light barely illuminating the darkness about the altar. We knelt down, one beside the other. Hania, broken by suffering, worn out through weeping, grief and lack of sleep, rested her poor head against me, and thus we remained. The hour was late. In the hall next to the chapel, a cuckoo on an old Gdansk clock called out hoarsely that it was two o'clock. A deep silence reigned everywhere, interrupted only by Hania's mournful sighs and the faint sound of a snow-storm, which shook the galena frames of the little windows in the chapel. I did not dare say one word of comfort to Hania; I only nestled her to me like a guardian or an older brother. But I could not pray; a thousand impressions and feelings rushed through my head and heart. A variety of pictures appeared before my eyes, but, slowly, one thought and one feeling emerged from this dissary—that this pale face with closed eyes, that this defenseless, poor little being resting against my arm is now my dear sister, for whom I would give my life and for whose sake, if necessary, I would challenge the world.

Meanwhile my younger brother Kazio came in and knelt behind us, and he was followed in short time by Father Ludwik and the servants. We said the evening prayers according to our custom. Father Ludwik read the prayers aloud, while we repeated them or answered them in a litany. The Virgin Mary looked down kindly at us; she seemed to share in our sorrow and affliction, and to bless all who were gathered at her feet. During the prayers, Father Ludwik started to name those who had passed away and we responded with "eternal rest," and when he added to that list Nicholas's name, Hania began to sob anew; at that point I made a silent vow that I would sacredly carry out the responsibilities that the deceased had set upon me, even at the greatest sacrifice to myself. This was a vow of an impassioned youth who did not yet understand the possible greatness of the sacrifice nor the responsibilities involved, but who was not without honorable impulses and who had a sensitive heart.

After the prayers were finished, we parted to retire for the night. I told the old housekeeper, Wegrowska, to conduct Hania to the room in which she would live from now on, and not to the dressing-room where she usually slept, and to spend the night with her. I, meanwhile, after warmly kissing Hania good-night, went to the outbuilding, in which I lived together with Kazio and Father Ludwik, and which was called at our home a "lodging house." I undressed and lay down to bed. Despite my grief for Nicholas, whom I loved sincerely, I felt proud and almost happy with my role as guardian. The fact that I, a sixteen-year-old boy, was to be the support of a weak and poor being raised me in my own eyes. I felt like a man. "You will not be disappointed in your young master," I thought, addressing Nicholas. "You left the future of your grandchild in good hands, and you can sleep peacefully in your grave."

In truth I had little worry over Hania's future. The thought that Hania would eventually grow up and that it would be necessary to give her away in marriage did not yet enter my mind. I thought that she would always remain beside me, surrounded with solicitude like a sister and loved like a sister; she would be sad perhaps, but at peace. According to a centuries-old custom the eldest son received five times as much of the wealth as his younger siblings; the younger sons and daughters always honored this custom and never opposed it, though in our family there was no right of primogeniture. I was the oldest son, and so the majority of the family wealth would one day be mine. Though I was still a student, I already considered this wealth as my own. My father was one of the richest men of the region. It is true that our family did not possess the wealth of magnates, but being of an old and affluent noble line, we did not lack for anything, a circumstance I could be sure of until the day I died.

Therefore I would be relatively rich, and I looked calmly at not only my future but Hania's as well, seeing that whatever would befall her, she would find peace and support in me should she need it.

With these thoughts, I fell asleep. The next morning I began to enact my role as guardian. But in what a ridiculous and childish manner I did this! And even today, when I recall it, I cannot help feeling a certain stirring emotion. When Kazio and I arrived for breakfast we found sitting at table Father Ludwik, Madame d'Yves, our governess, and my two little sisters, who, as usual, were on high bamboo chairs, swinging their legs and chatting merrily away. I sat down with great dignity in my father's chair, and throwing a dictatorial eye on the table, I turned to the serving boy and said dryly, yet authoritatively:

"Lay the table for Lady Hania."

I intentionally stressed the word "Lady."

This had never happened before. Hania usually ate in the dressing-room, for however my mother wished that she eat with us, old Nicholas would never allow it, saying: "What good can come of it? She should know her place. That's all that we need!" Now I introduced a new custom. Father Ludwik hid his smile with a pinch of snuff and a silk handkerchief. Madame d'Yves made a face, for, despite her good heart, she was, as a descendent of an old noble French family, an aristocrat. The serving boy, Franek, opened his mouth wide and looked at me in amazement.

"Lay the table for Lady Hania!" I repeated. "Do you hear?"

"Yes, lord," answered Franek, apparently impressed by the tone I used to address him.

I confess today that that "lord" could barely restrain a smile of satisfaction at the thought of that title given to him for the first in his life. Dignity, however, did not allow the "lord" to smile. Meanwhile the placement was quickly set, and the door opened and Hania came in, attired in a black dress, which the maid-servant and old Wegrowska had made for her during the night. She was pale, and her eyes showed traces of crying. Her long golden tresses, which fell over her dress, ended in ribbons of black crepe weaved among the brightness of her hair.

I got up and, hastening toward her, led her to the table. My efforts and all that splendor in front of her seemed only to embarrass, confuse and torment her. I did not understand yet that peace and a quiet, uninhabited corner are worth more in times of grief than the noisy ovations of friends, even if they come from the kindliest hearts. So I was tormenting Hania with the best of my intentions, thinking that I was carrying out my obligations to the letter. Hania was silent, and only from time to time replied to my questions as to what she would eat and drink:

"Nothing, if it please your lordship."

That "your lordship" hurt me, particularly as Hania had always been on more familiar terms with me and addressed me simply as "Master Henryk." But it was precisely that role which I had started to play since yesterday and the changed circumstances in which I had placed Hania that made her more timid and meek. Immediately after breakfast I took her aside and said:

"Hania, do not forget that from now you are my sister. From now on never say to me: 'Your lordship.'"

"Very well, your lord—very well, Master Henryk."

I was in an odd position. I accompanied her through the room, not knowing what to say. I would have been happy to console her, but in that case I would have had to bring up Nicholas and his death last night, and that would have made Hania cry again and renew her pain. It ended in this, that we both sat down on a low settee at the end of the room. The girl again rested her head on my arm, while I began to stroke her golden hair.

She nestled to me as if I were indeed her brother, and perhaps that sweet feeling of trust which rose in her heart elicited new tears in her eyes. She wept bitterly, while I tried to console her as best as I could.

"Are you crying again, Hania?" I said. "Your grandfather is in heaven, and I will try—"

Now it was I who could not speak, for tears came to my eyes also.

"Master Henryk, can I go to my grandfather?" she whispered. I knew that the coffin had been brought and that at that moment Nicholas's body was being placed in it, so I did not want Hania to go and see her grandfather before everything was prepared. Instead, I went.

Along the way I met Madame d'Yves, whom I requested to wait for me, for I needed to talk to her. After I had given the final orders for the burial and had prayed by Nicholas's body, I returned to the Frenchwoman and after a few preliminary words asked her if she would give French and music lessons to Hania after the first weeks of mourning would pass.

"*Monsieur Henri,*" replied Madame d'Yves, who apparently was angry that I was giving orders all over the place as if I were ruling the roost, "I would do this most willingly, for I love that girl very much, but I do not know if this is in keeping with the intentions of your parents, as I also do not know if they will agree to the role that you, of your own will, are trying to give this little one in this family. *Pas trop de zèle, monsieur Henri.*"

"She is under my care," I answered haughtily, "and I am responsible for her."

"But I am not under your care," responded Madame d'Yves, "therefore allow me to wait until your parents return."

The Frenchwoman's stubbornness angered me, but luckily it went much better with Father Ludwik. The good-hearted priest, who had already been teaching Hania, not only agreed to further and broaden her education but also praised me for my zeal.

"I see," he said, "that you are taking your task seriously, though you are young and still a child. But I praise you for this. Only remember to be as persevering as you are zealous."

And I saw that the priest was satisfied with me. The role of master of the house, which I had taken upon myself, amused rather than angered him. The old man saw that there was a lot of childishness in this, but that my motives were honest, therefore he was proud of me and happy that what he had planted in me had not died out. Besides, the old priest loved me very much; while I, as much as I had feared him with my whole soul when I was a child, now, in my adolescent years, found him more and more endearing. Having a weakness for me, he let himself be swayed by me. He also loved Hania and was glad to better her lot as far as it was in his power to do so. Therefore I met not the slightest resistance from him.

Madame d'Yves, in fact, had a good heart and, however angry she was with me, she likewise surrounded Hania with care. The orphan had no cause to complain of lack of loved ones. The servants began to treat her differently, not like an equal of theirs but as a young lady. The will of the oldest son of the family, even if he were just a child, was greatly respected among us. My father exacted this. The right of appeal existed to the elder lord and lady of the manor, but no one could oppose this will without authorization. It also was not permissible to address the oldest son other than "master" from his earliest years. The servants, as well as the younger members of the family, were trained to have respect for the oldest son, and later this respect lasted for a lifetime. "The family is upheld by this," my father would say, and in truth because of this, the voluntary, though not legally binding, family arrangement, on the strength of which the oldest had more wealth than the younger members of the family, had been kept up for a long time. This was a family tradition, passed on from generation to generation. People were accustomed to look at me as their future lord, and even old Nicholas, who was permitted everything and who was the only one to address me informally by my first name, could not help feeling this to a certain extent.

My mother kept a medicine-chest in our home and visited the sick herself. At times of the cholera she used to spend entire nights in peasant cottages together with the doctor, exposing herself to certain death, while my father, who feared for her yet did not forbid her, repeated: "Duty, duty!" Anyway, my father, though severe, helped his people. More than once he remitted arrears of labor; he forgave faults easily, despite his inborn hot temper; more than once he paid debts for the villagers; he gave weddings, he held babies at baptisms; he ordered us to respect the common folk; he tipped his hat when old farmers greeted him—ha! he even frequently sought their advice. And one cannot state just how much the peasants were attached to our whole family, which they proved frequently at a later date.

I am relating all of this, firstly, to faithfully record how it is and was with us; and secondly, to show that in creating a "lady" out of Hania I did not meet any great difficulties. The greatest resistance was presented by Hania herself, who, because of the way Nicholas had brought her up, was too timid and too worshipful of "their lordships" to be easily reconciled to her new position.

II

Nicholas's funeral took place three days after his death. Many of our neighbors came, wishing to honor the memory of the old man, who, though just a servant, was widely respected and loved. He was buried in our family plot, right next to my grandfather, the colonel. During the entire ceremony I did not leave Hania for a moment. She had arrived with me on a sleigh, and I wanted her to return with me, but Father Ludwik asked me to go and request our neighbors to come directly from the cemetery to our house to warm themselves and partake of some refreshments. Meanwhile Hania was attended to by my friend Selim Mirza-Dawidowicz, son of our neighbor Mirza-Dawidowicz, a Mohammedan of Tartar descent whose ancestors had lived here a long time and enjoyed the rights of citizenship and nobility. I had to sit with the Ustrzyckis, while Hania went with Madame d'Yves and the young Dawidowicz to another sleigh. I saw how the thoughtful lad wrapped her with his own fur and how he took the reigns from the driver and shouted at the horses; then they whisked away like a whirlwind. Upon our return home, Hania went to weep to her grandfather's room; I, however, could not hurry after her, for I had to entertain the guests along with Father Ludwik.

Finally everyone left except Selim Mirza. He was to spend the rest of the Christmas holidays with us and study a little with me, for we were both in the same class and exams awaited us; but mostly we would be engaged in riding horses, target practise, fencing and hunting, occupations which we both preferred to translating the *Annals* of Tacitus or the *Cyropaedia* of Xenophon. This Mirza was a merry fellow, a rascal and a great prankster; he was explosive as a spark but likeable to the highest degree. Everyone in our house liked him a lot, except my father, who was angered by the fact that the young Tartar shot and fenced better than I. But Madame d'Yves was crazy about him, for he spoke French like a Parisian; his mouth was never shut, he gossiped, made witty comments and amused the Frenchwoman better than any of us.

Father Ludwik had some hope of converting him to the Catholic faith, particularly since the boy joked about Mohammed on occasion and would have given up the Koran for certain if not for the fact that he feared his father, who, because of family tradition, held onto Islamism with both hands, saying that as an old noble he would rather be an old Mohammedan than a new Catholic. The elder Dawidowicz, however, had no other Turk-

ish or Tartar sympathies. His ancestors had settled in
these parts since the times of Duke Witold. The family
was quite wealthy and had lived in the same place for a
long time. Jan Sobieski had given the property which
they possessed to Mirza-Dawidowicz, a colonel of the
light horse who had performed wonders at Vienna and
whose portrait still hung at Chorzel. I remember that
this portrait always made a strange impression upon me.
Colonel Mirza was terrible man; his face was written
over by God knows how many sabres, as if with the
mysterious letters of the Koran. He had a swarthy complexion, prominent cheekbones and slanting eyes that
possessed a strange gloomy lustre, which had this singu-
lar feature that they looked at you no matter where you
stood in the room. But my friend Selim did not resemble
his ancestors in the least. His mother, whom the elder
Dawidowicz married in Crimea, was not a Tartar but
came from Caucasia. I do not remember her, but I know
that people said that she was a beauty beyond compare
and that the young Selim resembled her as one drop of
water does another.

Ah, that Selim was a handsome lad! His eyes were
barely slanted. They were not Tartar eyes, but the large,
dark, sad and watery eyes that apparently Georgian
woman possess. I have never seen and will never see eyes
so bestowed with inexpressible sweetness when calm.
When Selim asked for something, and he looked at you
with those eyes, it seemed that he was grabbing you by
your heart. His features were regular, noble and chiselled
as if by a sculptor's hand; his complexion was swarthy
but delicate, his lips were slightly protruding and red as
cherries; he had a sweet smile and pearly teeth. When,
however, Selim got into a fight with a friend, which
happened frequently enough, his sweetness vanished like
a deceptive dream, and he became almost frightful. Then
his eyes seemed to bulge out diagonally and gleam like

the eyes of a wolf; the veins in his face swelled; his complexion grew dark, and for a moment a real Tartar was awakened within him. This transformation was brief, however. A moment later and Selim would be weeping, kissing and begging forgiveness, and he was usually forgiven. He had the best of hearts and a great inclination toward noble impulses. He was, however, fickle, a bit thoughtless and a carouser with an unrestrained temperament. He rode, shot and fenced like a master; but in his studies he was not so successful, for despite his great abilities, he was a bit lazy. We loved each other like brothers, quarreled frequently, made peace just as often, and our friendship remained indestructible. At vacation time and on all holidays either I spent half the time at Chorzel or he half the time with us. And now, returning from Nicholas's funeral, he was to stay with us until the end of the Christmas holidays.

It was around four in the afternoon when the guests left. The short winter day was coming to a close. The great evening glow was looking through the windows; outside, on trees covered with snow and bathed in a red gleam, crows began to flutter and croak. Through the windows one could see whole flocks of them flying over the pond from the forest and basking in the evening light. In the room to which we passed after dinner, there was silence. Madame d'Yves went to her room to read fortunes, as was her want; Father Ludwik walked up and down the room with a measured step and took snuff; my two little sisters tumbled on the carpet under the table and, butting heads, tangled each other's golden curls; and Hania, Selim and I, sitting by the window on a sofa, looked at the pond on the garden side, at the forest beyond the pond and at the vanishing daylight.

Soon it became completely grey. Father Ludwik left to say the evening prayers; one of my sisters ran after the other to an adjoining room; we were alone. Selim cleared his throat and began to say something or another, when Hania moved over to me suddenly and whispered:

"Master Henryk, I feel strange. I'm afraid."

"Do not be afraid, Hania," I replied, drawing her to me. "Rest here, against me. While you are near me, nothing bad can happen to you. See, I am not afraid of anything, and I will always protect you."

All of what I said was not quite true, for, whether because of the darkness which filled the room or the effect of Hania's words and the recent death of Nicholas, I was also possessed by a strange feeling.

"Perhaps you would like to have a light brought into the room?" I asked.

"Very well."

"Mirza, ask Franek to bring a light."

Mirza jumped up from the sofa, and soon we heard an unusual tramping and noise outside the door. Suddenly the door opened with a bang and Franek rushed in like a whirlwind, and after him, holding him by the shoulders, was Mirza. Franek's expression was dazed and frightened, for Mirza, holding him by the shoulders, was spinning him round like a top and turning with him. Then he led him with that movement right up to the sofa, where he stopped and said:

"The master commands you to bring a lamp, for the lady is afraid. Which do you prefer: to bring the light or have your neck wrung?"

Franek went for the lamp and returned quickly with it; but it turned out that the light bothered Hania's tearful eyes, so Mirza extinguished it. Once again we were plunged in mysterious darkness, and once again there was silence among us. Now the moon threw its bright silvery light through the window. Evidently Hania was afraid, for she nestled closer to me, while I had to hold her hand at the same time. Mirza sat on a chair opposite us and, as was his custom, passed from a noisy to a pensive mood, which soon evolved to a dreamy mood. A great silence reigned among us; we felt a little scared but comfortable and cozy.

"Mirza, why don't you tell us a story," I said. "You tell a story so well. Is that all right with you, Hania?"

"Yes," the girl answered.

Mirza raised his eyes and thought a while. The moon lit up his handsome profile. Then he began to speak in his vibrating, sympathetic, but now subdued voice:

"Beyond the forests, beyond the mountains, there lived in Crimea a certain good fortune-teller named Lala. One day a sultan rode by her cottage. His name was Harun, and he was very rich. He had a coral palace with columns of diamonds; the roof of his palace was made of pearls, and the palace was so huge that it would take a year to go from one end to the other. The sultan wore real stars on his turban. His turban was made of the rays of the sun; on its top there was a crescent of the moon, which a certain wizard cut from the moon and presented to the sultan. So this sultan was passing by Lala's cottage and weeping, but weeping so that his tears were falling on the road, and wherever a tear fell, a white lily immediately sprang up."

"'Why are you crying, sultan Harun?' asked Lala.

"'Why should I not cry,' said sultan Harun, 'when I have only one daughter, as beautiful as the dawn, and I have to give her to the black Dev, who every year—'"

Mirza broke off suddenly.

"Is Hania asleep?" he whispered to me.

"No, I am not," answered the girl in a sleepy voice.

Mirza continued: "'How should I not weep,' said the sultan Harun to her, 'when I have only one daughter, whom I must give to the Dev.'

"'Do not cry, sultan,' said Lala. 'Get on a winged horse and ride to the grotto of Bora. Evil clouds will chase you along the road, but throw these poppy seeds at them and the clouds will immediately fall asleep...."

And thus Mirza went on; later he broke off again and glanced at Hania. The girl was asleep now. Extremely tired and worn out with sorrow, she slept soundly. Both Selim and I barely dared to breathe in fear of waking her up. Her breathing was even and peaceful, though at times interrupted by a deep sigh. Selim rested his forehead on his hand and fell into deep thought, while I raised my eyes to the sky, and it seemed to me that I was flying on angel wings to that heavenly space. I cannot relate the sweetness which overcame me when I felt that that dear little being was sleeping peacefully and with complete trust on my breast. A quiver passed through my entire body; some kind of celestial, new and unknown voices of joy were born in my heart, and they began to sing like a choir. Oh, how I loved Hania! How I loved her, with the love of a brother and guardian still, but without bounds and measure.

I neared my lips to Hania's hair and kissed it. There was nothing earthly in this, because my kiss and I were both equally innocent.

Mirza gave a sudden start and awoke from his reveries.

"How fortunate you are, Henryk!" he whispered.

"Yes, Selim."

We could not, however, stay in that position forever.

"Let us not wake her but carry her to her room," said Mirza.

"I will carry her myself, while you open the doors," I replied.

I delicately removed my arm from under the head of the sleeping girl and laid her head on the sofa. After which I carefully took Hania in my arms. I was still a boy, but I came from an unusually strong stock, while the girl was small and slender; so I carried her like a feather. Mirza opened the door to the adjoining room, which was lit, and proceeding thus, we reached the green room which I had selected as Hania's. The bed was already made up; an abundant fire crackled in the chimney, and by the chimney sat, poking the coals, old Wegrowska, who when she saw me burdened as I was, cried out:

"My goodness! so the master is carrying the girl. Couldn't you have woken her up so that she could come by herself?"

"Silence, Wegrowska!" I shot out angrily. "The lady— not 'the girl'—do you hear? The lady is tired. Please do not wake her up. Undress her and place her gently in bed. Do not forget that she is an orphan and that we must comfort her with kindness after the loss of her grandfather."

"An orphan, the poor little thing; indeed she is an orphan," the good-natured Wegrowska repeated with emotion.

Mirza kissed the old woman for this, after which we returned for tea. Mirza became his usual unrestrained self during tea, forgetting about everything; I, nevertheless, did not accompany him; firstly, because I was sad, and secondly, because I did not think it became a serious person, who was already a guardian, to frolic like a little child. That evening Mirza also got a scolding from Father Ludwik, for while we were saying prayers in the chapel, he dashed outside, climbed onto the low roof of the ice-house and began to howl. Naturally the dogs in the courtyard came running in from all sides and made such an uproar while accompanying Mirza that we could not continue on with our prayers.

"Have you gone mad?" Father Ludwik asked.

"Pardon, Father, but I was praying in Mohammedan fashion."

"Listen, you young stripling! Do not make fun of any religion!"

"But I, beg your pardon, want to become a Catholic, only I fear my father. What means Mohammed to me!"

Attacked on his weak side, the priest became silent, and we all went to bed. Selim and I had a room to ourselves, for the priest knew that we liked to chat, and he did not want to disturb us. When I had already undressed and noticed that Mirza had done the same, but without saying a prayer, I asked:

"Selim, don't you ever pray?"

"Of course I do. If you want, I will start right now."

And standing by the window, he raised his eyes to the moon, stretched his hands toward it and began to call out in a melodious voice: "O Allah! Allah Akbar! Allah Kerim!"

Dressed in his underclothing, with his face raised toward the heavens, he was so beautiful that I could not tear my eyes away from him. Afterward, he began to explain himself to me:

"What am I to do?" he said. "I do not believe in this prophet of ours, who forbade others from having more than one wife, but who himself had as many as it pleased him. Besides, I like wine. I am not allowed to be anything other than a Mohammedan, but I do believe in God and sometimes I pray as best as I know how. But do I know anything? I know that there is a God, but that's all."

Then he turned to another topic.

"Do you know what, Henryk?"

"What?"

"I have some excellent cigars. We are not children anymore; we can smoke."

"Get them."

Mirza sprang out of bed and took out a box of cigars. We lit up, lay down and smoked in silence, spitting away from each other behind our beds.

After a while, Selim spoke out:

"Do you know what, Henryk? I envy you very much. You are truly grown-up now."

"I should think so."

"For you are already a guardian. Ah, if only someone would let me be a guardian also!"

"It is not so easy, and besides, where would you find another girl in the world like Hania? But do you know what?" I continued in the tone of a serious adult. "I doubt that I will be going to school anymore. A person who has such responsibilities around the house as I have cannot go to school."

"Eh, you're talking nonsense. What, you'll stop learning? What about the University?"

"You know that I like to study, but duty comes first. Unless my parents send Hania with me to Warsaw."

"They won't even dream of it."

"While I am still in classes, of course not, but once I become an academic of the University they will give her to me. What, don't you know what an academic is?"

"Of course I do. Perhaps you are right. You will be her guardian, and then you will marry her."

I sat up in bed.

"Mirza, are you mad?"

"And why not? In school one is not allowed to get married, but an academic of a university can get married. Not only can he have a wife but children as well. Ha, ha!"

But at that moment the prerogatives and privileges of a university did not interest me in the least. Mirza's question illuminated, as with a flash of lightning, that side of my heart which was, even for me, still dark. A thousand thoughts, as if a thousand birds, continually flew through my head. To get married to my dearly beloved orphan—yes!—that was a lightning flash, a new flash of thought and feeling. It seemed to me that in the darkness of my heart someone had suddenly brought in a light. Love, deep but hitherto brotherly, had bloomed all at once from that light and was warmed by its unfamiliar heat. To get married to her, to Hania, to that bright-haired angel, to my dearest, my most beloved Hania....

In a weak and low voice I repeated, like an echo, my previous question:

"Mirza, are you mad?"

"I'll wager that you are already in love with her," he replied.

I made no answer. I put out the light, then grabbed the corner of my pillow and began to kiss it.

Yes! I was already in love with her!

III

On the second or third day after the funeral, my father arrived, summoned by a telegram. I was afraid that he might do away with my instructions concerning Hania, and my fears were to a certain extent justified. My father praised and embraced me for my zeal and conscientiousness in carrying out the duties of a master of the house; he appeared to be pleased. He even repeated several times "Our blood!"—something he only said when he was very pleased with me. He did not suspect how much that zeal was based on self-interest. But my instructions did not please him too much. It is possible that Madame d'Yves's exaggerated statements influenced him, though I have to admit that since that night when I became conscious of my true feelings toward Hania, that orphan became the most important person in the house. He also did not care for my idea of educating her in the same way as my sisters.

"I will not revoke or withdraw anything," he said to me. "That is your mother's affair. She will determine what she wants. This is her department. But it is worth-

while to consider what would be best for the girl herself."

"Getting an education cannot hurt, father. I have
frequently heard you say so yourself."

"Yes, in a man's case," he replied, "because education
gives a man a position, but it is different with women.
In a woman education should conform with the position
she will occupy in the future. Such a girl as Hania only
needs a moderate education. She doesn't need French,
music and things of that sort. With a moderate education Hania will not have a hard time finding a husband,
some worthy official—"

"Father!"

He looked at me in surprise.

"What's the matter with you?"

I was red as a beet. The blood almost burst from my
face. It grew dark before my eyes. To put Hania together
with an official seemed such a blasphemy against the
world of my dreams and hopes that I could not hold
back a cry of indignation. And the blasphemy hurt the
more since it came from my father's lips. This was the
first cold water thrown by reality on my youthful burning faith, the first blow aimed by life at the enchanting
edifice of illusions, the first such disappointment and
disenchantment, from the bitterness of which we defend
ourselves with pessimism and unbelief. But as a drop of
cold water merely hisses and soon turns to steam and
disappears when it falls on a red-hot iron, so, too, does
the first dose of reality hiss and soon disappear when
warmed by the passionate spirit of man.

The words of my father, therefore, hurt me for the
time being, and they hurt me in a strange manner, for I
felt resentment not against him but against Hania. Soon,
however, under the influence of that firm defiance one
has only in youth, I pushed those words away as far as
possible from my soul. My father understood nothing of

my feelings and ascribed them to excessive earnestness
concerning the duties that had been entrusted to me,
which was, after all, understandable at my age, and
which, instead of angering him, flattered him and weakened his disinclination toward a higher education for
Hania. I agreed to write a letter to my mother, who was
to be abroad for some time yet, and to ask her to make
the final decision in the matter.

I do not remember ever having written such a long or
such a heartfelt letter. I wrote of the death of old Nicholas, his last words, my desires, fears and hopes; I moved
the chords of compassion, which always quivered so
strongly in my mother's heart; I painted a picture of the
eternal remorse which would surely await me if we
would not do everything for Hania which lay in our
power—in a word, according to my opinion at that time,
I felt that my letter was a masterpiece of its type, which
must surely produce its intended effect. Pacified somewhat by this, I eagerly awaited my mother's response,
which arrived in two letters—one to me, the other to
Madame d'Yves. I won the battle on all points. Not only
had my mother agreed to Hania's higher education but
she strongly recommended it.

"If your father agrees to it," wrote my good mother, "I
should wish that Hania be considered in every respect as
being part of the family. We owe it to the memory of old
Nicholas, and to his devotion and faithfulness to our
family."

My triumph then was as great as it was complete, and
Selim shared it with me with his entire soul, for everything which touched Hania concerned him as if he
himself were her guardian. It is true that the sympathy
which he felt and the consideration which he showed
toward the orphan began to anger me a little, particularly since my relations with Hania had changed considerably since that memorable night in which I had

realized my true feelings. In her presence I felt inhibited.
That warmth and childish familiarity that I had with her
previously now disappeared. Barely a few days ago that
girl had quietly fallen asleep on my breast; now just the
thought of this made the hair stand on my head. Till a
few days ago whenever I would greet her in the morning
or bid her good-night I would kiss her pale lips like a
brother, now the touch of her hand burned me or sent a
delicious quiver over my body. I began to worship her, as
one usually worships the object of one's first love. And
when that innocent, unsuspecting girl cuddled up to me
as before, I felt anger at her, while I considered myself
sacrilegious.

Love brought me unknown happiness, but also unknown suffering. If I had had someone in whom I could
confide, if I had been able at times to weep on someone's
breast—a desire, incidentally, that I frequently had—I
would have for certain removed half the weight pressing
down upon me. I could have confessed all to Selim, but
I did not trust him. I knew that, at first, he would take
my words to heart, but who could assure me that the
next day he would not ridicule me with his particular
brand of cynicism, and with frivolous words desecrate
my ideal love, which I dared not touch with even one
inconsiderate thought? My character was such that I
kept my feelings to myself. Besides, there was one great
difference between Selim and me. I had always been a
trifle sentimental, while Selim had not one ounce of
sentiment in him. For me, love was mingled with sadness, while for Selim it was mingled with joy. So I
concealed my love from everyone, and almost from myself, and indeed no one noticed it. Within a few days,
without ever having seen anything I could pattern this
on, I had learned instinctively to hide all signs of that
love: the confusion which often came over me, the
blushes with covered my face whenever Hania was men-

tioned in my presence—in a word, I developed immense cunning, a cunning by the aid of which a boy of sixteen years will often deceive the most careful eye watching him. I had not the least intention of confessing my feelings to Hania. I loved her, and that was sufficient for me. Sometimes when we were alone, though, I felt a great urge to kneel before her and kiss the hem of her dress.

Meanwhile Selim went mad; he laughed, made jokes and was joyous for the both of us. He was the first to bring a smile to Hania's face when at breakfast one day he suggested to Father Ludwik that he turn Mohammedan and marry Madame d'Yves. Neither the Frenchwoman, who was easily offended, nor the priest, could get angry with him, for when he endeared himself to her, when he looked at her with his eyes and laughed, everything ended in a gentle scolding and in general laughter. In his conduct with Hania one could see a certain tenderness and care, but here, too, his inborn cheerfulness prevailed. With her he was far more unceremonious than I. It was apparent that Hania liked him a lot, for whenever he entered the room she became more cheerful. He made continual fun of me, or rather of my sadness, which he considered a forced pose of someone who wishes to appear grown up.

"He will become a priest, you will see!" he would say.

Then I would drop the first thing available to me, so that I could bend down for it and hide my blushing face, while Father Ludwik would take some snuff and respond:

"To the glory of God! to the glory of God!"

Soon the Christmas holidays came to an end. My faint hope of remaining at home was not realized. One evening it was announced to the great guardian that early the next morning he must be ready for the road. There was need of starting early because we had to go to

Chorzel, where Selim was to take farewell of his father. We rose at six o'clock when it was still dark. Ah, my soul was as gloomy then as that cold, dark, windy morning! Selim was also in a very bad mood. As soon as he got out of bed, he declared that the world was stupid and most wretchedly ordered, and I agreed completely; after which we dressed and left the lodging house for breakfast.

It was dark in the courtyard. Small flakes of icy snow, whirled by the wind, struck our faces. The windows of the dining-room were lit up. Before the porch stood a harnessed sleigh, on which our things were already packed; the horses were shaking the bells, and dogs were barking around the sleigh. All this, taken together, formed, at least for us, such a sad picture that it made our hearts bleed.

On entering the dining-room we found my father and Father Ludwik pacing about, their faces serious; Hania was not present. I kept on glancing toward the door of the green chamber, my heart pounding—would she come out or was I to go away without a farewell?

Meanwhile my father and the priest began to give us advice and to sermonize. Both started with this, that we were at that age where there was no need to repeat to us what work and learning meant—but they spoke of nothing else. I listened to everything absentmindedly, as I chewed toasted bread and swallowed with tightened throat the caudal. Suddenly my heart beat so strongly that I could barely sit in my chair, for I heard some rustling coming from Hania's room. The door opened, and out she came—Madame d'Yves, dressed in a morning wrapper, her hair in curl-papers. She embraced me warmly. For the disappointment which she had caused me I wanted to throw the glass of caudal at her head. She likewise expressed the hope that such good boys would surely learn perfectly, to which Mirza answered that the memory of the curl-papers in her hair would give him added strength and endurance in study. Hania, meanwhile, did not show herself.

But it was not destined that I should drain the bitter cup. When we rose from the breakfast table, Hania emerged from the other room, still sleepy, all rosy, her hair ruffled. When I pressed her hand to wish her good-morning, it was hot. My first thought was that she had a fever because of my departure, and I played a tender scene in my heart, but her warmth was simply due to sleep. After a while my father and Father Ludwik went for the letters that we were to take with us to Warsaw, while Mirza rode out through the door on a huge dog that had entered the room a moment earlier. I was left alone with Hania. Tears were welling in my eyes; from my lips tender and passionate words were bursting to come out. I had no intention of confessing my love for her, but I desperately wanted to say something like: "My dear, my beloved Hania!" and kiss her hands at the same time. This was the only convenient moment for such an outburst, for though I could do this in the company of other people, I dared not.

I wasted that moment most shamefully. I drew closer and closer, I stretched out my hand to her, but I did this awkwardly and unnaturally, and I said "Hania!" in such a strange tone that I immediately drew back and became silent. I wanted to slap my own face.

Meanwhile Hania herself began:

"My God, how sad it will be without you, Master Henryk!"

"I will be here for Easter," I replied curtly in a low, strange bass.

"But it is such a long time till Easter."

"Not at all," I muttered.

At that moment Mirza rushed in, followed by my father, Father Ludwik, Madame d'Yves and a few other

people. The words "To the sleigh! to the sleigh!" resounded in my ears. We all went to the porch. Here my
father and the priest embraced me. When the time came
to take leave of Hania, I had an irresistible desire to seize
her in my arms and kiss her as of old, but I could not
bring myself to do even this.

"Farewell, Hania," I said, giving her my hand, while
in my soul a hundred voices were weeping, and a hundred most tender expressions were on my lips.

Suddenly I saw that Hania was crying, and with equal
suddenness that irresistible, devilish impulse arose
within me to tear open my own wounds, an impulse I
would feel later in life more than once. So though my
heart was bursting, I said in a cold and curt manner:

"Do not cry needlessly, Hania."

And I sat down in the sleigh.

In the meantime Selim was taking farewell of everyone. Finally he rushed over to Hania and seized her two
hands, and though she tried to pull them away, he began
to kiss them passionately, first one and then the other.
Oh, what a desire I had to give him a thrashing at that
moment! After he had had enough of kissing Hania, he
sprang into the sleigh. My father cried out: "Off you go!"
Father Ludwik blessed us with a little cross. The driver
called "Gee up!" to the horses; the bells sounded, the
snow squeaked under the runners, and we were on our
way.

"Swine! idiot!" I berated myself in my soul. "So that is
the way you took farewell of your Hania! You upset her,
you scolded her for the tears of which you are unworthy,
for the tears of an orphan...."

I raised the collar of my fur coat and cried like a little
child, but quietly, for I did not want Selim to notice my
emotion. It appeared, however, that Selim saw everything perfectly, but since he himself was moved, he said

nothing for the time being. We still had not reached Chorzel, however, when he spoke:
"Henryk!"
"What?"
"Are you crying?"
"Leave me alone."
Again there was silence between us. But after a while Selim repeated:
"Henryk!"
"What?"
"Are you crying?"
I said nothing. Suddenly Selim bent down, grabbed a handful of snow, raised my cap, scattered the snow on my head and, putting the cap back down, said:
"That should cool you down!"

IV

I did not go home for Easter, because the approaching exams stood in the way. Besides, my father wished me to pass the entrance exam to the University, and he knew that I would not want to study while on vacation and that during that time I would undoubtedly forget at least one half of what I had learned. So I remained in Warsaw and studied very hard. Aside from regular school lessons and exam studies, Selim and I took private lessons from a student who, because he had entered the University recently, knew best what would be required of us.

Those were memorable times for me. Everything I had learned and thought previously, the entire edifice that had been so laboriously created by Father Ludwik, my father and the whole atmosphere of our quiet house, tumbled down. The young student we took lessons from was a great radical in every respect. While teaching us about Roman history and the reforms of the Gracchi, he was able to so well explain his disgust and contempt for

any oligarchy that my arch-noble convictions were easily
swept away. With what deep faith my young teacher
declared, for example, that a person who was soon to
occupy the serious and truly influential position of student at the University should be free from all "superstit-
tions," and not look on anything save with the eye of a
genuine philosopher. He was also of the opinion that a
man is best suited for the management of the world and
for exerting a strong influence on it between the ages of
eighteen and twenty-three, as later he gradually becomes
an idiot or a conservative.

Those who were neither students nor professors of the
University, he spoke of with pity. Nevertheless, he had
ideals, which never left his lips. I learned for the first
time of the existence of Moleschotte and Büchner—two
men of science whom he cited most often. You should
hear with what ardor our preceptor spoke of the con-
quests of science in recent times, of the great truths
which the blind and superstitious past had avoided, and
which, with unparalleled courage, the newest scholars
had raised "from the dust of oblivion" and proclaimed to
the world. While uttering such opinions he shook his
thick, curly head of hair and smoked an incredible number of cigarettes, assuring us as he did this that he was so
proficient in smoking that it did not matter to him
whether the smoke came out through his mouth or his
nostrils, and that there was not another man in Warsaw
who could smoke the way he did. Then he usually rose,
put on his overcoat, which lacked more than half of its
buttons, and declared that he had to rush, for he had
another "little meeting" that day. Saying this, he winked
mysteriously and added that Selim's age and mine did
not permit him to reveal anything more about this "little
meeting," but that later in life, and without his explanation, we would understand its meaning.

Despite all this, which would not have pleased our

parents very much, our young tutor did have his good points. He had a thorough knowledge of what he taught us and was a real fanatic of science. He wore boots with holes in them, a shabby coat and a cap which looked like an old nest; he was always broke, but he almost never thought about personal discomforts or poverty. He lived for science and not for himself. Mirza and I looked upon him as some higher supernatural being, as a sea of wisdom, as someone of unshakable authority. We truly believed that if anyone could save humanity in case of danger, it was surely he, that imposing genius, and he was of a similar opinion. And we adhered to his opinions as to glue.

In point of fact I went further in my rebelliousness, it seemed, than even my master. This was a natural reaction against my previous education. Besides, this young academic had really opened up for me new worlds of knowledge, in comparison with which my former ideas were too confining. Dazzled by these new truths, I did not have much time to think about Hania. At first, right after I arrived in Warsaw, I did not forget about my ideal love. The letters which I received from her fed the flame in my heart; but in the face of the extraordinary ideas of the young academic, our entire provincial world, so quiet and calm, began to recede, and Hania's figure, though it did not vanish, became enveloped, as it were, in a light mist.

As for Mirza, he went with me on an equal footing along the path of turbulent reforms; but of Hania he thought even less, for opposite our lodgings was a window in which sat a schoolgirl named Jozia. Selim began to sigh at her from first sight, and for days on end they looked at each other from their respective windows, like two birds in two cages. Selim maintained with absolute certainty that she was "the only one" for him. It frequently happened that he would lie on his back on his bed and study and study, and then suddenly fling his book to the floor, jump up, grab me and, laughing like a madman, cry out:

"Oh, my Jozia! how I love you!"

"Go to hell, Selim!" I would say to him.

"Oh, it's only you, not Jozia," he would answer roguishly, and return to his book.

Finally examination time arrived. Selim and I did very well on both the school exams and the entrance exam to the University; after that we were as free as birds, but we stayed on in Warsaw for three extra days. We used that time for acquiring student uniforms and for a celebration which our master considered essential—that is, an inauguration into drinking at the first good inn we came upon.

After the second bottle, when Selim's head and mine were turning, and when the cheeks of our master, and now our comrade, became flushed, a sudden and surprising tenderness came over us, together with an urge to unburden our hearts.

"Well, my boys," our master began, "you have come out among people, and the world is open before you. Now you can amuse yourselves; you can throw away money, play the lord, fall in love. But I tell you that these things are idiocies. A life that is superficial, a life without an ideal for which one lives, works and fights, is a waste. But in order to live wisely and to struggle wisely, one must look at things soberly. As for me, I think that I look at them soberly. I believe in nothing which I cannot touch, and I advise you to do the same. Jesus! there are so many different ways of living and so many ideas in the world, and all in such disarray, that one needs the devil knows what kind of head not to take the wrong path. But I hold fast to science, and that's that! I will not be trapped by trifles. Of course, life is foolish; you'll get no disagreement from me on that point. But we have science. Had we not, I would shoot myself. In my opinion, everyone has the right to take his own life, and I will surely shoot myself if science ever fails me. But it won't. You will be deceived in everything: if you fall in love, a woman will betray you; if you believe in God, a moment of doubt will come. But you can sit quietly until you die examining the alimentary canal of Infusoria, and you will not even notice how on a certain day everything will suddenly seem strange and darken—and that will be it for you! Then comes the obituary, your portrait in the paper, the more or less silly biography, and *finita comme-dia!* After that there will be nothing—I give you my word on that, my children. Don't believe in any of that religious nonsense. Science, my boys, is what matters! And there's another good thing about serving science. Without any misgivings you can walk about with holes in your boots and sleep on a straw mattress. It won't bother you at all. Do you understand?"

"To the health and glory of science!" shouted Selim, whose eyes were gleaming like live coals.

Our master pushed back his woolly hair and emptied his glass; then, inhaling smoke from his cigarette, he let out two lengthy streams of it through his nostrils and continued:

"Besides the exact sciences—Selim, you're drunk!— besides the exact sciences there is philosophy, and there are ideas. With these life can also be complete. But I prefer the exact sciences. Philosophy, and particularly the ideal type, I scoff at. It is just empty-headed talk. One supposedly goes after the truth, but the whole thing is like a dog chasing its own tail. I hate this type of chatter. I love facts. You cannot get something out of nothing. As to ideas—that's another thing. For them it is worthwhile to die, but you and your fathers go by silly ways. Mark what I say. Long life to ideas!"

We emptied our glasses again. We were drunk. The

dark room of the inn seemed darker; the candle on the table burned with a faint light; smoke hid the pictures on the walls. Outside a beggar was singing a religious hymn, and in between refrains he played a melancholic melody on a violin. Strange feelings filled my breast. I believed the words of the master, but I felt that he had not yet told us everything about what could make one's life complete. Something was missing. A sadness came over me. So, under the influence of my dreamy mood, the wine and a momentary excitation, I said in a low voice:

"What about the female sex, gentlemen! What about a loving, devoted woman—doesn't she matter?"

Selim began to sing:

> *"A woman changes her mind from day to day:*
> *A fool is he who trusts her in any way!"*

Our master looked at me with a peculiar expression, as if he were thinking of something else, but he soon shook himself free of this and said:

"Ha! you are a sentimentalist I see. Know that Selim will go much farther in the world than you. You will be damned. Guard yourself, guard yourself, I say, or else some petticoat will stand in your way and ruin your life. Women! women!" Here our master winked according to his custom. "I know that breed somewhat. I cannot complain; God knows, I cannot complain. But I know this too, that one does not give a finger to the devil, for he will seize the entire hand. Women! Love! Our entire misfortune is in this, that we make great things out of the small. If you wish to amuse yourself as I do, amuse yourself, but don't devote your life to it. Don't lose your mind, and do not lay down good money for false gods. Do you think that I complain about women? I do not even dream of it. On the contrary, I love them. But I do not let my imagination take over. I remember when I fell in love for the first time with a certain Lola, I thought, for example, that her dress was sacred, but it was calico. Don't you see! Was it her fault that she walked in mud instead of flying through the heavens? No! It was I who was stupid, for I put wings on her by force. Man is a rather limited beast. This one and that one carries God knows what ideal in his heart, and with this he feels a need of loving; so when he comes across the first nice goose he sees, he says to himself: 'This is the one.' Afterward he finds out that he has made a mistake, and because of that small mistake the devil takes him or he lives like a dolt all his life."

"But you acknowledge," said I, "that a man feels the need of loving. You must surely feel that need also?"

A fleeting and barely discernible smile came to his lips.

"Every necessity may be satisfied in a variety of ways," he answered. "I help myself in my own way. I have already said that I do not look on small things as great. I am sober, God knows, more sober than at this moment. But I have seen many men whose lives have become tangled up, like a thread, for one woman; so, I repeat, that it is not worthwhile to devote your life to that, and that there are better things, loftier aims. Love is a silly affair. To the health of sobriety!"

"To the health of women!" shouted Selim.

"Very good! let it be so," answered our master. "They are agreeable creatures if one doesn't take them too seriously. To the health of women!"

"To the health of Jozia!" I cried, touching Selim's glass.

"Wait! now it's my turn," he replied. "To the health of—of your Hania! One deserves the other."

My blood began to boil, and sparks flew from my eyes.

"Be quiet, Mirza!" I cried. "Do not mention that name in this place!"

Saying this, I threw my glass to the floor, and it broke into a thousand pieces.

"Have you gone mad?" cried our master.

I had not gone mad at all but was seething with anger. I could listen to everything which the master said about women and even take pleasure in it; I could rail against them along with the others. I could do that because I did not connect the words and the derision with anyone I knew, and because it did not enter my mind that the general theory was to be applied to persons dear to me. But when I heard the name of my immaculate orphan thrown out so frivolously in that inn, amid the smoke, dirt, empty bottles, corks and cynical conversation, I thought I had heard such a vile sacrilege, such a desecration and a wrong directed against Hania, that I almost lost self-control.

Mirza looked at me for a moment with astonishment. Then his face began to change in a flash also: his skin grew dark, his eyes glittered, the veins on his forehead stood out, and his features lengthened and became as defined as those of a real Tartar.

"Do you forbid me to say what I please?" he cried out in a choked voice, broken by his panting.

Fortunately our master jumped between us at that moment.

"You are not worthy of the uniforms you wear!" he exclaimed. "What kind of behavior is this? Are you going to fight or will you pull each other by the ears like schoolboys? Look at them! Philosophers who break glasses over each other's heads. Shame on you! How can one talk with you two about anything important! Shame on you! From a war of ideas to a war of fists. Now I will tell you that I propose a toast in honor of universities, and that you are drones if you will not clink your glasses together and drink to the last drop."

We calmed down. But Selim, though more drunk, was the first to regain his composure.

"I beg your pardon," he said in a tender tone. "I'm a fool."

We embraced heartily and emptied our glasses to the honor of universities. Then our master intoned that Latin song of students, "*Gaudeamus igitur.*" Through the glass doors of the inn, merchants began to look in. It was growing dark outside. We were all what one might call "sloshed." Our joyfulness had risen to a zenith and was now slowly descending. Our master was the first to fall into a pensive mood.

"All this is well and good," he said after a while, "but, when one considers everything, life is stupid. These are all artificial means. But as to what is happening inside one, that is another thing. Tomorrow will be like today: the same poverty, the same four bare walls, the same straw mattress, the same boots with holes in them, and so on, without end. Work and work, but happiness—pshaw! A man deceives himself as best he can and deadens his pain. Farewell!"

He put his torn cap on his head, made a few mechanical motions of fastening a coat which had no buttons, lighted his cigarette and, waving his hand, said:

"Say, why don't you pay for the wine—I'm broke, and be in good health. You may remember me or not. It doesn't matter to me. I am not sentimental. Be in good health, my fine lads. . . ."

He uttered the last words in an emotional and gentle voice, as if contradicting the statement that he was not sentimental. Just like every other heart, his poor heart needed love and was capable of it; but misfortune since childhood, poverty and the indifference of people had taught him to keep his heart locked up inside himself. Though ardent, he was proud, and therefore always fearful of being rejected should he get close to someone.

We remained alone for a while, under the influence of a certain sadness. Perhaps we had some bad premonition, for we were not to see our poor master alive again. Neither he nor we had any idea that in his chest he had been carrying for a long time the germs of a mortal disease from which there was no remedy. Poverty, too much exertion, long hours spent over books, sleepless nights and hunger hastened the illness.

In the autumn, at the beginning of October, our master died of consumption. Not many schoolmates followed his coffin, for it was vacation time, and only his poor mother, a dealer in holy pictures and wax candles, lamented aloud for the son whom she often had not understood during life, but whom, like a mother, she loved.

V

The day after our drinking-bout, horses came from the elder Mirza in Chorzel, and the following morning we set out for home. We had a long two-day ride ahead of us, so we rose early, at dawn. In our tenement-house everyone else was still asleep; but in the annex opposite, in a window amid geraniums, gillyflowers and fuchsias, glowed Jozia's face. Selim, when he had put on his knapsack and student's cap, stood in the window, ready for the road, in order to let it be known that he was leaving. Among the geraniums a melancholic glance answered him. But when he placed one hand on his heart and with the other sent a kiss, the little face between the flowers blushed and withdrew quickly into the dark interior of the room.

Below, on the flagstones of the yard, a britska, drawn by four sturdy horses, rattled in. It was time to take farewell and go to the carriage, but Selim kept on standing at the window, hoping to see something more. Hope deceived him, however, and the window remained empty. Only when we had gone downstairs and were passing the entrance hall of the annex, did we see on the steps within two white stockings, a walnut-colored dress, a bosom bent forward, and two bright eyes, shaded by a hand, looking out of the darkness into the daylight.

Mirza rushed at once to the hallway, while I took a seat in the britska nearby. I heard whispers and certain sounds very similar to the sound of kisses. After which a blushing Mirza came out, half laughing, half moved with emotion, and he sat by my side. The driver struck the horses; Mirza and I looked involuntarily toward the window; Jozia's face was glowing among the flowers again; just one moment remained—and a hand holding a white handkerchief came out; one more sign of farewell, and the britska rattled out onto the street, taking with it me and the beautiful picture of poor Jozia.

It was very early in the morning; the city was still asleep. The rosy light of dawn danced along the windows of the sleeping tenements. Only here and there a passerby—some early bird—awoke echoes with his steps; here and there a caretaker was sweeping the street; sometimes a cart loaded with vegetables clattered along from a village to the marketplace. Aside from these sounds, it was quiet, and the clear air was breezy and brisk, as is usual on a summer morning.

Our small britska, drawn by four Tartar horses, bounced along the flagstones like a nutshell pulled by a string. Soon our faces were bathed by the cool, bracing air of the river; the bridge rumbled under the hoofs of our horses, and half an hour later we were beyond the toll-gates of Warsaw and among wide fields and wheat and forests.

We breathed deeply the splendid morning air and feasted our eyes on the countryside. The earth was awak-

ening from its sleep. Pearly dew hung on the wet leaves
of trees and glittered on every ear of wheat. In the hedges
birds moved about joyously, greeting the beautiful day
with noisy chirping and twittering. The forests and
meadows were being exposed from morning mists, as if
from a baby's swathing. Here and there on the meadows,
water sparkled, and storks waded through it among gold-
en marigolds. Rosy smoke went straight up from the
chimneys of peasant cottages; a gentle breeze bent in
waves the yellow fields of ripened wheat, shaking from
them the dampness of the night. Joy overflowed everywhere. It seemed that everything was waking up, living,
and that the whole countryside was singing:

> *"When dawn causes night to flee,*
> *Yours, O Lord, is the land and sea—"*

What was taking place in our hearts at that moment
everyone will understand who remembers how in youth
he returned home on such a wonderful summer morning. The years of our childhood and our subordination
to school were behind us; a time of youth was spread out
expansively before us, a sort of rich, flowery steppe with
an endless horizon—a curious and unknown land into
which we had started on a journey with good omens: we
were young, strong, almost with wings on our shoulders,
like young eagles. Of all earthly treasures the greatest is
youth, and of that treasure, with its abundance of
wealth, we had not yet spent a single cent.

We proceeded along the road quickly, for at all the
main stopping-places relay horses were waiting for us.
Toward evening of the second day, after riding all night,
we came out of a forest and saw Chorzel, or rather the
pointed summit of the minaret of the house, shinning in
the rays of the setting sun. Soon we drove onto a dam,
lined with willows and privets, on both sides of which

were two immense ponds with gristmills and sawmills. The drowsy croaking of frogs, swimming among the overgrown banks in water warmed by the heat of the sun, accompanied us. It was evident that the day was ending. Herds of cattle and flocks of sheep, hidden in clouds of dust, were returning by way of the dam to the farm buildings. Here and there clusters of people with sickles, scythes and rakes on their shoulders were making for home, singing merry little tunes. These honest workers stopped the britska and kissed Selim's hands in warm greeting. Soon the sun inclined yet more toward the west and hid half of its bright disk behind the reeds. Only one broad golden strip of light still shimmered in the middle of the ponds, on the banks of which the trees looked into the smooth surface. We made a slight right turn; and soon, amid lindens, poplars, spruces and ash trees, shone the white walls of the manor house of Chorzel. A bell was heard in the courtyard calling the laborers to supper, and at the same time from the minaret came the melancholic but melodious voice of the muezzin of the house, heralding that a starry night was falling from the sky to the earth and that Allah is great. As if to accompany the muezzin, a stork, standing, like an Etruscan vase, in a nest on a treetop overlooking the roof of the manor, came out of his statuesque repose and raised to the sky a bill which seemed like a copper spear; then he dropped it onto his breast and clattered, shaking his head as if in greeting. I glanced at Selim. There were tears in his eyes, and his face shone with that incomparable sweetness peculiar to him alone. We drove into the courtyard.

Before the windowed porch sat the elder Mirza, and drawing blue smoke from his pipe, he gazed with a joyful eye at the calm and industrious life swarming on that charming landscape. When he saw his boy, he sprang up, caught him in his arms and pressed him long to his breast, for though he was stern to his son, he loved him above everything in the world. He asked at once about his examinations, after which came new embraces. All the numerous servants rushed over to meet the young lord, and the dogs jumped joyously around him. A tame she-wolf, a favorite of the elder Mirza, bounded from the porch. "Zula! Zula!" cried out Selim, and she leaped up and put her great paws on his shoulders, licked his face and then began to run around him as if mad, yelping and showing her fearsome teeth from joy.

We went to the dining-room. I looked at Chorzel and everything in it like a man who desires to be revived. Nothing had been changed. The portraits of Selim's ancestors, the captains of horse and standard-bearers, still hung on the walls. The terrible Mirza, Sobieski's colonel of light horse, looked on me as before with his ominous, slanting eyes; but his face, slashed with sabres, looked even more ugly and fearsome.

Selim's father had changed the most. The hair on his head, once black, was now grey; his bushy moustache was almost completely white; and his Tartar features were now more distinct. Ah, what a difference between the father and the son, between that stern, even harsh, bony face and that simply angelic face, which resembled a flower, so fresh and sweet! But it is difficult for me to describe the love with which the old man looked upon his boy and with which his eyes followed his every movement.

Not wishing to intrude, I kept my distance; but the old man, as hospitable as a genuine Polish noble, soon turned to me and began to embrace me and try to detain me for the night. I did not want to agree to spend the night in Chorzel, for I needed to be on my way, but I had to accept his invitation to stay for supper.

I rode out of Chorzel late in the evening, and when I was near my home the triangle had risen in the night sky, which meant that it was midnight. None of the windows in the village were lit up; but lights flickered from the wood-distillers a distance away, near the forest. Dogs were barking by the cottages. In the alley of linden trees, which ran up to our house, it was so dark that nothing could be seen. Someone with a few horses rode past me, humming a song, but I did not recognize him. I reached the porch; the windows were dark; clearly, everyone was already asleep. Dogs ran up from all sides and began to bark around the britska. I got off and knocked at the door, and kept on doing so for a long while. I felt hurt, for I had assumed that they would be waiting for me. Only after some time did a light begin to flit here and there through the window-panes, and finally a sleepy voice, which I recognized as Franek's, inquired:

"Who's there?"

I answered. Franek opened the door and immediately fell to kissing my hands. I asked him if everyone was well.

"Yes," answered Franek, "but the old lord has gone to the city and will not be back until tomorrow."

He conducted me to the dining-room, lit a hanging lamp over the table and went out to prepare tea. For a moment I was alone with my thoughts and my rapidly-beating heart. But that moment was of short duration, for Father Ludwik ran in, attired in his dressing-gown, and he was followed by Madame d'Yves, also in a dressing-gown and with her usual curl-papers; and then Kazio, who had arrived a month earlier from school for vacation. Those sincere hearts greeted me with emotion; they were amazed by how much I had grown; the priest insisted that I had grown manly, Madame d'Yves that I had grown more handsome. Only after some time did Father Ludwik, poor man, inquire rather timidly about the examinations I had taken and my school diploma; but when he heard of my successes he became so happy that he wept from joy and took me in his arms, calling me his dear boy. Suddenly from the adjoining room came the patter of small naked feet, and my two little sisters rushed in, in their night-dresses and little caps, repeating, "Henlik has come! Henlik has come!" and they sprang onto my knees. In vain did Madame d'Yves try to shame them, saying that it was an unheard of thing for two young ladies to show themselves to people in such "*dishabille*." The two, without asking me anything, put their little arms around my neck and nestled their pretty faces against my cheeks. After a while I inquired timidly about Hania.

"Oh, how she has grown!" answered Madame d'Yves. "She will come right away; she should be dressing now."

I did not have to wait long, for about five minutes later Hania entered the room. I looked at her—and, dear God, what had become of that skinny orphan of sixteen in just half a year? Before me stood an almost mature, or at least maturing, young lady. Her figure had filled and rounded out most wonderfully. She had a delicate but healthy complexion; her cheeks were ruddy, as if from the reflection of the morning dawn. Health, youth, freshness and grace were radiating from her, as from a rose when it blooms. I noticed that she looked at me curiously with her large blue eyes; but I saw also that she must have understood the impression which she had made on me, for a vague smile wandered along the corners of her lips. In that curiosity with which we both looked at each other there was a certain bashfulness of a young man and young woman. Oh, those simple heart-felt relations between a brother and sister, the relations of childhood, had vanished, never to return!

And how beautiful she was with that smile and that silent joy in her eyes!

The light from the lamp hanging over the table fell on her blonde hair. She was wearing a black dress with an equally dark cape hastily thrown over it, which she held at her breast underneath her white neck. But one could see in this attire a certain charming disorder, which came from the haste with which she had dressed. She glowed from the warmth of sleep. When I touched her hand upon greeting her, it was warm, soft, silky, and at the touch a shiver of pleasure rushed through me. When I went away she was a simple maiden, a half servant; now she was a young lady with a noble expression of face and a noble demeanor, which betrayed good breeding and the custom of keeping good company. One could read in her eyes that she had a moral and an intellectual foundation, that she had a soul. She had ceased to be a child in every respect. One could see this in her vague smile and the type of innocent coquetry with which she looked at me, and from which it was evident that she understood how much our relations had changed toward each other. I saw soon that she had a certain superiority over me. I was better educated, but in regard to life, in regard to understanding every situation, every word, I was still a rather simple lad. Hania was freer with me than I with her. My dignity of a guardian and a young lord had also vanished. On my journey I had been thinking on how I would greet Hania, what I would to say to her, and how I would be kind and forbearing toward her, but all these plans fell apart completely. The situation somehow developed that it was not I who was good and kind to her, but rather that it was she who seemed to be good and kind to me. At that moment I did not understand this clearly, but I felt it nevertheless. I had planned to ask her what she was studying and what she had learned, how she had passed the time, whether Madame d'Yves and Father Ludwik were satisfied with her; but meanwhile it was she who always asked me, with that smile playing around her lips, what I had been doing, what I had learned and what I intended to do in the future. In a strange way everything had turned out completely different than what I had wanted. In a word, our relationship had reversed itself.

After an hour's conversation it was decided that we would all go to sleep. I went to my room a little dreamy, a little astonished, a little disappointed and defeated, but under various impressions. Rekindled love began to come out, like a flame through the cracks of a burning building, and soon covered those impressions completely. Hania's figure, a maiden's figure, voluptuous, full of alluring charms, surrounded with the warmth of sleep, with her white hand holding the disordered dress at her bosom, and her hair falling freely, stirred my young imagination and veiled everything else before me.

I fell asleep with her image under my eyelids.

VI

I rose early and rushed out to the garden. The morning was beautiful, full of dew and the scent of flowers. I ran over to the hornbeam hedges, for my heart told me that I would find Hania there. But my too-eager heart was mistaken, for Hania was not there at all. I had to wait until breakfast was over before I could be alone with her, and I used the opportunity to ask her if she would like to go for a walk in the garden. She consented willingly and hurried off to her room, returning soon with a large russet hat on her head, which shaded her forehead and eyes, and a parasol in her hand. She gave me a playful smile from under the hat, as if she wanted to say, "See how pretty I look!"

We went to the garden. I turned toward the hornbeam hedges, thinking along the way on how to begin the conversation. I reflected that Hania, who certainly could start it better than I, had no desire to help me, but rather amused herself with my uneasiness. So I walked by her side in silence, cutting off with my riding-crop the flowers growing along the path, until Hania laughed all of a sudden.

"Master Henryk," she said, grabbing the whip, "what have these flowers done to you?"

"Oh, Hania, these flowers mean nothing to me! You see that I don't know how to begin a conversation with you. You have changed much, Hania. Oh, how you have changed!"

"Let us suppose that to be true. Does it make you angry?"

"I do not say that it does," I answered, half in sorrow; "but I cannot get used to it, for it seems to me that that little Hania whom I once knew and you are two different persons. That one is a part of my memory, a part of—my heart, like a sister, and so—"

"And so this one is a stranger, yes?" she asked in a low voice, pointing to herself.

"Hania! Hania! How can you even think such a thing?"

"Still it is quite natural, though perhaps sad," she answered. "You are seeking in your heart for the old brotherly feelings toward me and do not find them! That's all!"

"No, Hania! I'm not seeking the old Hania in my heart, for she is always there, but I am seeking her in you. And as to my heart—"

"As to your heart," she interrupted merrily, "I can guess what has become of it. It has remained somewhere in Warsaw with some other happy heart. That is easy to guess!"

I looked deeply into her eyes. I did not know whether she was testing me a little or, counting on the impression she had made on me yesterday and which I had been unable to hide, playing with me in a rather cruel manner. But all of a sudden a wish for defiance was awakened in me. I thought that I must have a extremely comical expression on my face when I looked at her, something like that of wounded doe; so I mastered my feelings and said:

"And if that is true?"

A barely discernible expression of surprise and something like dejection flashed across her face.

"If that is true," she answered, "it is you who have changed, not I."

Saying this, she frowned a little, and looking at me once in a while from the corner of her eye, she went on for some time in silence, while I endeavored to hide the joy her words had given me. "She says," I thought, "that if I love another, it is I who have changed; therefore, she has not changed, she—"

Overwhelmed with happiness, I dared not finish this wise deduction.

Despite all this, it was not I who had changed, not I, but she. Six months ago she was a little girl who knew nothing of God's world, who would never have thought of talking about feelings and emotions, and for whom a similar conversation would have been so much Greek, but now she carried on this conversation as easily and skillfully as if she were reciting a lesson. How much her formerly child-like mind had developed, how nimble it had become! But similar amazing things take place in girls. More than one falls asleep in the evening a child to awaken in the morning a woman, with another world of feelings and thoughts. For Hania—who by nature was quick-witted, intelligent and sensitive—six months, the passage of her sixteenth year, another sphere of society, learning, certain novels (read, perhaps, in secret)—all this was more than enough to render its effect.

Meanwhile we walked in silence, side by side. Hania was the first to break it.

"So you are in love, Master Henryk?"

"Perhaps," I said with a smile.

"Then you will miss Warsaw?"

"No, Hania! I would be happy if I never left this place."

Hania shot me a glance. She apparently wanted to say something but remained silent. After a while, however, she tapped her dress with the parasol and said, as if answering her own thoughts:

"Ah, what a child I am!"

"Why do you say that, Hania?" I asked.

"Oh, nothing. Let us sit on this bench and talk of something else. Is not the view beautiful from here?" she asked suddenly, with that by now familiar smile on her lips.

She sat down on the bench nearby the hedges under an immense linden tree, where the view was indeed very beautiful in the direction of the pond, the dam and the forest beyond. Hania pointed it out to me with her parasol, but I, however much I was an admirer of beautiful views, had not the least desire to look at it, because, firstly, I knew it perfectly, and secondly, I had before me Hania, a hundred times more beautiful than anything that surrounded her; and finally, I was thinking of something else.

"How wonderfully the water reflects those trees!" she said.

"I see that you are an artist," I answered, not looking at the trees nor the water.

"Father Ludwik is teaching me to sketch. Oh, I've learned much during the time you were away. I wanted—but what is the matter? Are you angry with me?"

"No, Hania, I am not angry. I could never be angry with you. But I see that you are evading my questions, and that—that we are both playing blindman's buff instead of speaking openly and with trust, as we used to

do. Maybe you do not feel this, but I do, and it pains me,
Hania!"

These straightforward words had only this result, that
they made both of us very embarrassed. Hania gave me
both hands, it is true; I squeezed those hands perhaps
too strongly, and—how awful!—bending over them
quickly, I kissed them in a manner not at all befitting a
guardian. Then we became both confused to the highest
degree. She blushed to the neck, and I did also. We did
not say a single word, both of us being unable to begin
a conversation that would be sincere and full of trust.

Then Hania looked at me, and I at her, and again we
hung out red flags on our faces. We sat side by side like
two dolls. It seemed to me that I heard the rapid beating
of my own heart. The situation was unbearable. At times
I felt that some hand was grabbing me by the collar to
throw me at her feet, and that another was holding me
by the hair and not letting me move. Suddenly Hania
sprang up.

"I must go," she said in a hurried, confused voice. "I
have a lesson at this hour with Madame d'Yves. It is
almost eleven."

We returned to the house by the same path we took
before, and, as before, we went on in silence, while I kept
cutting the heads off the flowers with my riding-crop.
This time, however, Hania had no compassion for the
flowers.

How splendidly our old relationship had returned—
there was no doubt about that!

"Jesus, what is happening to me?!" I thought when
Hania left me to myself. I was so in love that my hair was
standing on end.

Meanwhile Father Ludwik came over and led me to
the farm. Along the way he told me many things touching upon our estate, but these did not occupy my mind
in the least, though I pretended to listen attentively.

My brother Kazio, who, taking advantage of his vacation, spent his time out of doors engaged in a variety of activities from hunting to boating, was at that moment in the farmyard riding a young chestnut horse from the stud. When he saw us, he galloped up on the horse, which kicked and cavorted as if mad. He asked us to admire the horse's form, liveliness and walk; after which, he dismounted to join us. Together we visited the stables, the cow-sheds, the barns, and we were just on our way to the fields, when it was announced that my father had arrived, so we had to return to the manor.

My father greeted me more warmly than ever before. When he learned of the results of my university examinations, he took me in his arms and declared that from now on he would consider me an adult. Indeed, a great change had taken place in him in regard to me. He treated me more with confidence and an open heart. He began to immediately talk with me about our estate, and confided to me his intention of buying one of the neighboring estates, and asked my opinion. I realized that he spoke of this purposely, to show me how seriously he took my importance as a mature person and the first son in the family. At the same time I noticed to what degree he was pleased with me and my progress in school. His parental pride was flattered immensely by the testimonials which I had brought from my professors. I noticed also that he was testing my character, my manner of thinking, my ideas on honor, and that he was asking me various leading questions to see what I was all about. And one could see that this parental examination proved favorable, for however different my philosophic and social principles were from his, I did not reveal them, and in other things we did not differ at all. And so my father's stern, lion-like face was more radiant than I had ever seen it.

He covered me with gifts that day. He gave me a

couple of pistols, with which he had fought a duel not long ago with Zoll, the German, and on which were notched several other duels which he had fought during his younger days in the army. Then I received a splendid horse of Eastern stock and an old sabre handed down from my ancestors. The hilt was set with stones, and on the broad Damascus blade was an image of the Virgin Mary inlaid with gold and the inscription, "Jesus, Mary!" That sabre was one of our most prized family relics, and for many years had been the object of sighs from Kazio and me, for it cut through iron as if through butter. My father, when he presented it to me, unsheathed and swung it a couple of times so that the air whistled and there was a flash in the room; then he made a cross with it over my head, kissed the image of the Virgin Mary, and said, as he handed me the weapon: "Into worthy hands! I did not shame it; do not shame it either!" Then we threw ourselves into each other's arms, while Kazio seized the sabre with enthusiasm and— though he was only a fifteen-year-old boy, yet unusually strong—began to slash away at an imaginary enemy with a skill and a quickness that would not have shamed any trained master of fencing. My father looked at him with satisfaction.

"He will be someone to reckon with," he said; "but you will be able to hold your own, is that not so?"

"I will, father. I can even teach Kazio a thing or two. Of all the comrades with whom I have trained in fencing, only one has excelled me in the art."

"Who is that?"

"Selim Mirza."

My father made a wry face.

"Mirza! But you must be stronger?"

"And that is the only reason why I can hold my own against him. But what is the use of even thinking about such a thing? We will never fight."

"Life is full of surprises," answered my father.

After dinner we were all sitting on the wide, vine-covered porch where we had a view of the immense courtyard and, farther on, the shady road bordered by linden trees. Madame d'Yves was crocheting an altar-cloth for the chapel; my father and Father Ludwik were smoking pipes and drinking black coffee. Kazio was circling about in front of the porch, following with his eyes the turns of flying swallows, which he wanted to shoot at, an activity forbidden him at that moment by my father. Hania and I were looking at some drawings which I had brought home, and thinking very little about them. For me at least, they served only to conceal from others the glances which I cast at her.

"So, lord guardian, what do you think of Hania?" asked my father, glancing playfully at the girl. "Do you think she has lost her good looks?"

I began to examine a drawing most carefully and answered from behind the paper:

"I would not say that she has lost her good looks, but she has grown tall and has changed."

"Master Henryk has reproached me already for these changes," interjected Hania freely.

I admired her daring and presence of mind. I would not have mentioned those reproaches so casually.

"Oh, what does it matter how she looks!" said Father Ludwik. "What is important is that she learns quickly and well. Why doesn't Madame tell us how quickly she learned French?"

It should be known that Father Ludwik, though highly educated, did not know French and could not learn it, though he had spent many years under our roof with Madame d'Yves. But the poor fellow had a weakness for the French language and considered a knowledge of it an indispensable mark of a superior education.

"I cannot deny that Hania learns easily and willingly,"

answered Madame d'Yves. "But," she added, turning to me, "I still must complain of her to you, sir."

"Oh, Madame!" cried Hania, crossing her hands, "what new offence have I committed?"

"What offence? That you will explain in a moment," answered Madame d'Yves. "Just imagine, sir, that this young lady, the moment she finds any free time, picks up a novel right away. And I have strong reasons to suspect that when she goes to bed, instead of putting out the candle and going to sleep, she reads for hours on end."

My father, who liked to tease Madame d'Yves when he was in a good mood, said: "She does a very bad thing; but I know from another source that she follows the example of her teacher."

"Oh, I beg your pardon! but I am forty-five years of age," answered the Frenchwoman.

"Why, I would never have thought that!" my father replied.

"You are wicked, sir!"

"That I do not know; but I do know that if Hania gets novels from any place, it is not from the library, since Father Ludwik has the key to it. Therefore the blame falls on the teacher."

In fact, Madame d'Yves had read romance novels all her life, and having a passion to relate them to everyone, she must have also talked about them to Hania; that is why in the words of my father, said half in jest, a certain truth was concealed.

"Take a look! someone is coming!" cried Kazio suddenly.

We all looked at the shady linden alley, and, sure enough, at the other end of it, over a half mile away, we saw a cloud of dust approaching us with incredible speed.

"Who can that be?" said my father, rising up. "What

speed! There's so much dust that one can't make out anything."

Indeed, no rain had fallen for more than two weeks and the heat was great, so that along the roads clouds of white dust rose up at every step. We looked for a while longer at the rapidly approaching cloud, when suddenly a horse's head emerged from it, with distended, red nostrils, fiery eyes and flowing mane. The white horse was going at the swiftest gallop, his feet barely touching the ground; and on his back, leaning over his neck in Tartar fashion, was none other than my friend Selim.

"It is Selim, Selim!" shouted Kazio.

"What is that madman doing?" I cried out, springing up. "The gate is closed!"

There was no time to open the gate, for no one could run up to it in time. Meanwhile Selim pressed on like a maniac as if nothing were in front of him. It was almost certain that he would ram into the gate, more than two ells high and sharpened on top.

"God, have mercy on him!" cried Father Ludwik.

"The gate! Selim, the gate!" I screamed out, as if possessed, waving my handkerchief and running as fast as I could across the courtyard.

Suddenly, some fifteen feet from the barrier, Selim straightened himself in the saddle and measured the gate with a glance as quick as lightning. Then I heard the screams of the women sitting on the porch behind me and the rapid stamping of hoofs! The horse rose, suspended his forelegs in the air and went over the gate at the greatest speed without stopping for a moment.

Only when Selim reached the porch did he rein in his horse, so that the animal's hoofs dug into the earth. Then he tore off the hat from his head and began to wave it like a flag, shouting:

"How are you, my dear ladies and gentlemen? How are you? My respects to the lord benefactor!" he cried out, bowing to my father. "My respects to the dear priest, Madame d'Yves, Lady Hania! We are all together once again. *Vivat! Vivat!*"

Saying this, he sprang from the horse, and throwing the reins to Franek, who had just run out of the house, he embraced my father, the priest, and kissed the hands of the ladies.

Madame d'Yves and Hania were pale from terror, but it was precisely because of that that they greeted Selim as if he had been rescued from death. Meanwhile Father Ludwik spoke:

"Oh, madman, madman! You scared the life out of us! We thought that it was all over for you."

"Why is that?"

"Because of the gate. How can you race so blindly?"

"Blindly? Why, I saw that the gate was closed. Oho! I have my perfect Tartar eyes."

"And you did not fear to make the jump?"

Selim laughed.

"Not in the least, Father Ludwik. But the credit belongs to my horse, not to me."

"*Voilà un brave garçon!*" said Madame d'Yves.

"Oh, yes," added Hania, "not every man would have the courage to do that."

"You mean," I retorted, "that not every horse could clear the gate, for more such men could be found."

Hania stared at me for a moment.

"I would advise you not to try, Master Henryk," she said.

After which she turned toward Selim, and her look expressed admiration, for, in truth, after having done his daring Tartar deed, which was one of those risks that always please women, he was a sight to behold. His beautiful dark hair fell over his forehead, his cheeks were flushed and his sparkling eyes shone with gaiety and joy. As he stood there near Hania, looking her in the eyes with interest, no artist could have painted a more beautiful couple.

As for me, I was affected to the highest degree by her words. It seemed to me that that, "I would advise you not to try," had been spoken in a voice in which there was a tone of derision. I cast an inquiring glance at my father, who had been examining Selim's horse a moment before. I knew his parental ambition; I knew that he was jealous the moment that anyone surpassed me in anything, and that he had been annoyed with Selim for a long time because of this. That is why I presumed that he would not oppose me should I wish to show that I was not a worse horseman than Selim.

"That horse jumps well, father," I said.

"Yes, and that devil sits well," he muttered. "Could you do the same?"

"Hania has her doubts," I answered with a certain bitterness. "May I try?"

My father hesitated. He looked at the gate, at the horse, at me, and said:

"Let it rest."

"Of course!" I exclaimed in sorrow. "Let me be considered an old woman in comparison with Selim!"

"Henryk! what nonsense are you saying?" cried Selim, encircling my neck with his arm.

"Jump, jump, my boy! and give a good account of yourself!" said my father, whose pride was touched.

"Bring the horse here!" I called out to Franek, who was leading the tired horse slowly around the yard.

Suddenly Hania sprang up from her seat.

"Master Henryk!" cried she. "So I am the cause of this test. I do not wish it; I do not wish it, at all. Do not do it—for my sake!"

And while speaking, she looked straight at me, as if she wished to finish with her eyes what she could not express in words.

Ah! for that look I would have given the last drop of my blood at that moment, but I could not and would not withdraw. My offended pride was stronger at that moment than anything else; that is why I mastered myself and answered dryly:

"You are mistaken, Hania, in thinking that you are the cause. I'm going to make the jump for my own amusement."

Despite the protests of everyone save my father, I mounted and slowly moved forward into the alley of lindens. Franek opened the gate and closed it immediately after me. I had bitterness in my soul and would have jumped over the gate even if it had been twice as high. When I had ridden about three hundred yards, I turned the horse around and began at a trot, which I changed immediately to a gallop.

Suddenly I noticed that the saddle was moving.

One of two things had happened: either the girth had cracked during the previous leap, or Franek had loosened it to let the horse breathe and, through stupidity or perhaps forgetfulness, had not informed me.

Now it was too late. The horse was approaching the gate at the greatest speed, and I had no desire to stop him. "If I kill myself, I will kill myself," I thought. I was seized by a certain type of despair. I pressed the sides of the horse convulsively; the air whistled in my ears. Suddenly the gate flashed before my eyes; I thwacked my whip and felt myself being borne through the air. I heard a scream from the porch. It grew dark before my eyes— and after a while I regained consciousness on the lawn.

I sprang to my feet.

"What happened?" I cried. "Was I thrown? Did I faint?"

About me stood my father, Father Ludwik, Madame d'Yves, Selim, Kazio and Hania, white as a sheet and with tears in her eyes.

"How are you feeling? How are you feeling?" everyone cried out.

"Fine. I was thrown, but that was not my fault. The girth was cracked."

In fact, after my momentary faint I felt perfectly well and was only a little out-of-breath. My father began to feel my hands, feet and shoulders.

"Does it hurt?" he asked.

"No, I am perfectly fine."

My breath returned to me shortly. I was angry, however, for I thought that I seemed ridiculous. I must have looked ridiculous. In falling from the horse, I was thrown forcefully across the whole width of the road and landed on the lawn by its side. Because of this the elbows and knees of my brightly-colored clothing were green, and my attire and hair were disordered.

But the unfortunate incident had rendered me a service. A moment before, Selim was the object of our attention, both as a guest and as a guest newly-arrived; now I had taken from him that palm of victory, though, of course, at the expense of my elbows and knees.

Hania, who continued to think of herself—and justly, by the way—as the cause of this hazardous test, which might have ended badly for me, tried to make up for her indiscretion with kindness and sweetness. Under such an influence I soon recovered my good humor, which was communicated to all those present who a moment before had been terrified. We entertained ourselves splendidly. Afternoon tea was served, at which Hania was the hostess, and then we went to the garden. In the garden Selim played around like little boy; he laughed, frolicked, and Hania helped him with her whole heart. Finally Selim said:

"Oh, what a wonderful time all three of us will have now!"

"I am curious to know," said Hania, "who has the most joyful disposition?"

"Surely it is I," answered Selim.

"But perhaps it is I?" replied Hania. "I am also joyful by nature."

"But the least joyful is Henryk," added Selim. "He is serious by nature and tends to be melancholic. If he had lived in the Middle Ages, he would have been a knight-errant and a troubadour—only he cannot sing! But we," he continued, turning to Hania, "have looked for the seed of happiness and have found it."

"I don't agree," I answered. "In order to be well-matched to each other one nature has to be the opposite of the other, for, in such a case, one has the qualities which are lacking in the other."

"Thank you," replied Selim. "I assume that you are by nature fond of weeping, and Lady Hania of laughing. Very well, then; let us suppose that both of you get married to each other—"

"Selim!"

Selim looked at me and began to laugh.

"What do I see, my young lord? Ha, ha! Do you remember Cicero's discourse: *pro Archia?* —'*commoveri videtur juvenis,*' which in Polish means: the young man seems confused. But that signifies nothing, for you can become red as a boiled lobster for no apparent reason. Lady Hania, he boils lobsters wonderfully, and now he has boiled some for himself and for you."

"Selim!"

"Nothing, nothing! Let me go back to what I was saying. So you, Lord Weeper, and Hania, Lady Laughter, become husband and wife. And this is what will happen: He will begin to cry, and you will begin to laugh. You will never understand each other; you will never agree on anything, and disagree on everything. What kind of well-matched natures are these! Oh, with me it would be different! We would simply laugh throughout our lives, and that would be the end of the story!"

"Oh, what nonsense you are saying!" answered Hania, and both laughed as if nothing had happened.

As for me, I had not the least desire to laugh. Selim did not know what wrong he had done me in making Hania believe in the difference between her nature and mine. I was angry to the highest degree, and that is why I answered Selim with sarcasm:

"You have a strange view, and it surprises me all the more since I have noticed that you have a certain weakness for melancholic persons."

"I?" he said with genuine amazement.

"Yes. May I remind you of a certain window, several fuchsias in the window, and a little face between them. On my word, I never saw such a melancholic face!"

Hania clapped her hands.

"Oho! I am learning something new!" she exclaimed, laughing. "Is she pretty, Selim; is she pretty?"

I thought that Selim would become confused and get the wind knocked out of him, but he merely said:

"Henryk?"

"What?"

"Do you know what I do with those whose tongues are too long?"

And he burst out laughing.

Hania, however, insisted that he at least tell her the name of his chosen one. Without thinking long, he said: "Jozia!" But if he had made more out of it all, he would have paid dearly for his sincerity, because Hania gave him no peace from that moment until the evening.

"Is she pretty?"

"So-so."

"What about her hair, her eyes?"

"Pretty, but not the type that I prefer."

"And what kind of hair and eyes do you prefer?"

"Blonde hair and, if I may be so bold, blue eyes like those I am looking into at this moment."

"Oh, Selim!"

And Hania frowned, while Selim, joining his hands together in mock supplication, cajoled himself to her and, with that incomparable sweetness in his eyes, began:

"Lady Hania! do not be angry with me! What has this poor little Tartar done? Do not be angry! Give us a smile, please, please...."

Hania looked at him, and the more she looked at him, the more she became her former self. He simply enchanted her. A little smile played around the corners of her mouth; her eyes grew bright, her face radiant. Finally she answered in a soft, gentle voice:

"Very well, I will not be angry; but please behave yourself."

"I will, as I love Mohammed, I will!"

"And do you love your Mohammed very much?"

"As a dog loves a beggar."

And then both laughed again.

"But now tell me whom does Master Henryk love?" said Hania, picking up the conversation. "I asked him, but he did not want to tell me."

"Henryk? You know," here he looked at me from the corner of his eye, "I don't think he is in love with anyone yet, but he will be in love. Oh, and I know perfectly well with whom! As for me . . ."

"As for you—what?" inquired Hania, trying to conceal her embarrassment.

"I would do the same thing. But... Hold on! Perhaps he is in love already."

"Selim, please, I beg you to stop!" I cried out.

"My good fellow," said Selim, putting his arm around my neck. "Ah, Hania, if you only knew how good he is."

"Oh, I know that!" replied Hania. "I remember how kind he was toward me after my grandfather's death."

A cloud of sadness passed over us at that moment.

"I will tell you something," said Selim, wishing to change the subject. "After the university examination we shared a few bottles with our master—"

"You mean you drank wine?"

"Yes! A custom which cannot be avoided. So, after we had drunk a bit, I, being in a giddy state, raised a toast to you. I acted unwisely, of course, and Henryk sprang up. 'How dare you mention Hania in such a place as this?' he said to me. For we were in an inn. We almost came to exchanging blows. He will not let anyone offend you; it's out of the question."

Hania gave me her hand.

"Master Henryk, how good you are!"

"All right, all right," I answered, won over by Selim's words, "but, Hania, don't you think that Selim is just as good for telling you this?"

"Oh, I am most good, most good!" said Selim, laughing.

"But you are!" answered Hania. "Both of you are worthy of each other, and we will have such a wonderful time together."

"You will be our queen!" cried Selim with enthusiasm.

At that point Madame d'Yves called out from the garden veranda: "Gentlemen! Hania! Tea-time!"

All three of us went to tea in the very best humor. The table was set on the veranda. Candles flickered in glass balls, and moths circled around the lights, striking the glass; the leaves of wild grapevines, moved by the warm night air, rustled; and beyond the poplars rose a great golden moon. The last conversation between Hania, Selim and myself had put us in a mood that was wonderfully mellow and friendly. The calm and quiet evening also had its effect on the older persons. My father's face and Father Ludwik's were as serene as the sky.

After tea Madame d'Yves began to play solitaire, while my father started to talk of old times, which with him was always an indication that he was in a splendid mood.

"I remember," he said, "that we once stopped not far from a village in Krasnostawski. The night was pitch black." Here he drew smoke from his pipe and blew it out above the candlelight. "Everyone was as tired as an old nag. We were standing around in silence, when all of a sudden—"

And then began a narrative of wonderful and most wonderful happenings. Father Ludwik, who had heard this story more than once, slowly stopped smoking and began to listen more attentively, and, raising his spectacles to his forehead and shaking his head, repeated "Well! Well!" or called out, "Good Lord! and then what?" Selim and I, leaning against each other, our eyes fixed on my father, listened to his every word. But on no face was the expression depicted so prominently as on Selim's. His eyes were gleaming like coals; his face glowed red; his hot Eastern nature came to the surface like oil. He could hardly sit still. Madame d'Yves, glancing at him, smiled and showed him to Hania with her eyes. Then both began to observe him, for they were entertained by that face, which was like a mirror or the surface of water, in which everything is reflected.

Today, when I recall evenings like these, I cannot contain my emotion. Many waves in the sea, many clouds in the sky have passed since that time, but still my winged memory continually presents before me similar pictures of that country manor, those quiet summer nights and that family, harmonious, loving, happy; and a grey veteran telling of the ups and downs of his life; youths with their eyes sparkling; and, farther on, a face like a flower of the fields.... Yes, many waves in the sea and clouds in the sky have passed since that time!

Meanwhile the clock struck ten. Selim sprang up, for he had been told by his father to return home that night. All of us decided to accompany him as far as the cross which stood at the end of the lindens, while I would continue farther, on horseback, until Selim and I had passed the meadows. So we started off, all except Kazio, who had fallen asleep like a baby.

Hania, Selim and I moved on ahead. Selim and I led our horses by the reins, while Hania walked between us. The three older people trailed behind. It was dark in the alley, but the moon, breaking through the dense foliage, dotted the dark road with silver spots.

"Let us sing something," said Selim; "some old song, old but pretty. For example, that song about Filon."

"No one sings that anymore," replied Hania. "I know another one: 'Oh, autumn, autumn, the leaf is withering on the tree!'"

Finally the three of us agreed to begin with "Filon," which both the priest and my father liked much, for it reminded them of the old days, and then sing "Oh, autumn, autumn!" Hania rested her white hand on the mane of Selim's horse, and we began to sing:

> *"The moon has gone down, the dogs are asleep,*
> *But someone is trilling in woods so deep.*
> *Surely 'tis my dear Filon waiting for me,*
> *Under, under our favorite sycamore tree..."*

When we finished, the voices of the older people were heard behind us in the darkness: "Bravo! bravo! sing something more." I sang along as best I could, though I did not have a good voice, while Hania and Selim had beautiful voices, particularly Selim. Sometimes, when I went off key, they both laughed at me. Then they sang a few other songs, during which I thought, "Why is Hania resting her hand on the mane of Selim's horse and not the mane of mine?"

She seemed to have a special liking for that horse. At times she nestled up to its neck or, patting it, repeated, "Nice horse, nice horse!" And the gentle beast snorted and stretched out its open nostrils toward her hand, as if looking for sugar. All this caused me to become sad again, and I looked at nothing except that hand, which continually rested on the horse's mane.

Meanwhile we reached the cross at the end of the linden trees. Selim began to bid everyone good-night. He kissed the hand of Madame d'Yves and wanted to kiss Hania's also, but she would not allow it and glanced at me as if afraid. But when Selim had already mounted his horse, she approached him and spoke. In the light of the moon, unobstructed in that place by the lindens, I saw her eyes raised to Selim's and the sweet expression on her face.

"Do not forget Master Henryk," she said. "We will always entertain ourselves and sing together—meanwhile, good-night!"

Then she gave him her hand, after which she and the older people started on their way back, while Selim and I headed toward the meadows.

For some time we rode in silence along an open treeless road. It was so bright about us that one could count the needles on the low juniper bushes growing by the road. Occasionally the horses snorted or a stirrup struck against a stirrup. I glanced at Selim; he was sunk in thought, and he let his eyes wander over the dark distance ahead of him. I had an overpowering desire to speak of Hania: I desperately needed to speak of her; I needed to relate my impressions of the day, to talk about Hania's every word, but I could not begin such a conversation with Selim, not matter what. But Selim began it first. Suddenly, from neither here nor there, he leaned toward me and, embracing my neck, kissed me on the cheek and cried:

"Ah, my Henryk! What a charming and beautiful girl your Hania is! The devil take Jozia!"

This exclamation chilled me like a sudden breath of a winter wind. I did not say anything, but removed Selim's arm from my neck, and pushing him away coldly, I rode on in silence. My action unsettled him, and he grew silent also. After a while, turning to me, he said:

"Are you angry about something?"

"You are a child!"

"Perhaps you are jealous?"

I reined in my horse.

"Good-night, Selim!"

It was evident that he had no desire to bid me farewell just yet, but none the less he stretched out his hand mechanically for a handshake. Then he opened his mouth as if to say something, but at that moment I turned my horse about quickly and trotted toward home.

"Good-night!" Selim cried out after me.

He stood a while longer in the same spot, then slowly rode away.

Slackening my speed, I rode at a walk. The night was beautiful, calm and warm; the meadows, covered with dew, seemed like expansive lakes. I heard the voices of corncrakes coming from the meadows, and a bittern was calling out in the distant reeds. I raised my eyes to the vast starry sky. I wanted to pray and to cry.

Suddenly I heard hoofbeats behind me. I looked around. It was Selim. He caught up to me and then, blocking my way, said in an emotional voice:

"Henryk! I've come back because something is the matter with you. At first I thought: 'If he is angry, let him be angry!' But then I felt sorry for you. I have to know. Tell me what is wrong. Perhaps I spoke too much with Hania? Perhaps you are in love with her? Henryk?"

I felt a lump in my throat and could not say anything for the time being. If only I had followed my first inspiration and thrown myself on this fellow's honest breast and had a good cry and confessed everything! Ah! I have mentioned already that whenever it came time for me to reveal my heart in response to someone else's sincere outpouring, a kind of irresistible, perverse pride, which should have been broken like a stone with a pickaxe, froze my heart and held back the words on my lips. How many times has my happiness been ruined by that pride, how many times have I regretted it later! And yet I could never resist it in the first moment.

Selim had said, "I felt sorry for you." So, he took pity on me. That alone sufficed to keep my mouth shut.

Therefore I was silent, while he looked at me with his angelic eyes and spoke with a tone of entreaty and repentance in his voice:

"Henryk! Perhaps you love her? You see, I like her, but that's all. If you wish, I will not say another word to her. Tell me: are you in love with her? What do you have against me?"

"I am not in love and have nothing against you. I am a little weak. I was thrown from a horse; I got knocked about a bit. I am not at all in love—I only fell from a horse! Good-night!"

"Henryk! Henryk!"

"I repeat, I was thrown from a horse."

We parted again. Selim kissed me good-bye and rode away more at peace, for, indeed, it was quite possible that my fall would have such an effect on me. I remained alone, my heart constrained, in deep sorrow, tears in my eyes, a lump in my throat. I was moved by Selim's kindness, angry with myself, and cursing myself for having pushed him away. I let the horse go at a gallop, and soon I was before the manor.

The windows of the parlor were lit up; the sound of the piano came through them. I gave the horse to Franek and entered the room. Hania was playing a song unfamiliar to me, falsifying the melody with all of a dilettante's confidence, for she had begun to learn it not too long ago, but well enough so as to enrapture my spirit, which was much more in love than it was musical. When I entered, she smiled at me without stopping to play, while I threw myself into an armchair standing opposite the piano and began to look at her. Above the music-rack one could see her serene forehead and her symmetrically outlined brows. Her eyelashes were cast downward, for she was looking at her fingers. She played on for some time, then stopped and, raising her eyes to me, said in a gentle, caressing voice:

"Master Henryk?"

"What, Hania?"

"I wanted to ask you something.... Aha! Have you invited Selim over for tomorrow?"

"No. Father wishes us to go to Ustrzycki Hall tomorrow, for a package has come from mother for Lady Ustrzycki."

Hania was silent and struck a few soft chords; but it was evident that she did so only mechanically, while thinking of something else, for after a while she raised her eyes to me again:

"Master Henryk?"

"What, Hania?"

"I wanted to ask you about something.... Aha! Is that Jozia in Warsaw very pretty?"

That was enough! Anger mixed with bitterness rankled my heart. I approached the piano quickly, and my lips were trembling when I answered:

"Not prettier than you. Don't worry! You may use your charms on Selim without hesitation."

Hania was so shocked that she rose from the piano stool. A burning blush of offence covered her cheeks.

"Master Henryk! what are you saying?"

"What you are contemplating."

I grabbed my hat, bowed to her and left the room.

VII

It is easy to guess how I passed the night after such a day. After I had lain down in bed, I asked myself above all what had happened, and why I had behaved so badly during the day. The answer was simple. Nothing had happened; that is, I could not reproach either Selim or Hania with anything which might not be explained by the friendliness which bound us all equally, or by natural curiosity, or by mutual sympathy. That Selim liked Hania, and she him was more than certain; but what right had I to be angered because of that and destroy everyone's peace in the process? They were not at fault, but I. This thought should have calmed me, but it had the opposite effect. No matter how I explained their relations, no matter how much I repeated to myself that nothing had really happened, no matter how clearly I saw that I had acted unjustly to both, I still sensed a vague danger looming over me; and it was precisely its vagueness, the fact that it could not be put in the form of a reproach against Mirza or Hania, that made it all the more galling. Besides this, I thought of one other thing. Though I had no right to reproach them, I had still sufficient reason to be uneasy. These were all subtleties, matters intangible for the most part, in which my simple, unsophisticated mind became entangled and tormented, as if in a dark wilderness. Quite simply, I felt tired and broken, like a man who has made a long journey. Yet one more thought, the worst and most painful one, kept on coming back to me with persistence: that it was I, precisely I, who through my jealousy and tactlessness was forcing those two persons toward each other. Oh, how much awareness I had already, though I had no experience in these matters at all! Yet such things can be surmised. What is more, I knew that amid all these wrong paths, I would go not where I wished to go, but would be led by feelings and circumstances, perhaps temporary and insignificant, but important, nevertheless, and on which a person's happiness can depend. As for me, I was very unhappy; and if my sufferings seem trivial to some, I will say this, that the severity of any misery depends not on what it is in itself but on how one experiences it.

And yet nothing had happened! Yes, so far nothing had happened! Lying in bed, I repeated this to myself until my thoughts slowly began to grow dim, to scatter and fall into the usual disorder of sleep. Various strange elements intruded themselves upon me. My father's narratives, the persons and events in those narratives were interwoven with Selim, with Hania and with my love. Perhaps I had a slight fever, the more so since I had taken a fall. The wick of the burnt candle dropped suddenly into the candlestick: it grew dark, then a blue flame shot up, and it became smaller, until finally the expiring light shone brightly again before dying out. It must have been late; the cocks were crowing outside the window. I fell into a heavy and unhealthy sleep, out of which I woke up none too quickly.

I slept past the breakfast hour and also past the chance of seeing Hania before dinner, for she had lessons with Madame d'Yves until two. But at least I had a long sleep, and so gained courage, and did not look upon the world so bleakly. "I will be kind and courteous to Hania to make up for yesterday's gruffness," I thought. Meanwhile I had not foreseen one thing: namely, that my last words had not only annoyed but offended her. When she came down to dinner with Madame d'Yves, I hurried toward her; but suddenly, as if someone had poured cold water over me, I withdrew again into myself, taking my warm cordiality with me, not because I wanted to, but because I was spurned. Hania gave me a very polite, "Good-day," but so coldly that any desire I had for being kind and courteous left me at once. Then Hania sat down near Madame d'Yves, and throughout dinner she seemed not to notice my existence at all. I confess that at that point that existence seemed so wretched and pitiful in my eyes that if any man had offered two cents for it I would have told him that he was overpaying. What was I to do, though? A desire for defiance was awakened in me, and I determined to pay Hania in kind—a strange role in regard to someone whom one loves above everything. I could truly say, "My lips blaspheme, but my heart weeps!"

During the whole dinner we did not speak directly to each other once, only through the medium of others. For example, when Hania told Madame d'Yves that there would be rain toward the evening, I said, likewise to Madame d'Yves, and not to Hania, that there would be no rain. This mutual sulking and bantering even had a certain irritating charm for me. "I am curious to know, my young lady," I thought, "how we will treat each other at Ustrzycki Hall, for we must go there after all." I decided that at the manor I would ask her something purposely in the presence of others; she would have to answer me—and the ice would be broken! I promised myself much from this visit. True, Madame d'Yves would accompany us—but what of it? At present I was far more concerned that no one at the table should notice our anger. Should anyone notice it, I thought, that person would ask if we were angry, and right away everything would come out in the open! At the very thought of this, my face turned red, and fear pressed my heart. But, imagine! I saw that Hania feared this much less than I; furthermore, she saw my fear, and in her heart was amused by it. That made me feel humiliated, but for the time being there was nothing I could do. Ustrzycki Hall was waiting for me, so I latched onto that thought as my one salvation.

But apparently Hania was thinking of this too, for after dinner, when she brought black coffee to my father, she kissed his hand and said:

"If you please, sir, I would prefer not to go to Ustrzycki Hall."

Ah, what a scoundrel, what a rogue, that dear Hania was! My father, who was a little deaf, did not hear her clearly at first. Kissing her on the forehead, he asked:

"What do you want, my little lady?"

"I have one request."

"What is it?"

"That I not go to Ustrzycki Hall."

"But why? Are you ill?"

"If she says that she is ill," I thought, "all is lost, the more so since my father is in a good mood."

But Hania never lied, even innocently; and that's why, instead of laying the blame on a headache, she answered:

"I am well, but I have no desire to go."

"Ah! then you will go, for there is need of you to go."

Hania curtsied and left without saying a word. As for me, I was absolutely delighted, and had it been proper, I would have gladly pointed the finger of scorn at her.

After a while, when we were alone with my father, I asked him why he ordered Hania to go.

"I want the neighbors to get used to thinking of her as our relative. In going to the Ustrzyckis, Hania does this to some degree in the name of your mother. Do you understand?"

Not only did I understand, but I wanted to kiss my considerate father for this idea.

We were to start at five o'clock. While Hania and Madame d'Yves were getting dressed upstairs, I gave orders to harness horses to a light carriage for two persons, for I intended to go on horseback. It was several good miles to Ustrzycki Hall, so with the splendid weather we had a most pleasant drive ahead of us. When Hania came down—dressed in black, it is true, but with care and even elegance, for such was my father's wish—I could not take my eyes from her. She looked so beautiful that I felt my heart soften immediately, and my desire for resistance and artificial coldness flew by the wayside. But my queen passed me by in real regal fashion. She did not even look at me, though I had freshened up as best as I could. Incidentally, she was in a somewhat sullen mood, for she really had no desire to go, though not from a wish to annoy me, but from other, more reasonable causes, which I discovered later.

Punctually at five o'clock I mounted my horse, the ladies took their seats in the carriage, and we started off. During the journey I rode at Hania's side, wanting by all possible means to capture her attention. She looked at me once when my horse reared, and measured me with a calm eye from head to foot. I detected a faint smile, which cheered me up considerably; but then she turned to Madame d'Yves and began to talk with her in such a manner that excluded me from the conversation.

Finally we arrived at Ustrzycki Hall, where we found Selim. Lady Ustrzycki was not at home, but Lord Ustrzycki was present, along with his two daughters—Lola, a pretty, rather coquettish auburn-haired girl the same age as Hania, and her younger sister Marynia, a child yet. Also present were two governesses—one French, the other German. After the initial greetings were over, the ladies went straight to the garden for strawberries, while

Lord Ustrzycki took Selim and me to show us his new weapons and new hunting dogs, used for wild boars, which he had brought at great expense. I have mentioned already that Lord Ustrzycki was the most passionate hunter in the whole region, and moreover a very kind man, equally helpful as he was rich. He had only one annoying fault, which made him rather a bore: he laughed all the time, and after a few words he would slap his stomach with his hands and repeat, "What a farce, my good sirs! What's it called, eh?" Because of this people referred to him as "Neighbor Farce" or "Neighbor What's-it-called."

Well, Neighbor Farce took us to the kennel, not considering that perhaps we preferred a hundred times more to be with the ladies in the garden. We listened patiently for some time to his stories, until finally I mentioned that I had to tell Madame d'Yves something, while Selim said straight out:

"All this is very well, good sir. The dogs are wonderful, but what is to be done if both of us have a greater desire to go to the young ladies?"

Lord Ustrzycki slapped his stomach.

"Ah, what a farce, my good sirs! What's it called, eh? Well, go then; I will go with you."

And we went. It quickly became evident, however, that my hopes were for naught. Hania, who somehow kept apart from her companions, continued to ignore me and, perhaps purposely, occupied herself with Selim. Besides, it fell upon me to entertain Lady Lola. What I talked about with her, how I avoided talking nonsense and how I answered her polite questions, I do not know, for I followed Selim and Hania with my eyes all the time, catching their words, observing their looks and gestures. Selim did not notice me, but Hania did, and on purpose lowered her voice or looked with a certain coquettishness on her companion, who permitted himself to be carried away by that flood of favor. "Just you wait, Hania," I thought. "You are doing this out of spite, so I will do the same to you." And I turned to Lady Lola. I forgot to mention that Lady Lola had a special weakness for me, which she showed quite clearly. I began to be nice to her. I joked and laughed, though I wanted to cry instead, and Lola looked at me radiantly with her moist, dark-blue eyes, and began to fall into a romantic frame of mind.

Ah, if she had known how I detested her at that moment! But I was so absorbed in my role that I even did something thoroughly dishonorable. When Lady Lola, in the course of conversation, made some malicious remark about Selim and Hania, though in my soul I shook with rage, I did not answer her as I should have done but merely smiled rather stupidly and dismissed her in silence.

We spent about an hour in this fashion. Then afternoon tea was served under a weeping chestnut, which, touching the earth with the tips of its branches, formed, as it were, a green dome above our heads. It was then that I realized that Hania had far better reasons for not wanting to visit Ustrzycki Hall than just a disinclination for being in my presence.

The matter was simple. Madame d'Yves, as a descendant of an ancient noble French house, and being better educated than other governesses, considered herself superior to the Frenchwoman at Ustrzycki Hall, and especially superior to the German, while these two, in turn, thought themselves better than Hania because her grandfather had been a servant. But the well-bred Madame d'Yves did not exhibit this in front of them, while they clearly slighted Hania, even to the point of rudeness. These were typical female squabbles and vanities, but I could not allow my dear Hania, who was worth a hundred times more than all of Ustrzycki Hall, to be their victim. Hania endured their disrespect with tact and sweetness, doing honor to her character, but was still pained by it. Had Lady Ustrzycki been present, nothing of the kind would have ever happened, but at that moment both governesses took advantage of their golden opportunity. As soon as Selim sat near Hania, whispers and jests began, in which even Lady Lola took part, since she was jealous of Hania's beauty. I rebuffed those taunts several times sharply, perhaps even too sharply; but soon, to my consternation, Selim took my place. I saw a flash of anger shoot across his brow, but he quickly gained control over himself and, cooled down, turned a sneering glance on the governesses. Sharp, witty and possessing a ready tongue as few others at his age, he soon flustered them to such a degree that they did not know what to do with themselves. Madame d'Yves aided him with her noble bearing, as did I, who would have gladly given the two foreign women a sound thrashing. Lady Lola, not wanting to alienate me, came over to our side also and, though insincerely, showed Hania a kindness twofold greater than usual. In a word, our victory was complete, but unfortunately, and to my great mortification, the chief merit this time fell on Selim also. Hania, who, notwithstanding all her tact, could hardly restrain tears from coming to her eyes, began to look at Selim as her savior, with thankfulness and admiration. And so when we rose from the table and began to walk again through the garden in pairs, I heard her whisper to him in an emotional voice, as she leaned toward him:

"Selim! I am very—"

And she stopped suddenly, for she was afraid of weeping, as her emotion held sway over her.

"Lady Hania! let us not talk about that. Do not be concerned about it and—do not be troubled."

"You see how difficult it is for me to speak of this, but I wish to thank you."

"For what, Lady Hania? For what? I cannot stand to see tears in your eyes. For you I would gladly—"

Now it was his turn not to finish, for he could not find the correct expression, or perhaps he noticed in time that he allowed himself to be too carried away by the feelings which he kept hidden in his heart; so, confused, he turned away his face not to let his emotion be seen and was silent.

Hania looked at him with eyes bright from tears, while I did not ask what had happened.

I loved Hania with all the power of a youthful soul; I deified her; I loved her with a love which is only found in heaven. I loved her figure, her eyes, every strand of her hair, the sound of her voice. I loved every dress she possessed, the air which she breathed. And that love pervaded me through and through; it was not only in my heart but in my whole being. I lived only for it and through it. It flowed in me as my blood; it radiated from me as the warmth of my body. For others something else might exist besides love; for me the whole world existed in love; there was nothing beyond it. To the world I was blind, deaf and foolish, for my reason and senses were taken up by that one feeling. I felt that I was burning like a lighted torch, and that that flame was devouring me and that I was dying. What was that love? A mighty voice, a mighty voice from the soul that called out to another soul, "My goddess, my sacred one, my love, hear me!" I did not ask what had happened, for I understood that it was not to me, not to me, that Hania was answering that sincere entreaty. In the midst of indifferent people, a man yearning for love wanders as in a forest, and he shouts and calls as in a forest, waiting to see if some sympathetic voice will answer him. That was also why I did not ask what had happened, for through my own love and my own useless shouting, I sensed and heard two voices in sympathy: Selim's and Hania's. They were calling to each other with their hearts, and they did not know that I heard this calling too. One was to the other as a forest echo, and one followed the other as an echo follows a voice. And what could I do against this inevitability which they could call happiness—and I a tragedy? What could I do against the laws of nature, against the fatal logic of things? How could I win Hania's heart when some irresistible power was impelling it in another direction?

I separated myself from the company and sat on a garden bench, and thoughts like these flew around in my head like flocks of agitated birds. A frenzy of despair and suffering seized me. I felt that in the midst of my family, in the midst of well-wishing hearts, I was very much alone. The whole world seemed a barren desert, and the heaven above was so indifferent to the injustice inflicted on me that one thought above all others prevailed, consumed everything and covered me with its gloomy peace. Death. Only in death would there be an escape from this vicious circle, and an end to suffering, and the denouement of this entire sad comedy, and a severing of all the painful knots binding the heart, and repose after torture—ah, that repose for which I was so thirsty, a dark repose, a repose of nothingness, yet calm and eternal!

I felt like someone overcome by tears, suffering and sleepiness. If I could only sleep, sleep!—I thought—at any price, even at the price of my life. Then from that calm immense blue of heaven to which my former faith of childhood had fled, one more thought flew to me like a bird to settle in my mind. That thought was contained in the brief words: But what if? This was a new circle in which I became entangled in through the force of inexorable necessity. Oh, I suffered greatly, but there from the neighboring alley joyous words reached me, or soft, monosyllabic words. Around me was the perfume of flowers; on the trees birds twittered as they settled them-

102 The Little Trilogy

selves to rest; above me hung the clear sky, ruddy with the evening twilight. All was at peace, all was happy. I alone, in pain and with clenched teeth, desired to die amid this full flush of life.

Suddenly I gave a start: a woman's dress rustled before me. I glanced up. It was Lady Lola. There was a gentle and sweet look about her. She looked at me with sympathy and perhaps with more than sympathy. In the evening light and among the shadows cast by the trees, she seemed pale; her abundant tresses, streaming, as if by chance, fell over her shoulders.

At that moment I did not feel any hatred toward her. "Oh, my one compassionate soul," I thought, "have you come to console me?"

"Master Henryk, you seem sad, perhaps even in pain?"

"Oh, yes! I am suffering," I burst out; and seizing her hand, I placed it to my burning forehead, then I kissed it impetuously and ran off.

"Master Henryk!" she cried after me, in a low voice.

At the same time, at the turn in the path, appeared Selim and Hania. Both had seen my outburst. They had seen me kiss and press Lola's hand to my forehead. They had both seen everything, so, smiling, they exchanged glances, as if saying to each other: "We understand what that means."

Meanwhile the time had arrived to go home. Immediately beyond the gate Selim's road lay in another direction, yet I feared that he might wish to accompany us, so I mounted in haste and said aloud that it was late and that we had to leave. Upon our farewells, I received from Lady Lola an unusually intense pressure from her hand, to which I did not respond, and we moved off.

Selim made a turn immediately after we passed the gate, but he did, for the first time, kiss Hania's hand in good-night, and Hania did not forbid it.

She ceased to ignore me. Her mood was too mild for

her to remember the earlier angers, but I interpreted her mood in the worst possible way.

Madame d'Yves fell asleep after a few moments and began to sway in all directions. I looked at Hania; she was not asleep. Her eyes were opened wide and twinkling, as if from happiness.

She did not break the silence; she was evidently too much occupied with her own thoughts. Only when we were near the house did she look at me, and seeing that I was plunged in deep thought, she asked:

"What are you thinking about so? Lola?"

I did not say a word; I only gritted my teeth and thought: "Gnaw, gnaw away at me if it gives you pleasure, but you will not get a groan from me."

But, in reality, Hania did not even dream of gnawing me. She asked, for she had a right to ask.

Surprised at my silence, she repeated the question one more time. Again I said nothing. She thought, therefore, that this was a continuation of the sulking which had started in the morning and likewise became silent.

VIII

One morning, several days later, the ruddy light of early dawn came in through a heart cut in the window-shutter and woke me up. Shortly afterward someone knocked on the shutter, and in the rosy opening appeared, not the face of Mickiewicz's Zosia, who in a similar manner had awakened Tadeusz, nor of my Hania either, but the moustached face of Wach, the forester.

"Lord!" his deep voice boomed.

"What?"

"Wolves are chasing a she-wolf in the Pohorowa thickets. We were to lure them."

"Just a moment!"

I dressed, took my gun and hunter's knife, and went

out. Wach was waiting for me outside, all wet from the morning dew, and over his shoulder he had his gun, a long, rusty single-barreled firearm, from which, however, he never missed. It was early morning; the sun had not yet risen, nor had the people gone out to work, nor the cattle to pasture. In the east the sky was hued with the colors of blue, pink and gold, while in the west it was a deep grey. The old man hurried along.

"I have a horse and cart," he said. "We'll ride to the hollows."

We sat down in the cart and drove off. Just beyond the barns a hare sprang out of the oat fields, ran across our front and jumped into the meadow, marking its dew-silvered surface with dark tracks.

"A hare crossed our path!" said the old forester. "Touch wood!" Then he added: "It's late already. The ground will soon have shadows."

This meant that the sun would rise before long, for objects cast no shadows in the light of dawn.

"Is the hunting bad when there are shadows?"

"With long ones, so-so; but with short ones—useless!"

In hunter's language this meant that the later the hour, the worse the hunting, for, as is known, the closer one gets to midday, the shorter the shadows.

"Where will we begin?" I asked.

"At the hollows, right in the Pohorowa thickets."

The Pohorowa thickets were a part of a very dense forest, where one found "the hollows"—that is, holes made under the roots of old trees overthrown by storms.

"Do you think the luring will succeed, Wach?"

"I'll play the part of a she-wolf, and some wolf will come out."

"But he may not."

"Oh, he'll come out!"

We left the horse and cart at Wach's cottage, and then

continued on foot. After half an hour's walk, when the sun had begun to rise, we sat down in a hollow.

All around us were impenetrable thickets and, here and there, a few enormous trees, while the hole we were in was so deep that we could hide our heads in it.

"Now, back to back," muttered Wach.

We sat back to back, so that above the surface of the ground only the top of our heads and the barrels of our rifles appeared.

"Get ready!" said Wach. "I'm going to start."

Placing two fingers along his lips and modulating a drawn-out tone, Wach began to imitate a she-bitch—that is, to howl like a she-wolf when she entices the male.

"Listen!"

And he placed his ear to the ground.

I heard nothing, but Wach raised his head and whispered: "There is game, but over two miles away."

Then he waited a quarter of an hour, and again put his fingers to his lips and howled. The plaintive but ominous sound shot through the thickets and flew far, far away over the damp earth, rebounding from pine to pine.

Wach put his ear to the ground again.

"Game! but not farther than half a verst away."

Even I could now hear a distant echo of howling, still very far away and barely audible, but still discernible among the rustling of the leaves.

"From which direction will the wolf come out?" I asked.

"From yours, lord."

Wach howled a third time; now the other howling answered close-by. I grasped my rifle more firmly, while the both of us held our breaths. A breeze shook dewdrops from hazel-woods, and they fell pattering on the leaves; otherwise, the silence was immense. From afar, from the other edge of the forest, came the tooting of a wood grouse.

Suddenly, some two hundred yards distant, something appeared in the thickets. The juniper bushes shook quickly, and from among the dark needles emerged a grey triangular head with pointed ears and red eyes. I could not shoot, for the distance was too great, so I waited patiently, though my heart was pounding. Soon the whole beast emerged from the juniper bushes, and with a few short springs ran up toward the hole, smelling the ground carefully about himself. At one hundred yards the wolf stopped and pricked his ears, as if sensing something. I saw that he would not come closer, and I pulled the trigger.

The report of the rifle was mingled with the pained yelping of the wolf. I sprang out of the hollow, Wach after me, but we did not find the wolf at the place where I shot him. Wach, however, examined the spot carefully where the dew was rubbed away on the ground.

"He's bleeding!" he exclaimed.

Indeed, there were traces of blood on the grass.

"You didn't miss, though it was far! He's bleeding. Oh, yes, he is! We have to go after him."

And so we went. Here and there we came upon trampled grass and more traces of blood; it was clear that the wounded wolf was resting from time to time. Meanwhile an hour passed in the woods and thickets, then another. The sun was high now. We had gone over an immense part of the forest without finding anything except the wolf's tracks, which at times, though, disappeared altogether. Then we came to the edge of the forest; the tracks continued for about two versts more through a field toward the pond and finally disappeared in marshes overgrown with reeds and rushes. It was impossible to go farther without a dog.

"He will stay there," said Wach. "I'll find him tomorrow." Then we turned back.

Soon I stopped to think of the wolf, and of Wach, and of the rather unfortunate result of the hunt, and instead I returned to my usual circle of suffering. When we were approaching the forest, a hare sprang up almost from under my feet, and I, awakened from my meditations, merely trembled instead of shooting it.

"Ah, lord!" cried Wach in indignation, "I would shoot my own brother if he jumped up that way in front of me."

I merely laughed and went on in silence. While crossing the forest road, the so-called "auntie's way," which led to the road that went to Chorzel, I saw on the wet ground fresh tracks of a shodden horse.

"Wach, do you know whose tracks these are?" I asked.

"It seems to me that they are made by the young lord from Chorzel on his way to the master's manor," he replied.

"Then I will go to the manor also!" I answered. "Farewell, Wach!"

Wach requested somewhat timidly that I stop by his cottage, which was not far away, for a bite to eat. I saw that if I refused I would cause him great pain, but still I refused, promising, however, to come the following morning. I did not want to leave Selim and Hania alone without my presence. During the five days which had passed since the visit to Ustrzycki Hall, Selim had visited our home almost every day. The mutual sympathy both had for each other blossomed quickly before my very eyes. But I never lost sight of them, and today was the first time that an opportunity presented itself for them to be alone with each other for any greater length of time. "What if," I thought, "they will declare their love for each other?" And I felt that I was growing pale as one who loses all hope.

I feared this as if it were some great disaster, an unavoidable sentence of death which one knows is coming but which one delays as long as possible.

Upon reaching home, I met Father Ludwik in the courtyard; he had a bag on his head and a wire net protecting his face. He was going to the beehives.

"Is Selim here, Father Ludwik?" I asked.

"He is. He arrived about an hour and a half ago."

My heart trembled uneasily.

"And where will I find him?"

"He went to the pond with Hania and Evunia."

I ran quickly to the garden and to the edge of the pond where the boats were. Indeed, one of the largest was missing. I surveyed the pond, but at first I could see nothing. I surmised that Selim must have turned right, toward the alder trees, and consequently the boat and those in it were concealed by the reeds growing along the bank. I seized an oar and, jumping into a small one-seat boat, pushed out quietly into the pond, keeping to the reeds so that I would not be seen while spying on them.

And I soon saw them. On a wide part of the pond free of reeds stood a motionless boat, its oars hanging. At one end sat my little sister, Evunia, turned away from Hania and Selim; at the other end were the two. Evunia, bent over the boat, was striking the water joyously with her hands and completely occupied with this activity, while Selim and Hania, almost leaning shoulder to shoulder, seemed absorbed in conversation. Not the slightest breeze rippled the clear blue surface; and the boat, Evunia, Hania and Selim were reflected in it as in a mirror, calm and motionless.

That was a very pretty little picture perhaps, but at the sight of it the blood rushed to my head. I understood everything. They had taken Evunia with them, for the child could not be in their way or understand any declarations of love. They had taken her for appearance' sake.

"It's happened!" I thought. "It's happened!" rustled the reeds. "It's happened!" mumbled the ripples, striking the side of my boat. And it grew dark before my eyes. I felt cold and then hot. I felt a deathly pallor covering my face! "You've lost Hania! you've lost her!" cried voices above me and within me. Then I heard the same voices crying, "Jesus, Mary!" And then these voices went on: "Push up nearer, hide in the reeds—you will see more!" I obeyed and edged closer with the boat, as quiet as a cat. But even at that distance I could not hear their conversation, though I saw them more clearly. They were sitting side by side on one bench, but not holding each other's hands; Selim was turned toward Hania. For a moment I thought that he was kneeling before her, but in this I was mistaken. He was turned toward her and was looking at her entreatingly, while she was not looking at him but seemed to be glancing everywhere else uneasily, before raising her eyes to the sky. I saw that she was confused; I saw that he was pleading. Finally I saw that he clasped his hands before her, as she slowly, slowly turned her head and eyes toward him, as she began to lean toward him, until suddenly, coming to her senses, she gave a start and withdrew to the very edge of the boat. He seized her hand at that moment, as if fearing that she might fall into the water. I saw that he did not let go of her hand.

After that I saw nothing, for a cloud covered my eyes. I let the oar drop out of my hand, and I fell to the bottom of the boat. "O God, help me! help me" I cried out in my soul; "they are killing me!" I gasped for air. Oh, how I loved her, and how unhappy I was! Lying on the bottom of the boat and tearing my clothing from rage, I felt all the helplessness of that rage. Yes, I was helpless, helpless as an athlete with bound hands, for what could I do? I could kill Selim, myself; I could drive my boat against theirs and sink both in the water; but I could not tear from Hania's heart her love for Selim and take it for myself alone!

Ah, that feeling of powerless rage, that conviction that there was no help, seemed almost worse at that moment than at any other! I had always been ashamed to cry, even before myself. If suffering squeezed tears from my eyes by force, pride kept them back with a force not inferior. But now my helpless rage gave way to despair, rending my heart, and in the presence of my loneliness, in the presence of that boat with that loving couple, whose image was reflected in the water, in the presence of that calm sky and those reeds rustling plaintively above my head, in the presence of the silence beyond, and my unhappiness and misery, I burst into a great weeping, into one great flood of tears, and lying on my back with my hands pressed over my face, I almost wailed with great, inexpressible sorrow.

Then I became weak. A numbness came over me. I almost stopped thinking. The ends of my fingers and toes became cold. I grew weaker and weaker. With my remaining thoughts it seemed that death and a great, icy calm were drawing near. It seemed that that dark queen of the grave was taking me into her arms, so I greeted her with a calm, glassy eye. "It's over!" I thought, and a great weight, as it were, fell from my chest.

But nothing was over. How long I lay on the bottom of the boat, I could not tell. At times light, fluffy clouds moved across the vault of the sky; at other times lapwings and cranes, chirping sadly, flew by in succession. The sun had risen high in the sky and burned strongly. The wind had gone down; the reeds had ceased to rustle. I woke up, as if from sleep, and looked around. The boat with Hania and Selim was no longer there. The silence, peace and delight which reigned in all of nature were in strange contrast to the sleepy torpor from which I had awakened a moment before. Everything about me was calm and smiling. Dark-sapphire crickets were sitting along the boat and on the leaves of water-lilies, which were as flat as plates; little grey birds flew about the reeds, twittering sweetly; here and there one could hear the busy buzzing of a bee that had wandered in over the water; sometimes from the rushes wild ducks were heard; teals led their young to a clear patch of water. Before my eyes, the bird kingdom drew aside the curtains concealing its daily life, but I ignored everything. My torpor had not passed. The day was sweltering, and I had a terrible headache, so, leaning over the boat, I took water into my hands and drank it with parched lips. That gave me back some strength. Grabbing the oar, I moved among the rushes toward home, inasmuch as it was late, and they must have been inquiring about me there.

Along the way I tried to calm myself. "If Selim and Hania have declared their love for each other," I thought, "it may be for the better. At least the cursed days of uncertainty would be over." Misfortune had raised its visor and stood before me with clear face. I knew it and must struggle with it. Strangely enough this thought began to have a certain painful charm for me. But I was still uncertain, and I resolved to query Evunia deftly, at least as far as was possible.

I reached home in time for dinner. I greeted Selim coldly and sat down at the table without saying a word. My father looked at me and called out:

"What's the matter with you—are you sick?"

"No. I'm just tired. I got up at three in the morning."

"What for?"

"I went with Wach to hunt wolves. I shot one. Later, I lay down to sleep, and now I have a slight headache."

"You should see yourself in the mirror."

Hania stopped eating for a moment and looked at me carefully.

"Perhaps yesterday's visit to Ustrzycki Hall has had an effect on you, Master Henryk," she said.

I looked her straight in the eye and asked her, almost sharply:

"What do you mean by that?"

Hania became confused and began to mutter some vague explanation. Selim came to her aid:

"Well, it is very natural. Whoever is in love looks haggard."

I began to look now at Hania, now at Selim, and replied slowly, clearly, stressing every syllable:

"I do not see that you are looking haggard, either you or Hania."

Both of their faces turned red. A moment of very awkward silence followed. I myself did not know whether I had gone too far. Luckily my father had not heard everything that was said, while Father Ludwik took it as the usual banter of young people.

"Oh, that is a wasp with a sting!" he cried, taking some snuff. "He really gave it to you! You'd better not start with him."

O God, how little that triumph comforted me, and how gladly I would have changed places with Selim!

After dinner, in passing through the parlor, I glanced into the mirror. In truth I did look like one of the undead. I had blue circles under my eyes, and my face was sunken. It seemed to me that I had turned amazingly ugly, but at that point it made no difference to me.

I went to find Evunia. Both of my little sisters had dined earlier and were now in the garden, where a gymnasium for children had been set up. Evunia was sitting carelessly on a wooden board hung by four ropes to a crossbeam. She was talking to herself and shaking the locks of her golden head from time to time as she swung her feet.

When she saw me, she laughed and stretched out her little hands. I took her hand and led her down the path.

Then I sat on a bench and, placing Evunia before me, asked:

"What has Evunia been doing all day?"

"Evunia went on a trip with her husband and Hania," answered the little girl boastfully.

Evunia called Selim her husband.

"And was Evunia good?"

"She was."

"Splendid! for good children always listen to what older people say and pay attention so that they can learn something. And does Evunia remember what Selim said to Hania?"

"I forgot."

"Eh, perhaps Evunia remembers something?"

"I forgot."

"You are not being a good girl! Let Evunia remember right away or I will not love Evunia."

The girl began to rub one eye with her fist, while she looked from under her brow with the other tearful eye; and frowning, as if to cry, the corners of her mouth turned down, she said in a quivering voice:

"I forgot."

What could the poor thing say? In truth, I thought myself foolish, and I became ashamed of having spoken with a duplicitous tongue to that innocent angel—asking about one thing but wishing to learn another. Besides, Evunia was the pet of the whole house, and my pet, so I did not wish to torment her any further. I kissed her on her cheek, stroked her hair and let her go. The girl ran immediately to the swing, and I walked off as well-informed as before, but still with the conviction in my heart that Selim and Hania had already declared their love for each other.

Toward evening Selim said to me:

"I will not see you for a week; I am going away."

"Where to?" I asked indifferently.

"My father wants me to visit my uncle in Szumna," he answered. "I have to amuse myself there about a week."

I glanced at Hania. This information made no impression on her. Evidently Selim had already informed her about the visit.

Instead, she smiled, raised her eyes from her work and looked at Selim somewhat playfully, somewhat contrariwise, after which she asked:

"Are you glad to be going?"

"As glad as a dog on a chain!" he answered quickly; but he caught himself in time, and seeing that Madame d'Yves, who could not endure anything trivial, was making a face, he added:

"I apologize for the expression. I love my uncle, but you see—it is nicer here—near Madame d'Yves."

Saying this, he cast a flirtatious glance at Madame d'Yves, which elicited general laughter, not excluding that of Madame d'Yves, who, though she was easily offended, had a special weakness for Selim. She took him gently by the ear and said with a kindly smile:

"Young man, I could be your mother!"

Selim kissed her hand, and there was harmony. But I thought to myself, what a difference between that Selim and me! If I had been the beneficiary of Hania's love, I would merely dream and gaze at the sky. There would be no joking around. But he laughs and jokes and is merry, as if nothing had happened.

Even when radiant with happiness, Selim was always joking and fooling around.

Right before he was about to leave, he said to me:

"Say, why don't you come with me?"

"I don't think so. I have no inclination to go."

Selim was struck by the cold tone of my response.

"You've become strange lately," he said. "I almost don't recognize you. But…"

"Go ahead."

"But everything is forgiven those who are in love."

"Unless they cross our path," I answered with the voice of a pitiless commander.

Selim shot me a glance as sharp as lightning, which pierced me to the bottom of my soul.

"What did you say?"

"I say that I will not go and, furthermore, that one does not forgive everything!"

Had it not been for the fact that all were present at this conversation, Selim certainly would have clarified the whole issue then and there. But I did not wish to make it clear until I had more positive proof. I saw, however, that my last words had disturbed Selim and alarmed Hania. He loitered about a while, putting off his departure under trivial pretexts, and then, choosing an appropriate moment, he said to me in a low voice:

"Mount a horse and go with me. I wish to speak to you."

"Another time," I answered aloud. "Today I feel somewhat weak."

IX

Selim did indeed go to his uncle, and he stayed there not a week, but ten days. The days passed sadly for us in Lithuania. Hania seemed to avoid me, and when she was in my presence she gazed at me with a measure of hidden fear. In truth, I had no intention of speaking sincerely with her about anything, for pride stopped the words on my lips; and she, I know not why, so arranged things that we were never alone even for a second. Besides, she seemed to really miss Selim. She wasted away to the point of becoming thin, while I looked at her yearning with distress, and thought, "This is no passing fancy of a girl, but, unfortunately, a genuine, deep feeling!"

I myself was irritable, morose and sad. In vain did my father, Father Ludwik and Madame d'Yves ask what was troubling me. Was I sick? I answered in the negative; their concern simply annoyed me. I spent my days alone, either on horseback, in the woods or in a boat among the rushes. I lived like a savage. Once I spent a whole night in a forest, with a rifle and a dog, before a fire which I had kindled. Sometimes I spent half a day with our shepherd, who was a healer and who had grown wild through continual solitude. He was always collecting various herbs and testing their properties, and he initiated me into the fantastic world of witchcraft and superstitions. Who would have believed how I behaved during this time? But there were moments when I missed Selim and my "circles of suffering," as I typically called them.

One day the idea came to me of visiting the elder Mirza in Chorzel. The old man, captivated that I visited him for his own sake, received me with open arms. But I went there for another reason. I wanted to look at the eyes of that terrible Mirza, that colonel of the light horse from Sobieski's time, whose portrait hung on the wall. And when I looked at those sinister eyes, which stared at one wherever one stood, I recollected my own ancestors, whose counterfeits hung at our home in the parlor; they were equally stern and iron-like.

Under the influence of such impressions, my mind reached a state of strange exultation. Loneliness, the silence of night, life with nature—all these should have had a soothing effect; but I carried within me a poisoned arrow, as it were. At times I surrendered to dreams, which worsened my condition. More than once, while lying in some remote corner of the forest or in a boat among the rushes, I imagined that I was in Hania's room, kneeling in front of her and kissing her feet, her hands, her dress, as I called her by the most loving names, until finally she would place her divine hands on my feverish forehead and say: "You have suffered enough; let us forget everything that has happened! It was just a bad dream! I love you, Henryk!" But then came the awakening and grey reality, and a future as gloomy as a cloudy day, a future the more terrible because it would be without her, to the end of my days. I became more and more unsociable, and avoided people, including my father, Father Ludwik and Madame d'Yves. Kazio, with his boyish talkativeness, his curiosity, his eternal laughter and endless pranks, annoyed me to the highest degree.

And yet those honest people tried to divert me, and they suffered in secret over my condition, not knowing how to explain it. Hania, whether she suspected something or not—for she had strong reason to believe that I was in love with Lola Ustrzycki—did what she could to cheer me up. But I was so surly even toward her that she could not free herself of a certain fear when talking to me. My father, yes, even my father, who was usually stern and despotic, strove to divert me and interest me in anything whatsoever, and at the same time to examine me. More than once, he began a conversation which, he supposed, would be of interest to me. One day after dinner we went out to the courtyard, and he said, studying my face:

"I've wanted to ask you about something for a while. Do you not think that Selim is circling a little too much about Hania?"

Normally I would have become confused and let myself be caught, as they say, in the very act. But I was in such a state of mind that I did not betray by one twitch the effect my father's words had on me, and replied calmly:

"No, I know that he is not."

It piqued me that my father took part in these things.

I felt that, since the affair touched me alone, I alone should decide it.

"Can you vouch for that?" asked my father.

"Yes. Selim is in love with some schoolgirl in Warsaw."

"For, you see, you are Hania's guardian after all, and it is your duty to watch over her."

I knew that my father said this only to rouse my own love so that I would be occupied with something that would tear my thoughts away from that gloomy circle in which I seemed to be turning; but I answered, as if in spite, indifferently and gloomily:

"What kind of guardian am I! You were not present when old Nicholas died, so he left her in my care. But I am not her real guardian."

My father frowned. Seeing, however, that he could not straighten me out using this path, he chose another. He smiled under his grey moustache, winked in a soldierly fashion, took me gently by the ear and asked, half familiarly and half in irritation:

"Perhaps Hania has turned your own head? Speak up, my boy!"

"Hania? Not in the least. Ha, that would be amusing!"

I lied as if possessed, but it went more smoothly than I expected.

"Then perhaps it's Lola Ustrzycki? Eh?"

"Lola Ustrzycki! That coquette!"

My father became impatient.

"Then if you are not in love, why the devil do you walk around like a recruit after his first drill?"

"Do I know? Nothing is the matter with me."

But similar examinations, which in their solicitude my father, Father Ludwik and even Madame d'Yves did not spare me, tormented me and made me more and more impatient. Eventually my relations with them became unendurable. The least thing angered or annoyed me. Father Ludwik saw in this certain traits of a despotic character coming to the surface with age, and glancing at my father, he would laugh meaningfully and say: "The apple doesn't fall far from the tree!" But even he lost patience with all of this at times. Between my father and me arose several unpleasant incidents. Once at dinner, when during a dispute about nobility and democracy, I forgot myself to such a point that I declared that I should prefer a hundred times not to have been born a noble, my father ordered me to leave the room. The women wept, and everyone in the house walked around in a sour mood for two days. As for me, I was neither an aristocrat nor a democrat at that time; I was simply in love and unhappy. There was no place in me for principles, theories or social convictions; and if I fought in the name of some against others, I did so only through vexation, to spite it is unknown whom or why, just as, out of spite, I entered into religious disputes with Father Ludwik, which ended with the slamming of doors. In short, I made not only my existence miserable but everyone else's; that is why, when Selim returned after a ten-day absence, a weight seemed to fall from everyone's chest.

When he arrived, I was not at home, for I was riding about the surrounding areas on horseback. I returned only toward evening and went straight to the farm buildings, where a stable-boy said, while taking my horse:

"The lord from Chorzel has come."

At that moment Kazio ran up and repeated the same news.

"I know that already," I answered roughly. "Where is he now?"

"In the garden with Hania, I think. I will go and look for him."

We both started toward the garden, but Kazio ran ahead, while I walked slowly after him, purposely taking my time in greeting Selim.

I had not gone fifty steps when I saw, at the bend of
the alley, Kazio hastening back.

As soon as I saw him, Kazio, who was a great clown
and a joker, began to make strange gestures and grimaces
like a monkey; aside from this, his face was red, he held
his finger to his lips and laughed while trying not to
laugh. When he came up to me, he shot out in a low
voice:

"Henryk! Ha! ha! ha! Shhh!"

"What are you doing?" I asked, in a bad mood.

"Shhh! Upon my word! Ha! ha! Selim is kneeling
before Hania in the hop arbor. Upon my word!"

I seized him at once by the arms and dug my fingers
into them.

"Be quiet! Stay here! Not a word to anyone, do you
understand? Stay here! I will go myself; but be quiet, and
not a word to anyone, if my life means anything to you!"

Kazio, who had considered the whole affair a sort of
joke at first, seeing the corpse-like pallor of my face,
became alarmed and stood on the spot, his mouth open,
while I ran like a madman toward the arbor.

Crawling forward among the barberry bushes surrounding the arbor as quickly and silently as a snake, I
went right up to the very wall. The wall was a grille made
of thin pieces of wood, so I could hear and see everything. The repugnant role of an eavesdropper did not
seem repugnant to me at all. I pushed aside the leaves
delicately and strained my ears.

I heard Hania's low, suppressed whisper: "There is
someone nearby!"

"Those are leaves rustling on the branches," answered
Selim.

I looked at them through the green veil of the leaves.
Selim was not kneeling by Hania now, but was sitting
next to her on a low bench. She was as white as a sheet;
her eyes were closed, her head was inclined and resting

on his shoulder, while he had his arm about her waist and was nestling her to him with love and rapture.

"I love you, Hania! I love you! I love you!" he repeated in passionate whispers, and he sought her lips with his. She drew back, as if to ward off the kiss, but, despite this, their lips met and remained pressed and joined against each other for a long, long time—ah, it seemed to me for an eternity!

And then it seemed to me that all which they had to say to each other they said in that kiss. Some sort of shame checked their words. They had daring enough for kisses but not enough for speech. A deathlike silence reigned, and amid that silence I could hear their quick and passionate breathing.

I seized the wooden grating of the arbor, fearing that I might crush it into bits and pieces with that convulsive grasp. It grew dark before my eyes; I felt dizzy; the ground disappeared from under me. But even at the price of my life I wanted to hear what they were saying. So I mastered myself again, and catching the air with parched lips, my forehead pressed to the grating, I listened, counting every breath they drew.

The silence lasted for some time, until finally Hania whispered:

"Enough already, enough! I dare not look you in the eye. Let us leave this place!".

And turning her head aside, she tried to tear herself out of his arms.

"Oh, Hania!" cried Selim. "What is happening to me? I am so happy!"

"Let us go. Someone will come."

Selim sprang up, his eyes glittering, his nostrils distended.

"Let the whole world come," he said. "I love you, and I will say so right to anyone's face. I myself do not know how this happened. I struggled with myself. I suffered,

for it seemed to me that Henryk loved you, and you him.
But now I do not care. You love me, and so it is a
question of your happiness. Oh, Hania! Hania!"

And once again there was the sound of a kiss; after
which Hania began to speak in a soft and, as it were,
weakened voice:

"I believe you, Selim, I do; but I have many things to
tell you. They want to send me abroad to the Lady.
Madame d'Yves spoke of this to the Lord yesterday.
Madame d'Yves thinks that I am the cause of Master
Henryk's strange conduct. They think that he is in love
with me. I myself do not know if this is so. There are
times when it seems to me that he is. I do not understand
him. I fear him. I feel that he will stand in our way, that
he will separate us, but I—"

And she finished in a barely audible whisper:

"I love you so very, very much!"

"Listen, Hania," replied Selim. "No earthly power will
separate us. Should Henryk forbid me to come here, I
will write to you. I have someone who will always bring
a letter. I will come too, from the direction of the pond.
At dusk, go always to the garden. But you will not go
abroad. I will not permit it, as God is in heaven. Do not
say such things, Hania, or I will go mad. Oh, my beloved, my beloved!"

Seizing her hands, he pressed them passionately to his
lips. She sprang up quickly from the bench.

"I hear voices—they're coming!" she cried with fear.

Both went out of the arbor, though no one was coming and no one came. The evening rays of the sun cast
gleams of gold on them, but to me those gleams seemed
as red as blood. I walked slowly toward the house. Just
at the turn in the alley I met the waiting Kazio.

"They've left," he whispered. "I saw them. Tell me
what I am to do?"

"Shoot him in the head!" I burst out.

Kazio's cheeks turned red, and his eyes glowed.

"Very well!" he said.

"Stop! Don't be an idiot. Do nothing. Don't meddle in anything, and on your honor, Kazio, not a word to anyone about this! Leave everything to me. I will tell you when you are needed. But not a word to anyone!"

"No one will get a peep out of me, even if they kill me."

We went on in silence for a while. Kazio, taken up with the importance of the affair and sensing something serious afoot, toward which his heart was racing, glanced now and then at me with sparkling eyes, after which he said:

"Henryk?"

"What?"

We both whispered, though no one was listening.

"Will you have a duel with Selim?"

"I do not know. Perhaps."

Kazio stopped and suddenly threw his arms around my neck.

"Henryk! my dear brother! My one and only! Permit me to take your place. I can manage him. Let me try. Oh, please, Henryk, please!"

Kazio was simply dreaming of knightly deeds, but I felt the brother in him as never before; therefore I pressed him to my breast with all my strength and said:

"No, Kazio, I still don't know what will happen. Besides, he would not accept you as an opponent. I still don't know what will happen. Meanwhile have a horse saddled for me. I will go before he does, meet him on the road and have a talk with him. Meanwhile watch them both; but don't let them suspect that you know anything. Have the horse saddled."

"Will you take arms?"

"Kazio! Why, he has nothing on him. No! I only wish to speak to him. Don't worry. Go now to the stable."

Kazio sprang away immediately according to my instructions, while I returned slowly to the house. I was like a man struck on the head with a hammer. I can truly say that I did not know what to do, nor how to act. I just wanted to scream.

Until I was absolutely certain that I had lost Hania's heart, I desired to have that certainty. I thought that, come what may, a weight would fall off my chest, while now misfortune had raised its visor, and I was looking at its cold, icy face and stony eyes. A new uncertainty was born in my heart—not uncertainty as to my misfortune, but the hundred times worse feeling of my own helplessness: the uncertainty as to how I was to deal with my misfortune.

My heart was filled with gall, bitterness and rage. Voices of denial and self-sacrifice, which had formerly called out to my soul: "Renounce Hania for the sake of her happiness!—You should think of her happiness above all!—Sacrifice yourself!"—those voices were completely gone now. The angels of silent sadness, tenderness and tears had flown far away from me. I felt like an insect that had been trampled upon, but of which people had forgotten that it still possessed a sting. Up until now I had let myself be chased by misfortune as a wolf by dogs; but, pushed too far and finally cornered, I had begun like a wolf to show my teeth. A new active force, whose name was revenge, rose in my heart. I began to feel hatred for Selim and Hania. "I will lose my life," I thought, "I will lose everything that can be lost in this world, but I will not let those two be happy." Taken up with this thought, I grasped it like a condemned man grasps a crucifix. I had found a reason for living; the horizon brightened up before me. I breathed deeply, very deeply and freely, as never before! My scattered thoughts arranged themselves in order and were focused in one direction, an ominous one for Selim and Hania. When I reached the house, I was almost calm and cool. In the parlor were sitting Madame d'Yves, Father Ludwik, Hania, Selim and Kazio, who had already returned from the stable and was keeping close to the two.

"Is there a horse from me?" I asked Kazio.

"Yes."

"Will you ride with me?" asked Selim.

"I can. I'm going to the hay stacks to check for damage. Kazio, let me have your place."

Kazio got up, and I sat down near Selim and Hania, on the sofa by the window. I could not help but remember how we had sat like that so very long ago, right after Nicholas's death, while Selim told the Crimean tale about Sultan Harun and Lala the soothsayer. But at that time Hania, still small and with tears in her eyes, had rested her golden head on my breast and fallen asleep; now that same Hania, taking advantage of the darkness descending into the room, was pressing Selim's hand in secret. At that time a sweet feeling of friendship had joined all three of us; now love and hate were soon to contend with each other. But on the outside all was calm: the lovers were smiling at each other; I was more merry than usual. But no one suspected the source of my cheerfulness.

Madame d'Yves asked Selim to play something. He rose, sat at the piano and began to play a Chopin mazurka, leaving me alone for a while on the sofa with Hania. I noticed that she was gazing at Selim as at a rainbow and that she was flying away on the wings of the music into a land of dreams, so I decided to bring her back down to earth.

"Selim has many talents, does he not?" I said. "He plays, he sings."

"Oh, how true!" she answered.

"And, besides, what a beautiful face! Just look at him!"

Hania followed the direction of my eyes. Selim was

now in darkness, but his head was illuminated by the last
light of the evening, and in those gleams, with his raised
eyes, he seemed inspired, and at that moment he truly
was inspired.

"Is he not beautiful, Hania?" I repeated.

"You must love him very much."

"That means nothing to him, but women love him.
Ah, how that schoolgirl Jozia loved him!"

Anxiety marked Hania's smooth forehead.

"And he?" she asked.

"Eh, he loves one today and another tomorrow! He can
never love one woman for long. Such is his nature. If he
ever tells you that he loves you, do not believe him."
Now I stressed my words. "For him it will be a question
of your kisses, not your heart—do you understand?"

"Master Henryk!"

"You're right! What am I saying! Why, this doesn't
concern you at all. Besides, you are so modest that you
would never kiss a guest. Hania, I beg your pardon, for
it seems to me that I have offended you with just the
suggestion. You would never allow something like that
to happen. Am I not right, Hania, am I not right?"

Hania sprang up to leave, but I seized her by the hand
and forcibly detained her. I tried to be calm, but rage was
throttling me, as if with pincers. I felt that I was losing
self-control.

"Answer me!" I said with restrained fieriness, "or I will
not let you go!"

"Master Henryk! What do you want? What are you
saying?"

"I'm saying—I'm saying," I whispered through set
teeth, "I'm saying that you have no shame! That is what
I am saying!"

Hania sank down on the sofa. I looked at her: she was
as white as a sheet. But pity for the poor girl had fled

from me. I grasped her hand and, squeezing her small fingers, continued:

"Listen to me! I was at your feet! I loved you more than the whole world—"

"Master Henryk!"

"Be quiet. I saw and heard everything! You have no shame—both you and he!"

"My God! Oh, my God!"

"You are shameless! I would not have dared to kiss the hem of your skirt, and he kissed you on the lips. You yourself were eager for those kisses! Hania, I despise you! I hate you!"

The voice died within me. I began to breathe quickly and catch for air, which was lacking in my breast.

"You've guessed," I said after a while, "that I will separate you. Even if I had to lose my life, I will separate you; even if I had to kill him, you and myself. What I said a moment ago is not true. He loves you, he would not leave you; but I will separate you."

"Of what are you talking about with such liveliness?" asked suddenly Madame d'Yves, sitting at the other end of the room.

For a moment I wanted to spring up and reveal everything aloud; but I pulled myself together and said in a seemingly calm, though somewhat broken, voice:

"We were disputing which arbor in the garden is the more beautiful, the rose or the hop arbor."

Selim stopped playing suddenly, studied us and then said with the greatest calmness:

"I would give all others for the hop arbor."

"Your taste is not bad," I replied. "Hania is of the opposite opinion."

"Is that true, Lady Hania?" he asked.

"Yes," she said in a low voice.

Once again I had the feeling that I could not hold out any longer. Red circles began to flash before my eyes. I sprang up, and running through several rooms to the dining-room, I seized a decanter of water standing on the table there and poured the water over my head. Then, without knowing what I did, I flung the decanter to the floor, where it broke into a thousand bits. I dashed to the entrance-hall.

My horse and Selim's were standing before the porch, saddled.

I rushed to my room to wipe the water from my face in some manner; and having done this, I returned to the parlor.

In the parlor I found Father Ludwik and Selim in the greatest terror.

"What has happened?" I asked.

"Hania has fainted."

"What? how?" I cried, seizing the priest by the arm.

"Right after you left she burst into loud weeping and then fainted. Madame d'Yves has taken her to her room."

Without saying a word, I ran to Madame d'Yves's chamber. Hania had truly burst into loud weeping and fainted, but the paroxysm had passed. When I saw her I forgot everything and fell on my knees before the bed like a madman.

"Hania, my precious, my love!" I cried out, ignoring the presence of Madame d'Yves. "What is the matter with you?"

"Nothing, nothing now," she replied in a weak voice and tried to smile. "Nothing now. Truly, nothing."

I sat with her for a quarter of an hour. Then I kissed her hand and returned to the parlor. It was not true! I did not hate her! I loved her as never before! Instead, when I saw Selim in the parlor, I wanted to choke him. Oh, him, him I hated at that moment from the bottom of my heart. Both he and the priest ran up to me.

"Well?"

"Everything is fine now."

And turning to Selim, I whispered in his ear:

"Go home. Let us meet tomorrow at the mounds near the edge of the forest. I want to speak to you. I do not want you to come here anymore. Our friendship is over."

The blood rushed to Selim's face.

"What does this mean?"

"I will explain tomorrow. I do not wish to do so today. Do you understand? I do not wish to today. Tomorrow morning at six."

Having said that, I returned to Madame d'Yves's chamber. Selim ran some steps after me but stopped at the door. A few minutes later, looking through the window, I saw him ride away.

I sat about an hour in the room next to the one where Hania had been taken. I could not go in, for, weakened by crying, she had fallen asleep. Madame d'Yves and Father Ludwik went to consult with my father. I sat alone until tea-time.

During tea I saw that my father, the priest and Madame d'Yves had mysterious and serious expressions. I confess that I became a bit uneasy. Had they guessed something? That was probable. Say what you will, things had occurred today between us young people which were quite unusual.

"Today I received a letter from your mother," my father said.

"How is mother's health?"

"Perfectly good. But she is troubled by what is happening here. She wants to return soon, but I will not allow it. She has to remain where she is two months longer."

"What is mother concerned about?"

"You know that there is small-pox in the village. I was careless enough as to inform her."

To tell the truth, I did not know that small-pox was in

the village. It may be that I had heard of it, but the information had certainly fallen on deaf ears.

"Will father go to her?" I asked.

"I'll see. We will talk about that."

"It is now nearly a year since that dear woman has been abroad," said Father Ludwik.

"Her health requires it," replied my father. "She will be able to spend the coming winter at home. She writes that she feels much better, but that she misses us and is worried." Then, turning to me, he added, "After tea, come to my room. I wish to speak with you."

"Very well, father!"

I rose and, with all the others, went to Hania. She was perfectly well now. She even wanted to get up, but my father would not allow it. Around ten in the evening a britska rumbled up before the porch. Doctor Stanislaw, who had been seeing the peasants in their cottages since midday, had arrived. After he had examined Hania carefully, he declared that she was not sick at all but needed rest and recreation. He forbade study; instead, he prescribed fun and games.

My father asked his advice on whether my little sisters could stay at home during the small-pox epidemic. The doctor assured him that there was no danger and added that he himself had written to my mother to set her mind at rest. Then he went to bed, for he was about to drop from fatigue. I led him by the light of a candle to the other building, where he was to spend the night with me. I myself needed to go to sleep, for I was completely worn out by the day's events, when Franek entered and said:

"The lord wishes to see the young master."

I went to his room at once. My father was sitting by his desk, on which lay the letter from my mother. Father Ludwik and Madame d'Yves were present also. My heart beat rapidly like that of an accused man who has to appear before a court of judgment, for I felt almost certain that they wished to question me about Hania. But my father began to speak of things of far greater importance. For my mother's peace of mind, he had determined to send my little sisters, along with Madame d'Yves, to his brother at Kopczan. In that case Hania would have to be alone with us. This my father did not wish. He also said that he knew that certain things were happening among us young people which he did not want to look into but which he did not approve of, and that he expected that the departure of Hania would put a stop to them.

At that point everyone looked at me inquiringly, and they were not a little surprised when, instead of desperately opposing Hania's departure, I approved of it gladly. I had calculated simply that her departure would be equivalent to breaking all relations with Selim. And besides, a certain hope, like a will-o'-the-wisp, flickered in my heart, that it would be I, and no one else, who would take Hania to my mother. I knew that my father could not leave home, for the harvest was at hand; I knew that Father Ludwik had never been abroad; so only I was left. But this was a faint hope, and soon it was extinguished like a will-o'-the-wisp when my father said that Lady Ustrzycki would be leaving for sea baths in a couple of days, and that she had already consented to take Hania with her and accompany her to my mother. The day after tomorrow Hania was to set out in the evening. This saddened me not a little, but I preferred that she should go even without me rather than stay. Besides, I must confess that immense delight rose in my mind at the thought of how Selim would receive this information when I would tell him tomorrow.

X

I arrived at the mounds at six on the following morning. Selim was already waiting for me. While riding there, I promised myself to be calm.

"What did you want to tell me?" asked Selim.

"I wanted to tell you that I know everything. You love Hania, and she loves you. Mirza, you have acted dishonorably in ensnaring Hania's heart! I wanted to tell you this above all."

Selim became pale; everything in him was boiling over. He rode up so closely to me that our horses almost touched each other.

"How have I acted dishonorably?" he asked. "Be brief."

"Firstly, because you are a Muslim, and she is a Christian. You cannot marry her."

"I will change my religion."

"Your father will not permit that."

"Oh! he will permit it. And—?"

"And there are other obstacles. Even if you changed your religion, neither my father nor I will give you Hania. Never, never! Do you understand?"

Selim bent toward me from his saddle, leaned against me and answered, stressing every syllable:

"I will not ask you! Do you understand?"

I was still calm, for I was keeping the news of Hania's departure till the end.

"Not only will she not be yours," I answered coolly and with equal emphasis, "but you will not see her again. I know that you wanted to send her letters. But I say that I will be on the look-out for your messenger and will have him flogged. You yourself will not come to us anymore. We forbid you!"

"We will see!" he replied, panting with rage. "Permit

me now to have my say. It is not I who have acted
dishonorably, but you. I see that clearly now. I once
asked you if you were in love with her. You answered:
'No!' I wanted to withdraw while there was still time;
you rejected my offer. Who is to blame? You lied when
you said that you were not in love with her. Through
vanity, through egotistical pride, you were ashamed to
confess your love. You loved in darkness, I in light. You
loved secretly, I openly. You poisoned her life, I tried to
make it happy. Who is to blame? I would have with-
drawn. God knows I would have. But today it is too late.
Today she loves me. So listen to this: You may forbid me
to enter your house, you may intercept my letters, but I
swear that I will not give up Hania, I will not forget her,
I will love her always and find her anywhere she goes. I
act directly and honorably. I am in love. I love Hania
above everything else in this world; my whole life is in
this love, and I would die without her. I do not wish to
bring unhappiness into your house, but remember that
there is in me now something that I myself fear. I am
ready for anything. Oh, if you do Hania any wrong—"

He said all this quickly, his face pale, his teeth
clenched. A great love had taken hold of his fiery Eastern
nature, and it radiated from him like heat from a fire.
But I paid no attention to this and answered with icy
resoluteness:

"I have not come here to listen to your confession of
love for Hania. And I laugh at your threats and repeat
again: Hania will never be yours."

"Listen once more, then," said Selim. "I will not try
to tell of my love for Hania, because I could not express
it and you could not understand it. But I swear that in
spite of my love, if she loved you now, I would still find
in my soul enough noble feelings to renounce her forever. Henryk, why should we fight over her? You have
always been honorable. So renounce her, and afterward

ask even my life of me. Here is my hand, Henryk! The question is of Hania—of Hania, do not forget that!"

And he bent toward me with open arms, but I reined back my horse.

"Leave the issue of Hania's care to my father and me. We have already thought about her. I have the honor to inform you that the day after tomorrow Hania will go abroad and that you will not see her again. And now farewell."

"Ah! if so, then we will see!"

"We will see!"

I turned my horse and rode home without looking back.

During those two days before Hania's departure, a gloom descended over our house. Madame d'Yves and my sisters left on the day following the conversation with my father. Besides myself, there remained only my father, Kazio, Father Ludwik and Hania. The poor girl already knew that she would leave, and she received this news with despair. Apparently she thought to seek help and the last plank of salvation in me; but I, foreseeing this, made sure that I would not be alone with her for one moment. I knew myself well enough, and I knew that with tears she could do whatever she liked with me and that I would not refuse her anything. I avoided even her glance, for I could not endure that plea for pity which was depicted in it whenever she looked at my father or me.

On the other hand, even had I wanted to intercede for her, I knew that it would be of no avail, for once my father made a decision he never retreated from it. Besides this, a certain shame kept me a good distance from Hania. In her presence I was ashamed of my last conversation with Selim, of my recent harshness, of my entire role in the affair and, finally, of this, that without approaching her I nevertheless followed her from a distance. But I had reason to follow her. I knew that Selim was circling about our house day and night like a bird of prey. On the second day after our conversation I saw Hania quickly hide a piece of paper with writing on it, beyond doubt a letter to or from Selim. I even guessed that perhaps they would see each other, but as much as I was on the lookout for Selim, I could not catch him. Meanwhile the two days passed as quickly as an arrow through the air. On the eve of the day when Hania was to go and spend the night at Ustrzycki Hall, my father went to the market in town to buy horses, and he took Kazio along to test them out. Father Ludwik and I were to accompany Hania.

I noticed that as the decisive moment drew closer, Hania became seized by a strange disquiet. The look in her eyes changed, and her whole body trembled. At times she gave a start, as if something had momentarily frightened her. Finally the sun set, but in a dreary sort of way, behind thick, billowing clouds the color of yellow, which threatened hail and storm. Several times from the western horizon one could hear a distant rumble, like the dangerous growl of an approaching storm. The air was humid, sultry and filled with electricity. The birds had hidden under roofs, trees, and only swallows were rushing uneasily through the air. The leaves ceased to rustle on the trees and hung limply as if in a faint; from the direction of the farm came the plaintive bellowing of cattle, returning from pasture. A type of gloomy unease came over all of nature. Father Ludwik ordered all the windows closed. I wish to reach Ustrzycki Hall before the outbreak of the storm, so I sprang up to go to the stable and order the carriage to be brought up. At the moment when I was leaving the room Hania sprang up also, but immediately sat down. I glanced at her. Her face turned alternately red and white. "It is so humid! so humid!" she called out; and sitting near the window, she

began to fan herself with a handkerchief. Her strange
disquiet seemed to have increased. "Perhaps we should
wait," Father Ludwik said to me. "The storm will burst
forth in half an hour or so!" "In half an hour we will be
at Ustrzycki Hall," I answered; "besides, who knows if
our fears are not in vain." And I ran to the stable. My
horse was saddled already, but there was the typical delay
with the carriage. Half an hour had passed before the
coachman drove up to the porch with the carriage, with
me following on horseback. The dark clouds of the
storm seemed to be right overhead, but I did not want
to delay any longer. Hania's trunks were brought out at
once and strapped to the rear of the carriage. Father
Ludwik was already waiting on the porch. He was
dressed in a white linen smock and had an umbrella,
equally white, in his hand.

"Where is Hania?" I asked him. "Is she ready?"

"She is ready. She went to pray in the chapel half an
hour ago."

I went to the chapel but did not find her there. Then
I went to the dining-room and from there to the parlor.
Hania was nowhere to be found.

"Hania! Hania!" I began to call out.

No one answered.

Somewhat alarmed, I went to her room, thinking that
she might have become weak. In her room old Wegrowska was sitting and crying. When she saw me, she
asked:

"Is it time to take farewell of the young lady?"

"Where is she?" I asked impatiently.

"She went to the garden."

I ran to the garden.

"Hania! Hania! It is time to go."

Silence....

"Hania! Hania!"

As if in answer the leaves began to rustle uneasily

under the first breath of the storm; several large drops of rain fell, and silence set in again.

"What is this?" I asked myself, and felt the hair rising on my head from fright.

"Hania! Hania!"

For a moment it seemed to me that from the other end of the garden I heard an answer. I breathed out a sigh of relief. "Oh, what a fool I've been!" I thought, and I ran in the direction from where the voice originated.

I found nothing and nobody.

On that side the garden ended at a fence, beyond which was a road toward a sheepfold in the field. I grabbed the fence and looked down the road. It was empty; but Ignas, a farm-boy, was herding geese in a ditch nearby.

"Ignas!"

Ignas took off his cap and ran toward me.

"Have you seen the young lady?"

"Yes. She was riding in a carriage this way just a few moments ago."

"What? how? Where was she going?"

"Toward the forest with the young lord from Chorzel. Oh, and how they rode, as fast as the horses could gallop!"

Jesus, Mary! Hania had fled with Selim!

It grew dark in my eyes, and then a lightning-flash, as it were, flew through my head. I remembered Hania's disquiet, the letter I had seen in her hand. So all of this had been planned? Mirza had written to her and had seen her. They had chosen the moment right before our departure, for they knew that everyone in the house would be occupied at that time. Jesus, Mary! A cold sweat covered me, and my hair stood on end. The next thing I remember I was standing on the porch.

"My horse! my horse!" I cried out in a terrible voice.

"What has happened? What has happened?" cried Father Ludwik.

But he was answered only by a roar of thunder.

The wind whistled in my ears from the mad rush of my horse. Dashing into the alley of linden trees, I crossed it toward the road which they had taken; I jumped across one fence, then another, and sped on. Their trail was clear. Meanwhile the storm burst forth: it grew dark; against the black billowing clouds fiery zigzags of lightning shot out; at times the whole sky was one great blaze, and then an even deeper darkness descended; rain poured down in one torrent. The trees along the road swayed in all directions. My horse, struck by the frenzied blows of my whip and pressed by spurs, was snorting and groaning, and I also snorted, but from rage. Bent over the neck of my horse, I followed the tracks on the road, not seeing nor thinking about anything else. Thus I rushed into the forest.

At that moment the storm became even more intense. A kind of rage took hold of the earth and the sky. The forest bent like wheat in a field and brandished about its dark branches; in the darkness the echoes of the thunder traveled from pine-tree to pine-tree; the peals of lightning, the noise of the trees, the cracking of breaking limbs were all mingled into one hellish concert.

I could not see their trail now, but I flew onward like a whirlwind. Only beyond the forest, by the light of the lightning flashes, did I make out their tracks again; but I noticed with dismay that the snorting of my horse was increasing and his speed lessening. I redoubled the blows of my whip. Just beyond the forest began a real sea of sand which I could avoid by going to one side but which Selim had to pass through. That would delay his flight.

I raised my eyes to the sky. "O God!" I cried out in despair; "let me overtake them, and then kill me, if it be your will!" And my prayer was answered. Suddenly a red flash of lightning rent the darkness, and by its bloody light I saw an escaping small britska. I could not distinguish the faces of those who were fleeing, but I was sure that the pair was Selim and Hania. They were about a half a verst ahead, but they were not going very fast, as Selim was forced to drive cautiously because of the darkness and the floods created by the downpour. I gave a cry of both rage and joy. Now they could not escape me.

Selim looked around, cried out too, and fell to beating the frightened horses with his whip. By the light of the lightning-flashes Hania also recognized me. I saw that she grasped Selim in despair and that he said something to her. In a few seconds I was so near that I could hear Selim's voice: "I have weapons!" he shouted in the darkness. "Do not come closer or I will shoot." But I cared for nothing and pressed my horse on and on. "Halt!" cried Selim; "halt!" I was barely fifteen feet away, but the road began to get better now, and Selim lashed his horses into a full gallop. The distance between us increased for a moment, but I began to overtake them again. At that point Selim turned and aimed his pistol. He was glaring, but he aimed calmly. One more moment, and I might have touched the carriage with my hand. Suddenly, however, the report of a pistol was heard—my horse threw himself to one side, reared a few times, then knelt on his forelegs. I raised him. He crouched on his hind legs and, snorting heavily, fell on the ground, bringing me down with him.

I sprang up at once and ran as fast as I could, but my effort was vain. The britska went farther and farther away from me; then I saw it only when lightning rent the clouds. It disappeared in the distance and the darkness like a last hope. I tried to shout out; I could not: my breath failed me. The rattle of the britska became fainter and fainter. Finally I stumbled against a rock and fell.

In a moment, I was up again.

"They've escaped! they've escaped!" I repeated loudly, not knowing what was happening to me. I was helpless, alone in the storm and the night. That devil Selim had won. Ah, if Kazio had not gone with my father, if we had both pursued them! But now? What will happen? "What will happen now?" I shouted loudly, so as to hear my own voice and not go mad. And it seemed to me that the whirlwind was laughing at me and whistling: "Sit on the road, without a horse, while he is with her." And thus the wind howled and laughed and giggled.

I returned slowly to my horse. From his nostrils flowed a stream of dark coagulating blood; but he was still alive: he panted and kept turning his expiring eyes toward me. I sat near him and rested my head on his side; it seemed to me that I, too, was dying.

Meanwhile the wind whistled above my head and laughed and called out, "He is with her!" It seemed to me that at times I heard the hellish rattle of that britska flying off in the darkness along with my happiness. And the whirlwind whistled, "He is with her!"

A strange torpor came over me. How long it lasted I do not know. When I came to, the storm had passed. Across the sky raced bright flocks of soft, whitish clouds; but in the intervals between them an azure sky was visible, and the moon shone brightly. From the fields, mists were rising. My dead horse, already cold, reminded me of everything that had happened. I looked around to see where I was. To my right I saw faint lights in some distant windows, so I hurried in that direction. It turned out that I was close to Ustrzycki Hall.

I decided to go to the manor and see Lord Ustrzycki, which I could do the more easily as he lived not in the manor itself, but in his own little house, in which he usually spent his time and slept. The light was still shining in his windows. I knocked at the door.

He opened it himself and started back in fear.

"What a farce!" he said. "How you look, Henryk!"

"Lightning killed my horse not far away. I could do nothing but come here."

"In the name of the Father and Son! How wet and cold you are! How late it is! What a farce! I will have some food brought to you and some dry clothes."

"No! no! I want to go home immediately."

"Well, well. But why is Hania not with you? My wife will start tomorrow at two. We thought that you would bring her here to spend the night."

At that point I determined to tell him everything, for I needed his help.

"Lord!" said I. "Something terrible has happened at our place. I pray that you will not mention this to anyone, neither to your wife, nor your daughters, nor the governesses. The honor of our house is at stake here."

I knew that he would tell no one, but I had little hope that the affair would be concealed; therefore I preferred to forewarn him, so that he could explain what had happened when necessary. And I told him all, except that I was in love with Hania.

"So you must fight with Selim?" he said, hearing me out to the end. "What a farce! Eh?"

"Yes; I want to fight with him tomorrow. But today I must still go after them, and that is why I'm requesting your best horse immediately."

"You don't have to chase them. They must not have gone far. They probably rode and rode along various roads and then returned to Chorzel. Where else could they go? What a farce! They returned to Chorzel and fell at the feet of old Mirza. They could do nothing else. Old Mirza surely locked up Selim in the granary, and the young lady—the young lady he will take back to your house. A farce, eh? But Hania! Hania! Well, well!"

"Lord Ustrzycki!"

"Well, well! my child, do not get angry! I do not take it ill of her. My women, that is different! But why waste time?"

"You are right; let us not waste time."

Lord Ustrzycki reflected for a moment.

"I'll tell you what. I will go immediately to Chorzel, while you go home, or, better yet, stay here. If Hania is in Chorzel, I will take her and go to your house. But perhaps they will not give her to me? What a farce! But I prefer to be with old Mirza when we take her, for your father is hot-tempered. He will be ready to challenge the old man, but the old man is not to blame. No?"

"My father is not at home."

"So much the better! So much the better!"

And Lord Ustrzycki clapped his hands.

"Janek! over here!"

The servant entered.

"Horses and a britska for me in ten minutes. Do you understand"

"And a britska for me?" I said.

"And horses and a britska for the young lord! What a farce, lord benefactor!"

We were silent for a time, after which I said:

"Will you permit me to write a letter to Selim? I wish to challenge him by letter."

"Why?"

"I'm afraid the old man will not let him fight a duel. He will lock him up for a while and think that is enough. But for me that is not enough, absolutely not! If Selim is locked up already, you will not see him; in that case the letter should be handed over to someone else, since this can't be done through the old man. Besides, I will not tell my father that I want to fight. He might challenge old Mirza, but Mirza is not to blame. But if Selim and I fight to begin with, there will be no reason for them to fight. Why, you said yourself that I must fight with him."

"I should think so! Fight, fight! That is always the best means for a noble; it doesn't matter whether he is old or young. For someone else, a farce! But not for a noble. Well! write that letter! You are right!"

I sat down and wrote the following:

"You are a scoundrel. With this letter I slap you in the face. If you will not appear tomorrow near Wach's cottage with pistols or with a sabre, you will be the greatest of cowards, which most probably you are."

I sealed the letter and gave it to Lord Ustrzycki. Then we went out, for the britskas were already waiting for us. Before I got into mine, a terrifying thought came to my head.

"But, sir," I said to Lord Ustrzycki, "what if Selim did not take Hania to Chorzel?"

"If he did not go to Chorzel, then he has gained time. It is night; there are fifty roads in every direction and— well, it's like looking for the wind in a field. But where could he have taken her?"

"To N."

"So many miles with the same horses? Then don't worry. What a farce, eh? I will go to N. tomorrow, even today, but first I'll go to Chorzel. I repeat, don't worry."

An hour later I arrived home. It was late at night, very late even, but lights were flicking everywhere in the windows. Apparently people were running about with candles through various rooms. When my britska rumbled up to the porch, the door squeaked, and Father Ludwik came out, lamp in hand.

"Quiet!" he whispered, putting his finger to his lips.

"Hania?" I asked feverishly.

"Keep your voice down. Hania is already here. Old Mirza brought her here. Come to my room. I will tell you everything."

We went to the priest's room.

"What happened to you?" he asked.

"I pursued them. Selim shot my horse. Is my father here?"

"He came right after old Mirza left. Oh, what a tragedy! what a tragedy! The doctor is with him now. We thought that he would have an apoplectic stroke. He wanted to go and challenge old Mirza immediately. Don't go to your father, for it might harm him. But beg him tomorrow not to challenge Mirza. That would be a great sin, and besides, the old man is not to blame. He beat Selim and locked him up and brought Hania back himself. He commanded his people to silence. It is fortunate that he did not find your father here."

It turned out that Lord Ustrzycki had foreseen everything.

"How is Hania?"

"Wet to the bones. She has a fever. Your father gave her a terrible scolding. The poor child!"

"Did Doctor Stanislaw see her?"

"He did and ordered her to go straight to bed. Old Wegrowska is with her now. Wait here for me. I will go to your father and tell him that you have arrived. He already sent out men after you in every direction. Kazio is not at home also, for he has gone to look for you. O God! O Almighty God, what has happened here!"

Having said this, the priest went to my father. But I could not wait in his room and ran to Hania. I did not want to see her—oh, no! That would have cost her too much. Rather I wanted to be sure that she had really returned, that she was safe once again under our roof, near me, sheltered from the storm and the terrible events of that day. Strange feelings swirled within me when I approached her room. My heart was not filled with anger, nor hatred, but with an oppressive, deep sorrow and a great, inexpressible compassion for that poor and unfortunate victim of Selim's madness. I thought of her as of a dove which a hawk had swept away. Ah! how much humiliation the poor thing must have felt, through what shame she must have passed in Chorzel in presence of the elder Mirza! I swore immediately that I would not reproach her today or ever, and would act with her as if nothing had happened.

At the moment when I reached the door to her room, it opened and Wegrowska came out. I stopped her and inquired:

"Is the young lady sleeping?"

"She is not, she is not, the poor thing," replied the old woman. "Oh, my precious young master, if you had seen what was happening here! When the old lord yelled at the young lady"—here old Wegrowska raised her apron and began to wipe away her tears—"I thought the poor thing would die on the spot. And she was so terrified and so wet. O Jesus! Jesus!"

"But how is she now?"

"You will see that all of this will make her very sick. It is lucky that the doctor is here."

I ordered Wegrowska to return at once to Hania and not to close the door after her, for I wished to look at Hania, even if from a distance. Looking from the dark room through the open door, I saw her sitting on the bed, dressed in her night-clothing. A deep flush was on her face, and her eyes were sparkling. I also saw that she was breathing quickly.

Apparently she had a fever.

I was trying to decide whether to go in when Father Ludwik touched my shoulder.

"Your father wants you," he said.

"Father Ludwik, she is sick!"

"The doctor will see her again right away. Meanwhile you must talk to your father. Go, go; it is late already."

"What time is it?"

"One in the morning."

I struck my forehead with my hand. I had to fight with Selim at five in the morning.

XI

After the talk with my father, which lasted half an hour, I returned to the lodging house, but I did not lie down at all. I calculated that to reach Wach's hut at five I would have to leave by four at the very latest, therefore I had not quite three hours ahead of me. Shortly afterward, Father Ludwik came in to see if I was not ill from my mad ride and if I had put on some dry clothes. It made no difference to me, though, whether I was wet or not. The priest urged me to go to bed at once, but meanwhile he himself became engrossed in talking, and so an hour went by.

He told me the details about what old Mirza had said. According to the old man it seemed that Selim had simply committed an act of madness, but, as he told his father, he saw no other way out. He assumed that after the flight his father would have no other avenue open to him but to bless him, and we none but to give him Hania. It was also revealed that, after talking with me, not only did he write to Hania, but he had a meeting with her, and it was at that point that he persuaded her to flee with him. The girl, though she did not realize the consequences of this step, resisted him instinctively with all her might; but Selim overcame this with his pleas and his love. Besides, he represented the flight as a simple drive to Chorzel, after which they would be united forever in happiness. He assured her that afterward he himself would bring her to us, but as his betrothed; that my father would agree to everything, while I must agree, and would, more importantly, console myself easily with Lola Ustrzycki. Finally he entreated, begged and implored Hania. He said that for her he would sacrifice everything, even his life; that he could not endure a separation and would drown, shoot or poison himself in such an event. And then he threw himself at her feet and made such a fuss that she agreed to everything. But just as soon as the flight began, and they were starting off, Hania became frightened and begged him with tears to return; but he would not, for, as he told his father, he forgot the whole world at that time.

This was what old Mirza told Father Ludwik, and he told it, perhaps, to show that though Selim had ventured on a mad deed, he had done so in good faith. Taking everything into consideration, Father Ludwik did not share the anger of my father, who was indignant at Hania's ingratitude. According to the priest, Hania was not ungrateful; she had been simply led astray by sinful worldly love. Then the priest moralized to me about worldly feelings, but I did not take it ill at all of Hania that her love was worldly; I would have been willing to pay with my life had that love been aimed in a different direction. I felt the greatest compassion for Hania, and besides, my heart had become so attached to her that had I wished to tear it away I would have had to tear it apart. Therefore I begged Father Ludwik to take her side before my father and to explain her actions as he had explained them to me. Then I took farewell of him, for I wished to be alone.

After the priest had gone, I took down that famous old sabre, given to me by my father, and two pistols, to prepare everything for the morning duel. Of that duel I had neither the time nor the inclination to think about. All I wanted was to engage in a fight for life and death. As to Selim, I was certain that he would not disappoint me.

I wiped my sabre carefully with soft cotton. Despite it being about two hundred years old, the wide blue blade had not the slightest defect, though in its day it had cut open not a few helmets and breastplates, and had drunk no little Swedish, Tartar and Turkish blood. The golden inscription, "Jesus, Mary," shone distinctly. I tried the edge: it was as fine as the edge of a satin ribbon. The blue turquoises on the hilt seemed to be smiling, as if requesting a hand to grab and warm them.

When I was done with the sabre, I turned my attention to the pistols, for I did not know what weapons Selim might choose. I dropped oil on the locks and put bits of linen cloth to the bullets, after which I loaded both pistols carefully. It was getting grey outside. It was three o'clock. When I had finished the work, I threw myself into an armchair and began to think. From the course of events and from what Father Ludwik had told me, one thing became more and more evident: I was to blame not a little for all that had happened. I asked myself if I had fulfilled properly the duty of guardian which old Nicholas had imposed on me, and I answered: No. Had I thought of Hania, and not of myself? I answered: No! Of whom had I been thinking in this entire affair? Quite simply of myself. And meanwhile Hania, that gentle, defenseless creature, was among us, like a dove among birds of prey. I could not stifle the immensely bitter thought that Selim and I had torn her apart, as if she were tempting plunder, and that in that struggle, during which the plunderers were thinking primarily of themselves, she had suffered most who was least to blame. And now in a couple of hours we were to have our last battle over her. These were sad, grievous thoughts. It turned out that our entire world of nobles was too harsh for Hania. Unfortunately my mother had not been home for a long time, and we men had hands that were too rough, and we had crushed that delicate flower thrown among us by fate. Blame hung over our entire house, and this blame must be expiated with my blood or Selim's.

I was ready for either event.

Meanwhile the light of day had begun to look in through my windows with greater and greater force. Outside, swallows greeted the dawn with chirps. I extinguished the candles burning on the table. The hour three-thirty struck clearly in the parlor of the house. "Well, it is time!" I thought; and throwing an overcoat over my shoulders to hide the weapons in case someone met me, I went out of the lodging house.

While passing by the manor, I noticed that the main door of the entrance, usually closed at night by the jaws of an iron lion, was open. Evidently someone had gone out; therefore I needed to take every precaution not to meet up with that person. Silently stealing along the edge of the courtyard toward the linden trees, I looked carefully about, but the world seemed to be still asleep. Only when I found myself in the alley did I fully raise my head, certain that now I could not be seen from the manor.

The morning was clear and beautiful after yesterday's storm. The honey-like smell of wet lindens was strong in the alley. I turned left toward the forge, the mills and the dam, as that was the way to Wach's cottage. Sleep and weariness fled far away from me under the influence of the fresh morning and fine weather. I was full of hope, and some internal presentment told me that in the fight to come, I would be the victor. In truth Selim used pistols like a master, but I was no less a shot; and though in handling a sabre he surpassed me in skill, I was far stronger than he, to such a degree that he could hardly hold back my onslaught. "Besides," I thought, "come what may, this is the end, and if not the unraveling, then the cutting, of the Gordian knot which has bound and stifled me for so long." Moreover, whether in good or bad faith, Selim had committed a great wrong against Hania, and so must pay for it.

Thus meditating, I reached the bank of the pond. Mists were descending over the water. Daylight had painted the azure surface of the pond with the colors of dawn. The early morning had now begun in truth. The air was growing more and more transparent; everywhere it was calm, rosy and quiet, except from the direction of the reeds, where wild ducks quacked. I was near the sluices and the bridge, when I stopped suddenly, as if driven to the ground.

On the bridge stood my father, his arms crossed behind him and an extinguished pipe in his hands. He stood leaning against the railing of the bridge, and was looking thoughtfully at the water and the morning dawn. Apparently he, like I, had been unable to sleep, and he had gone out to breathe the morning air or perhaps to look about the estate.

I did not see him at first, for I was walking along the side of the road where the willows hid the railing of the bridge from me; but I was not more than thirty feet away. I hid behind a willow, unsure of what to do.

My father continued to stand in the same place. I looked at him. Worry and sleeplessness were depicted on his face. He looked around at the pond and muttered the morning prayer. I clearly heard:

"Hail Mary, full of grace! The Lord be with Thee!" The rest he whispered and then said aloud again: "And blessed be the fruit of Thy womb. Amen!"

I became impatient at standing behind the willow and decided to sneak by quietly over the bridge. I could do that, for my father was turned toward the water; and besides, as I have already mentioned, he was a little deaf, for during his army days he had been deafened by the extreme noise of cannon. Treading carefully, I was passing the bridge beyond the farther willows, when, unfortunately, a badly mounted board squeaked, and my father looked around.

"What are you doing here?" he asked.

I turned red as a beet.

"I'm just taking a walk, father."

But my father approached me, and lifting up slightly the overcoat with which I had covered myself carefully, he pointed to the sabre and pistols.

"And these?" he asked.

There was no help for it. I had to confess.

"I will tell you everything, father," I said. "I am going to fight with Selim."

I thought that he would burst out in anger, but to my surprise he merely asked:

"Who was the challenger?"

"I."

"Without consulting your father, without saying a word?"

"I challenged him yesterday in Ustrzycki Hall, immediately after the pursuit. I could not ask about anything, father; and besides, I was afraid that you would forbid me to fight."

"You are right on that point. Go home. Leave the whole affair to me."

My heart was compressed in me with such pain and despair as never before.

"Father," I said, "I beg you by all that is holy and by the memory of my grandfather, do not forbid me to fight with the Tartar. I remember how you called me a democrat and were angry with me because of that. But now I remember that your blood as well as grandfather's is flowing in me. Father, he did Hania wrong! Should he get away with that? Let not people say that our family let an orphan be wronged and did not avenge her. I am very much at fault here. I loved her and did not tell you. But I swear that even if I had not loved her, I would for the sake of her orphaned state, our house and our name do what I am doing now. My conscience tells me that this is an honorable thing to do, so do not deny me this, father. If what I say is true, then I cannot believe that you would forbid me to act honorably. I cannot! I cannot! Father, remember that Hania is wronged, and I gave the challenge, I gave my word! I know that I am not a man yet; but does not an adolescent have the same feelings of honor as a grown-up? I made the challenge; I have given my word; and you have taught me more than once that honor is the first duty of a noble. I gave my word, father! Hania was wronged; there is a stain on our house, and I have given my word. Father, father!"

And lowering my lips to his hand, I cried my eyes out and very nearly prayed to my father. As I spoke, his severe face became softer and softer. He raised his eyes, and a large heavy tear, truly a parental one, fell on my forehead. He fought a grievous battle within himself, for I was the apple of his eye, and he loved me above all things on earth; therefore he had the greatest concern for me. Finally he bent his grey head and said in a low, barely audible voice:

"May the God of your ancestors conduct you! Go, my son, go to fight with the Tartar!"

We fell into each other's arms. My father pressed me long to his breast. Eventually, however, he shook himself out of his emotion and said with force and a measure of joy:

"Now then, fight, my son, so that it'll be heard in the heavens!"

I kissed his hand, and he asked:

"With swords or pistols?"

"He will choose."

"And the seconds?"

"Without seconds. I trust him; he trusts me. Why do we need seconds?"

Again I threw myself around his neck, for it was time to go. I looked back a few minutes later. My father was still on the bridge and blessed me from afar with a sign of the cross. The first rays of the rising sun fell on his lofty figure, encircling it with a kind of bright aureole. And thus in the light, with upraised hands, that grey-haired veteran seemed to me like an old eagle blessing from afar its young for such a vigorous and winged life as he himself had once enjoyed.

Ah, how the heart rose in me then! I had so much courage, faith and zeal that if not one but ten Selims had been waiting for me at Wach's cottage, I would have challenged all ten of them at once.

Finally I reached the cottage. Selim was waiting for me at the edge of the forest. I confess that when I saw him I felt in my heart something like that which a wolf feels when he sees his prey. We looked each other in the eye threateningly and with curiosity. Selim had changed during the last two days; he had grown thin and ugly, but maybe it only seemed to me that he had grown ugly. His eyes gleamed feverishly, the corners of his lips quivered.

We went immediately to the interior of the forest, but we did not speak one word to each other along the entire way. At last, when I found a little opening among the pines, I stopped and asked:

"Here. Agreed?"

He nodded his head and began to unbutton his overcoat, so as to throw it down before the duel.

"Choose!" I said, pointing to the pistols and the sabre.

He pointed to a sabre which he had with him: it was a Damascus blade highly curved toward the point.

Meanwhile I threw off my coat; he followed my example, but first he took a letter from his pocket and said:

"If I die, I ask you to give this to Lady Hania."

"I will not receive it."

"This is not a confession; it is an explanation."

"Very well."

Thus speaking, we rolled up our shirt-sleeves. Only now did my heart begin to beat more rapidly. At last Selim seized the hilt of his sabre, straightened himself and assumed the position of a fencer—challenging, proud.

"I am ready," he said, holding his sabre high.

I assumed the same position and touched my sabre to his.

"Ready?"

"Ready."

"Begin!"

I struck at him immediately and pressed so hard that he had to retreat several steps while receiving my blows on his sabre with difficulty. He answered each blow with a blow, however, and with such swiftness that both stroke and counterstroke were heard almost simultaneously. A flush covered his face; his nostrils distended; his eyes stared out slantingly in Tartar fashion and began to glint. For a while nothing was to be heard but the clink of blades, the hollow sound of steel and our whistling breaths. Selim quickly understood that if the fight would go on, he must fall, for neither his lungs nor his strength would hold out. Large drops of sweat popped out on his forehead; his breathing grew hoarser and hoarser. But also a certain rage possessed him, a certain madness of battle. His hair, tossed around by his movements, fell over his forehead; his clenched white teeth glittered in his open mouth. You would have said that his Tartar nature had become thoroughly roused in him when he felt the sabre in his hand and smelled blood. Still I had the advantage of equal fury with greater strength! One time he was not able to effectively ward off my blow, and blood squirted out from his left arm; a few seconds later, the point of my sabre touched his forehead. He was terrible then, with that red trail of blood, mixed in part with sweat, trickling down his face. But this only seemed to stir him further. He sprang up to me and sprang away like a wounded tiger. The point of his sabre circled about my head, arms and breast with the terrible swiftness of a fiery thunderbolt. I parried these mad blows with difficulty, all the more since I was thinking of giving rather than taking. At times we came so near each other that breast almost struck breast. Suddenly Selim sprang away; his sabre whistled right near my temple, but I warded it off with such force that his head was momentarily unprotected. I aimed a blow capable of splitting his skull in two, when a thunderbolt, as it were, struck my head all of a sudden. I cried, "Jesus, Mary!" The sabre dropped from my hand, and I fell toward the earth.

XII

For a long time I did not know what was happening to me or around me. When I woke up, I was lying on my back in my father's bed, while my father was sitting next to me in an armchair, his head bent back, his face pale, his eyes shut. The shutters were closed. Candles were burning on the table, and in the great silence of the room, I heard only the ticking of the clock. I stared vacantly for some time at the ceiling, gathering my lethargic thoughts; then I tried to move, but a terrible pain in my head prevented me. This pain reminded me a little of what had happened, so I called in a low, weak voice:

"Father!"

My father gave a start and leaned over me. Joy, mixed with tenderness, was expressed on his face.

"O God," he said, "thanks to You he has recovered consciousness. What, my son? what?"

"Father, did I fight with Selim?"

"Yes, my love! Do not think of that!"

The silence continued for a while, then I asked:

"Father, who brought me to this room from the forest?"

"I brought you in my arms; but do not speak, do not exert yourself."

Not five minutes had passed before I spoke again. This time I spoke very slowly:

"Father?"

"What, my child?"

"What happened to Selim?"

"He likewise fainted from loss of blood. I had him taken to Chorzel."

I still wanted to inquire about Hania and my mother, but I felt that consciousness was leaving me again. It seemed to me that black and yellow dogs were dancing on their hind legs around my bed, and I gazed at them. Then again I seemed to hear the sounds of village pipes; at moments, instead of the clock which hung opposite my bed, I saw a face peer out of the wall and then withdraw into it again. This was not a condition of complete unconsciousness but one of fever and a confusion of thought; however, it must have lasted quite long. At times I was a little better, and then I recognized in part the faces around my bed: now my father, now the priest, now Kazio, now Doctor Stanislaw. I remember that among those faces one was missing, but I could not make out which one; but I know that I felt the absence of that person, and I sought that face instinctively. At one point in the night I fell into a deep sleep, and I woke up toward morning. The candles were still burning on the table. I was very, very weak. All of a sudden I noticed someone bending over the bed whom I did not recognize at first, but at the sight of whom I felt so much bliss that it was as if I had died and was taken into heaven. This person's face was angelic, but so angelic, so sacred and kind, with tears flowing quietly, that I felt as though I

were ready to weep also. Then a spark of consciousness
returned to me. It grew bright in my eyes, and I called
out weakly:

"Mother!"

The angelic face bent to my emaciated hand, lying
motionless on the bedspread, and kissed it. I tried to
raise myself, but the pain in my temples returned, so I
called out only:

"Mother! it hurts!"

My mother, for it was she, began to change the bandages on my head, which contained ice. This dressing
had always caused me much suffering; but now those
sweet, loving hands moved with such careful delicacy
about my poor slashed head that, not feeling the least
pain, I whispered:

"That feels good, so good!"

Afterward I had more consciousness; but toward evening I fell into a fever. At that point I began to see
Hania, though when I was conscious I never saw her
near me. But now I saw her always in some danger. At
one time a wolf with red eyes was rushing at her; at
another time someone was carrying her away—Selim,
perhaps, but perhaps not, for the face was grown over
with black bristles, and horns topped the head. Then I
would cry out or request the wolf, or the horned one,
very politely and humbly, not to carry her away. At those
moments my mother placed her hands on my forehead,
and the evil visions vanished immediately.

Finally the fever left me for good, and I regained
complete consciousness, though that did not mean that
I was in better health. Another type of sickness came
upon me, a certain unusual weakness, under the influence of which I seemed to be dying. For entire days and
nights I stared at one point on the ceiling. I was conscious but indifferent to everything. Nothing concerned
me: not life, nor death, nor the persons watching over

my bed. I received impressions, saw everything that was happening around me, remembered everything, but I had not enough strength to collect my thoughts or to feel. One evening it appeared that I was dying. A great yellow candle was placed near my bed. Then I saw Father Ludwik in his vestments. He gave me the Sacrament, then he put holy oil on me, but sobbed so during the process that he came near to leaving because of losing consciousness. They carried my mother out in a faint. Kazio was howling near the wall and tearing at his hair. My father was sitting with clasped hands, as if made of stone. I saw all this perfectly, but I was completely indifferent to everything; and, as usual, I looked with dead, glassy eyes at the ceiling, or at the railing at the foot of the bed, or at the window, through which entered milky and silvery beams of moonlight.

Then the servants began to push into the room through all the doors; a cacophony of cries, sobs and howls, led by Kazio, filled the whole room; only my father sat motionless as before. But finally when all had knelt down, and the priest began the Litany but stopped, for he could not go on because of his tears, my father sprang up suddenly and roared, "O Jesus! O Jesus!" Then he threw himself full length onto the floor. At that moment I felt that the ends of my fingers and my toes were beginning to grow cold; a certain strange drowsiness seized me, and I began to yawn. "Ah! I am dying!" I thought, and I fell asleep.

But instead of dying, I had really fallen asleep, and I slept so well that I did not wake up until twenty-four hours later, and so greatly strengthened that I was unable to understand what had happened. My indifference had vanished; my powerful young constitution had conquered death itself and was awakening to a new life with renewed strength. Now there were such scenes of delight at my bed that I will not attempt to describe them. Kazio simply went mad from joy. They told me later that right after the duel, when my father carried me wounded to the house and the doctor could not vouch for my life, they had to lock up Kazio, for he was ready to hunt Selim as if the Tartar were a wild beast, and he swore that if I died he would shoot Selim on sight. Fortunately Selim, also wounded somewhat, had to stay in bed for some time.

Meanwhile each new day brought me greater relief. My desire for life returned. My father, my mother, the priest and Kazio watched night and day over my bed. How I loved them then; how I missed anyone who left the room even for a moment! But with life the old feeling for Hania began to speak in my heart again. When I woke from that sleep which all had considered initially an eternal one, I asked right away about Hania. My father answered that she was well, but that she had gone with Madame d'Yves and my sisters to my uncle's, for the small-pox was spreading in the village. He told me, moreover, that he had already forgiven her, that he had forgotten everything, and asked me to be quiet and rest. Nevertheless, I spoke frequently of her with my mother, who, seeing that that subject occupied me more than all others, soon initiated a conversation on the topic herself and finished it with the angelic, though vague, words that when I got well she would speak with my father of many things which to me would be very agreeable, but that I must rest and try to recover as quickly as possible. While saying this, she smiled sadly, but I wished to weep from joy.

Once in a while, however, something would happen in the house which would disturb my peace and even fill me with fear. For example, one evening, when my mother was sitting by my side, the servant Franek came in and asked her to Hania's room.

I sat up immediately in bed.

"Has Hania returned?" I asked.

"No, she has not!" answered my mother. "He asks me to Hania's room, for they are whitewashing there and re-upholstering the furniture."

At times it seemed to me that a heavy, though badly-concealed, cloud of sadness hung over the persons about me. I did not understand what was happening, and my inquiries were dismissed with trivial answers. I sounded out Kazio; he answered as did the others, that in the house all was well; that our sisters, Madame d'Yves and Hania would return soon; and, finally, that I must rest.

"But where does this sadness come from?" I asked.

"I will tell you everything. Selim and old Mirza call here every day. Selim is in despair throughout the day. He weeps; he wants desperately to see you, but our parents are afraid that this would harm you."

I smiled.

"Smart fellow that Selim!" said I. "He came near to splitting my skull, and now he is crying for me. So, is he thinking of Hania all the time?"

"Eh, how could he be thinking of Hania? I don't know, and I did not ask, but I think that he has renounced her completely."

"That is the question!"

"In any case someone else will get her, don't worry!"

Here Kazio made a wry face, student fashion, and added with a roguish expression:

"I know even who. If only God grants that—"

"That what?"

"That she return as soon as possible," he added hastily.

These words calmed me down completely. A couple of days later, in the evening, my father was sitting near me with my mother. He and I began to play chess. After a while my mother went out, leaving the door open. A whole row of rooms was visible now, at the end of which was Hania's room. I looked there but could not see anything, for all the rooms, except mine, were not lighted, while Hania's door, as far as I could see in the darkness, was closed.

Then someone went in, whom I thought was Doctor Stanislaw, and did not close the door.

My heart beat uneasily. There was light in Hania's room.

This light fell in a bright streak to the dark neighboring hall; and on the background of that bright streak it seemed to me that I saw a delicate line of smoke, curling as dust curls in the sunlight.

Gradually an indefinable odor struck my nostrils, which became stronger and stronger with every moment. Suddenly the hair rose on my head. I recognized the odor of juniper.

"Father! what is that?" I cried madly, throwing the chessmen and chessboard to the floor.

My father sprang up, confused; and also sensing that cursed odor of juniper, he closed the door of the room as quickly as possible.

"It is nothing, nothing!" he said hastily.

But I was already on my feet; and though I staggered, I moved forward quickly toward the door.

"Why are they burning juniper there?" I cried. "I want to go there!"

My father seized me by the waist.

"You will not go there! you will not! I forbid you!"

Despair seized me; so grasping the bandages around my head, I cried fiercely:

"Very well! But I swear that I will tear off these bandages and open my wound with my own hands. Hania has died! I want to see her!"

"Hania is not dead—I give you my word!" cried my father, seizing my hands and struggling with me. "She was sick, but she is better! Calm down! Calm down! Have we not had enough tragedy already? I will tell you everything, but you must go back to bed. You cannot see her. That would kill her. Calm down! Go back to bed. I swear to you that she is better."

My strength failed me, and I fell on the bed.

"My God! My God!" I repeated.

"Henryk, take hold of yourself! Are you a woman? Be a man. She is no longer in danger. I have promised to tell you everything, and I will do so, but on the condition that you collect your strength. Lay you head on the pillow! Yes, that way. Cover yourself, and lie quietly."

I obeyed.

"I am calm now; but hurry up, father, hurry up. Let me know everything. Is she really better? What was the matter with her?"

"Listen, then. That night when Selim took her there was a storm. Hania had on only a thin dress which got wet to the last thread. Oh, that mad step cost her much! In Chorzel, where Selim took her, she had no change of clothes, so she returned in the same wet dress. That very night she got the chills and a violent fever. The next day old Wegrowska could not hold her tongue and told her about what had happened to you. She even said that you had been killed. Of course that harmed her. In the evening she was unconscious. The doctor did not know for a long time what was the matter, until.... You know that there was, and still is, small-pox in the village. Hania caught the small-pox."

I thought I was losing consciousness and closed my eyes.

"Go on, father," I finally said. "I am calm."

"There were moments of great danger," he continued. "That same day on which we considered you as lost, she, too, was almost dying. But the both of you had a fortunate turning point. Today she is recovering, as are you. In a week or so she will be perfectly well. But what has been happening in the house! What has been happening!"

My father finished and looked at me carefully, as if in fear that his words might have shocked my still weak mind. I was lying motionless. The silence lasted a long time. I was collecting my thoughts, as I was looking at this new tragedy. My father rose and began to walk with long strides about the room, glancing at me from time to time.

"Father?" I said, after a long silence.

"What, my boy?"

"Is she—is she—greatly marked?"

My voice was calm and low, but my heart was beating loudly in anticipation of the answer.

"Yes!" answered my father. "As is usual after the smallpox. Perhaps there will be no marks. There are marks now, but they will disappear. To be sure, they will disappear."

I turned to the wall. I did not feel so good.

A week later, however, I was on my feet, and in two weeks I saw Hania. Ah! I will not even attempt to describe what had happened to that beautiful, ideal face. When the poor girl came out of her room, and I saw her for the first time, though I had sworn to myself that I would not show the least emotion, I became weak all of a sudden and fell into a dead faint. Oh, how terribly marked she was!

When they brought me back to consciousness, Hania was weeping aloud, certainly over herself and me, for I still looked more like a shadow than a man.

"This is all my fault!" she repeated, sobbing. "My fault!"

"Hania, my dear sister, do not weep; I will always love you!" I cried, and I seized her hands to raise them to my lips as I used to do.

Suddenly I shivered and drew back my lips. Those

hands, once so white, delicate and beautiful, were horrible now. Black spots covered them completely, and they were rough, almost repulsive.

"I will always love you!" I repeated with an effort.

I lied. I had immense, tearful compassion in my heart and the love of a brother; but the old feeling had flown away, as a bird flies away without leaving a trace.

I went to the garden, and in that same hop arbor where the first confession of love had taken place between Selim and Hania, I cried, as if after the death of some dear one.

For, in truth, the former Hania had died for me, or rather, my love had died; and in my heart there remained only emptiness and pain, as if from an unhealed wound, and also a memory that elicited tears from my eyes.

I sat there for a long time. The twilight of the quiet autumn evening began to redden the treetops. They searched for me in the house. Finally my father entered the hop arbor.

He looked at me and respected my sorrow.

"Poor boy!" he said. "God has made you go through a lot, but trust in Him. He always knows what He does."

I rested my head on my father's breast, and for some time we were both silent.

After a while, my father spoke:

"You were greatly attached to her, so tell me, if I were to say to you: 'I give her to you; will you give her your hand for a lifetime?'—what would you answer?"

"Father," I replied, "love may fly from me, but honor never! I am ready."

My father kissed me warmly.

"May God bless you! I appreciate your gesture, but it is not your duty nor your obligation; it is Selim's."

"Will he come here?"

"He will come with his father. His father knows everything."

Selim came about dusk. When he saw Hania, he grew red and then turned as white as a sheet. For a moment one could see a great struggle within him between his heart and his conscience. It was clear that for him that winged bird, whose name is love, had flown also. But the noble youth conquered himself. He rose, stretched out his arms and then fell on his knees before Hania, crying:

"My Hania! I am the same as always; I will never desert you—never, never!"

Abundant tears were flowing down Hania's face, but she gently pushed away Selim.

"I do not believe, I do not believe that it is possible to love me now," she said; and then covering her face with her hands, she cried: "Oh, how kind and honorable you all are! I alone am less honorable, more sinful; but now everything is over. I am another person!"

And despite the insistence of old Mirza, despite Selim's pleas, she refused to give him her hand. The first storm of life had broken that beautiful flower when it had barely opened. Poor girl! After that storm, she now needed some holy and peaceful harbor, where she could alleviate her conscience and calm her heart.

She found that quiet and holy harbor—she became a Sister of Charity. Later, new events and one terrible storm caused me to lose sight of her for a long time.

After several years, however, I saw her unexpectedly. Peace and calm were depicted on those angelic features, and all traces of the terrible disease had vanished. In the black robe and white head-dress of the cloister she was beautiful as never before. Now, however, it was a beauty not of this earth, but one more angelic than human.

SELIM MIRZA

I

It was spring during the Franco-Prussian War. Belfort was besieged by the Prussians, while a detachment of volunteer riflemen, in which I served along with Selim, my companion from my younger days, moved around at their rear, fighting almost every day, seizing their messengers and falling upon their convoys.

This detachment was made up of all sorts of trouble-makers, mostly foreigners, people disposed to robbery, plundering and all types of abuses, people for whom life meant nothing, who had nothing to lose and who had been made half-savage by continually fighting with the instinct and passion of wild animals. We even called ourselves hunters of men, though it was difficult to tell who the hunter was and who the hunted, for we were tracked down with thorough Germanic stubbornness and persistence. We did not give the enemy any rest, but we also did not have it ourselves, day or night. During the day we lay mostly in thickets, forests and vineyards; at night, particularly if it was raining, we came out on the prowl. We crept right up to the Prussian camps to carry off men from their outposts; we fought with patrols and lay in ambush for trains along the ditches by the railway lines—or we tore out rails, destroyed telegraph wires, and so on.

No one ever knew, not even the government of Leon

Gambetta, the one-eyed French dictator, where we were, what we were doing and where we would show up. We did not take any pay; we ate mostly what we took from the Prussians; we drank the vodka of the Prussian uhlans who surrounded us on all sides. Closed off, one could say, by a wall of guns and bayonets, we hardly ever lit a campfire; soaked from the rain, we dried ourselves in the sun; chilled to the bone, we warmed ourselves by the fire of a rifle.

"We're living right at the Prussians' doorstep," our men would say.

Indeed, the France that fought and fled was far behind us, as were French cities, the French government, its army, the one-eyed dictator, manifestos, generals in golden uniforms, newspapers, army hospitals, provisions. Closer by were Prussian, Bavarian and Saxon detachments, and we were right in the middle.

Once in a while the iron hand of some Prussian general would come down on us stealthily, like the hand of someone who wants to grab a weary insect. That hand would pause for a moment, then fall like lightning and seize only empty air—we were already someplace else.

Sometimes, though, we would place a bayonet under such a hand; then that hand would withdraw, and its owner would utter a cry of rage.

Incessant fighting, betrayals and ambuscades developed in our men a truly wolf-like instinct. They almost did not need a leader; they operated quietly, efficiently, cautiously. When they were hunted, they did not stop for a moment to hunt themselves; they knew how to lie in wait throughout the night and suppress their breathing and strain their eyes in the direction from where the prey was expected.

Risking everything, they were able to maintain a cat's caution. At times, while we were lying in the thickets, Prussian detachments passed by so closely that I could hear the voices of their officers; yet if the detachments were too strong, not one shot fell.

A regiment going through the sun's rays casts a shadow.

"We were always certain that you were hiding in our shadow," a prisoner once said to us.

Indeed, we were the Prussians' shadow.

Little by little our people lost all human feeling. I would not say that they fought for France, they just fought for the sake of fighting. They did not care for France. They could not stand the regular French troops almost as much as they could not stand the Prussians. They even had more contempt for them. When we met—which happened rarely, by the way—it always came to quarrels and fights.

"The Prussians would run away if they saw your faces," our soldiers would say to the others, "but they always see your backsides."

To put it simply, it was a detachment that was in every way exceptional. But it was not large. On the contrary, its numbers dwindled more and more through continual fighting as well as through hardships almost beyond human endurance. Besides this, the fate of our wounded and the sick was horrible. They were simply left in the woods. Once, one of our men fell from nervous exhaustion and begged to be finished off; I heard as he was answered:

"Don't worry, little lamb, the wolves will find you here."

New candidates were lacking because such a service was not alluring. On the other hand, it gave abundant promise of plunder. Our people had so many watches, coins and rings, taken from dead bodies, that they did not know what to do with them. But they were also indifferent to these things. Card-playing was forbidden; there was nothing to buy and nowhere to buy it; and it was not worthwhile to hide anything for each man knew that sooner or later he would die.

So the detachment became smaller with each passing day. Candidates were also lacking because there was no promotion. A soldier had death in his pocket, not a marshal's baton. The Defense Department mentioned us very rarely in its bulletins.

"They do not know that we exist," said our leader, who could not stand this French government.

The one-eyed dictator wanted to see us, however, and he sent an order to La Rochenoire, our leader, to appear at a particular place, but La Rochenoire ignored the order, and instead of turning up where requested, he went off on an ambush.

"If he wants to see us," he said, "let him come to us by balloon; he knows how."

Besides, our detachment would not have presented a good appearance on review. The men were gaunt, their faces blackened through smoke, their eyes bloodshot. Their uniforms were in tatters, and some had their heads wrapped in kerchiefs stained with dried-up blood. They were unkempt and unwashed—more like animals than men.

I found myself in this detachment not through any desire of my own. Selim persuaded me to join it. When the war broke out and both of us were leaving Paris, I wanted to join the regular army, but Selim said:

"We will join up with La Rochenoire."

"Who is he?"

"He is forming a detachment of riflemen."

"Do you know him?"

"Yes."

He never wanted to tell me how he knew him, and my conjectures on this part were just that, conjectures. I knew that Selim, who had more money than he could spend, had made a fuss in Paris before the war; I knew that he had a duel with someone who belonged to the French aristocracy and that he knocked the sword from that person's hand three times, but I did not know any of the details of this duel nor his opponent's name. Those were times in which Selim and I were not close. Firstly, because he was rich, and secondly, because, say what you will, the memory of Hania separated us. In truth, Selim had acted toward Hania as a man of honor, yet I could not forget that if it had not been for him my beloved Hania would not have passed through her horrible illness and would not have put on a nun's dress. Furthermore, if it had not been for him, I would have been happy. I would not have in my soul an emptiness which I had been carrying for eight years, and—quite possibly—instead of wandering around in foreign countries, I would be ploughing my family land in peace.

Finally, I was still hurt by the fact that while I, who had wronged Hania the least, bore myself with sadness and a certain reproach in my soul, Selim had forgotten about her completely. Arriving in Paris, he gave himself over to the boisterous, passionate life of that city with the entirety of his hot Eastern blood. Selim did not know the meaning of the word restraint. His wealth, the family name of Mirza-Dawidowicz, his proud nobility, his education, his wit and humor, and finally his beauty, inherited from his mother, opened all doors of pleasure to him in the world's capital. He was accepted everywhere and amused everywhere. Oh! for this boy was beautiful, like an artistic ideal, with his angelic eyes, which simply grabbed you by the heart, with his head, which seemed as if chiselled by a sculptor, with his lofty, supple figure, winged with youth and a richness of life so boundless that the more he experienced, the more he conquered.

And he was not your typical handsome man of the Parisian boulevards. Everything, beginning with his mind, his abundance of life, which he himself did not know what to do with, and ending with his facial features, was in him original and uncommon.

This young Tartar—with his angelic features, athletic strength, lion-like courage and knightly nobility—was for Paris a flower of unknown color and fragrance. It is easy to understand how the marquises of the Seine paled beside him. They were tired by the life of the salon; he found it rejuvenating. They were dead spirits, like burned-out lamps, while he was a bright flame. They had outlived their days, while he did not know what he should do with his; they were disillusioned, while he was enchanting and saw everything around him as enchanting. For them an orgy was a stimulant of dulled nerves, for him—a cooling down of excessively heated blood. Furthermore, the dregs lying at the bottom of the cup of life did not touch his lips, and evil fell from his noble nature like dry sand from a rock.

This individual was formed before my eyes; I saw how he developed almost from day to day. That is why I knew him inside out. This was the same Selim as from our younger days, only raised to the nth power.

His conviction of his own powers gave him self-assurance, while his conviction, based on an innate knowledge of the baseness and false appearance of most people's souls, taught him to treat people with disregard. The germs of unrestrained energy and enterprise that had resided in him since his younger days, now burst forth to the highest degree, toughened him and, to a certain extent, made him dangerous.

His old liveliness and a little of his former recklessness were still there, and considering his passionate nature, they could easily change into frenzy and madness. But he was protected from this frenzy and madness by an awareness of self, which gives people education and a subtle, and to some extent philosophical, sense of every act, word, position and idea. He was never sentimental, and if anything similar to sentimentality existed within him during his adolescent years, even if in minute form, it disappeared now without a trace. That is why the memory of Hania did not leave in him even a shadow of sadness or remorse. He knew how to love with laughter, kisses, joy and partying, but he was unfamiliar with sighing and pinning away for a loved one.

Such a disposition, however, agreed with the character and nature of the women of the world's capital; that is why these women went crazy for him, though they knew that he would desert them easily and without regret. When I spoke to him on the subject one day, he said to me:

"I have no obligations here and am merely playing around. I would give my right arm to find a true love. If such a creature exists, you will seek her the longest out of the both of us, and you will probably find her."

"So you are deceiving a woman when you say that you are in love?"

He smiled.

"No! I know that later I will deceive her; but when I say it, I mean it."

The men whom he met were divided into two groups: those that really liked him, and those that could not stand him. As for Selim, he had a most interesting opinion concerning them.

"I prefer those that like me, but I have more respect for those that do not; they are more their own men."

Later he would frequently add:

"Besides, I don't care for everyone."

He was an excellent companion, however. He had a good, kind heart and lent a helping hand to anyone he could and whenever he could. But he did not enter into friendships easily. Yet at the moment when he shared with someone everything as if with a brother, he loved that person also like a brother; and then his feeling was sincere, almost naive, flowing from the depths of his soul. Later, though, he would treat the relationship lightly. Selim treated everything a little lightly.

But when I removed myself somewhat from him and began to live more to myself, because of the reasons I have already mentioned, Selim fretted over this for some time. In the beginning, he would frequently ask:

"What do want from me, madman?"

Later he stopped asking me, but that did not stop his hurt. Once in a while, escaping his turbulent, joyful and exuberant life, he would rush to my little room on Montmartre and, sitting by the window, follow me solicitously with his angelic eyes, as if wanting to find out what was hidden in my heart. As for me, I did not stop loving him; and maybe precisely because our natures were completely different, I had toward him as much weakness as attachment. But the memory of Hania, who stopped to exist for him, separated us. I had other reasons as well.

I could not live on an equal level with him. Besides, he was merry, while I was sad. Oh, yes, I had a lot of reasons to live apart from Selim, but I could not reveal them to him because I feared his condolences. My nature was such that I did not share my bitterness with any soul. When I felt a thorn in my heart, I closed myself up like a shell in which falls a grain of sand. Likewise, I did not talk about my happiness to anyone. Whoever does this, does so out of some internal necessity. I did not feel this need.

And so we lived under these circumstances for several years in Paris. I vegetated, he blossomed. Meanwhile war broke out. We met it with indifference. All of Paris considered it some sort of military parade at first. It was presumed that the very sight of bearded zouaves and black Africans would scatter the Germans to the four

corners of the earth. Those zouaves and Algerian riflemen proceeded east like flocks of birds of prey. They
breathed with the craving for battle and blood, they
trembled with impatience, eager for the smoke, noise
and dust of war. Paris became intoxicated and was calm
about the future.

"One more triumph," it was supposed, "and that will
be the end of it."

But when the smoke cleared at Wissembourg, Grav-
elotte and Sedan, the terrified eyes of the French saw the
most horrible disaster which had ever befallen them.
Those colorful red and black regiments took flight before the iron German legions like forest birds before a
flock of hawks, and a dark and dangerous wall of Prussian warriors tightened around the world's capital. At the
gates of Paris, the neighing of Atilla's horse began to
reverberate night after night. From time to time, amid
the silence of the city, the clatter of a galloping dispatch-
rider was heard and a voice calling out: "They defeated
our men! Another defeat!" Paris bent its knees momentarily, like a bull hit with an axe-head between the legs,
but later it raised itself up and bellowed.

The entire nation rose up in defence. The dangerous
one-eyed dictator sailed away from the city in a balloon.
The scales of war began to waver once again. In the
north, the south, the east and the west of France detachments were formed; armies grew up from under the
ground like mushrooms. The country bristled with
bayonets.

During those days, Selim dropped by one evening, his
face flushed, his eyes sparkling. He fell about my neck.

"We will go and fight!" he cried out.

I had wanted to do this for a long time, so I received
his words coolly. He assumed that this was my old
coldness, which for several years had distanced us, so he
said quickly:

"There was something between us, but—by the Prophet!—let it be forgotten. Henryk, once again stirrup to stirrup!"

I remembered what my father had said to me when I was to have a duel with Selim:

"Now then, fight, my son, so that it'll be heard in the heavens."

So I replied similarly to Mirza:

"Yes, we will fight, Selim, so that it will be heard in the heavens."

Then we embraced, and then we began to quarrel. I wanted to stay in Paris and fight along its walls; Selim wanted to get out of Paris and join the volunteer riflemen.

"Here the city-folk will cut and run," he stated.

Then he began to tell me about La Rochenoire, assuring me that under his command we would find what we were looking for.

"He doesn't care for me," he said, "but he is quite special. I've never met anyone like him. I would give my life for him."

I have already mentioned that I had asked him in vain about the details concerning his duel with La Rochenoire. I surmised that La Rochenoire was that marquis who had his weapon knocked out three times by Selim, but since Selim had had a lot of duels, it was difficult to determine anything exactly.

"He is an exceptional person; there are perhaps only three such people in the whole world," he repeated to me with insistence.

Finally I gave in, for I usually gave in to Selim, but I did this with regret. There were enough rifles in Paris and enough fighting beyond the walls, as much as one wanted, in fact—but to get out of Paris one had to go by balloon. The prospect of such an aerial sailing did not please me. Besides, I wanted to join the cavalry, while La

Rochenoire's detachment was a foot one. Selim was ada-
mant, however—and I gave in.

And so we took flight in a balloon two days later,
taking with us a significant number of dispatches for the
dictator. The day was cloudy and rainy. Our craft, which
inside the city immediately soared up several thousand
feet, fell a considerable distance outside the city and
floated along lethargically above the Prussian camp itself. I saw the entire camp as if it were in the palm of my
hand—the white sea of tents, the redoubts, the divisions, the guards in their pointed helmets, standing
motionless like statues around the camp. Clusters of
soldiers, both large and small, pointed up at us; generals
looked at us through field-glasses. The entire camp came
to life so noisely that we heard its uproar. Our craft was
shot at by a light field gun, but we did not even hear the
whistle of the projectile. Monsieur Vaucourt, the captain
of our balloon, who was a brave aeronaut but a great
coward, was dying of fright at the bottom of the basket.
Selim was laughing like a child and clapping his hands;
he bowed to the Germans and called out to them in
every language, shaking the basket in the process, which
had the effect of increasing Vaucourt's fear. I, meanwhile, held my rifle to see if I could get off a good shot,
but the distance and the rocking of the basket prevented
this.

When we reached the last outposts of the camp, the
balloon went down even more. Now Selim also grabbed
a rifle, and his eyes sparkled like a wolf's. He strained his
eyes in one direction and a moment later said to me:

"Look!"

I glanced in the direction he was pointing at, and
through the transparent fog, through which we sailed at
that moment, I saw several dozen figures on horses
emerge, as if from a large black mass of people, and begin
to head toward us.

Soon we could see with the naked eye the square caps of the uhlans, their uniforms and lances and the colors of their banners. We heard their cries; then they were directly below us. Meanwhile our craft went down still further and floated more and more freely.

"Those are uhlans!" cried out Selim.

"Nous sommes perdus!" groaned Vaucourt.

Meanwhile the uhlans vied with one another to get us, but without the least order. At the front dashed an officer, a stalwart man with a white beard. His chestnut-colored horse, which one could see was farther ahead than the others, was running like mad right under our balloon, kicking up the earth with his hooves. The officer, not paying attention to where he was going, was looking at our craft as if at a rainbow and shouting in German:

"We got you! We got you!"

"Then hold onto us!" Selim replied, laughing.

We floated over a meadow overgrown with clusters of rushes and somewhat marshy. The horses of the uhlans started to get stuck in the mud and fall; barely half of them continued on in the chase, and soon even that group began to diminish; the officer, however, and about twenty other uhlans, held fast to the chase magnificently.

"What brave horses!" I said to Selim.

"One can shoot now," he said.

Indeed, we were not higher than four hundred feet above the ground, but shooting was difficult because of the rocking of the basket, which, at times, came close to collapsing.

"Can't you stop this devilish basket from dancing like a ballerina?" cried out Selim in a loud voice, as if Vaucourt were deaf.

"Nous sommes perdus!" groaned Vaucourt.

Then Selim, holding onto a rope with one hand,

raised himself up in the basket, and with the other hand
he aimed his rifle toward the officer, as if he were about
to shoot from a pistol.

"Too difficult a shot," I said.

"I'll give it a try."

The hollow report of the shot rang out, immediately
eliciting a shout of anger below. I glanced down. The
officer was not looking up anymore. He had fallen face
down on the horse's mane and soon tumbled to the
ground.

At the same time, however, we descended so low that
the trail line, which usually hung under the balloon,
almost touched the ground. Luckily, the uhlans had
stopped by their dead officer, as a result of which we
were able to distance ourselves from them by several
hundred feet.

Vaucourt, pulling himself together, threw out of the
basket everything he possibly could, but apparently the
gas was seeping through a wet lute, or perhaps holes had
formed in the upper portion of the balloon, and now
enough gas had escaped so that one-third of the trail line
began to hit the ground, causing the basket to rock
wildly.

The uhlans noticed this and once again began their
chase, but their tired horses could not gallop after us for
any length of time, and soon only five remained; and
then, after about ten minutes, another horse fell from
under a rider and did not rise.

"There are only four left," said Selim.

"Shoot, and there will be three."

"The distance is too great; besides, this basket has
gone crazy."

"But we don't have to flee anymore."

"Very well, then! Monsieur Vaucourt, open the valve,
let the gas out; we want to get off."

"Gentlemen!" cried out the Frenchmen with despair,

"have you lost your senses? How's that—four devils are after us, and we will voluntarily give ourselves up? Never!"

"Monsieur Vaucourt, open the valve and lower the anchor," Selim repeated threateningly.

"Never."

Mirza turned to me and said calmly:

"Will you be so kind as to place the barrel of your rifle against Monsieur Vaucourt's head. Let him choose."

I turned and, holding onto a line with one hand, I directed the rifle at Monsieur Vaucourt's head with my other hand.

"I will give you a minute to think about it, monsieur."

Monsieur Vaucourt started to curse our nationality, the moment he was born, himself, Paris, the Prussians, but he lowered the anchor and with shaking hands opened the valve with such speed as if the salvation of France rested on it. We started to fall to the ground like a ball.

"Hold on!" cried out Selim.

We did not count on one thing, however. One does not get out of a balloon basket as if from a carriage. The anchor did indeed hook into a cluster of rushes, but the basket hit the ground so hard that we flew out in three different directions. What was worse, the rifle fell out of my hand, while I myself fell face down on the ground.

I started up immediately, but I was unable to look around for my rifle, for right at my ear I heard the snorting of a horse and the whirr of an uhlan's banner.

"To the right, to the right!" shouted Selim.

I was able to jump in that direction, when a shot rang out and the rider, who had already reached me with his lance, blinked his eyes and tumbled heavily from the saddle as if struck by lightning.

Ah, Mirza had not let go of his rifle upon falling!

I grabbed mine and glanced around. Now it was Selim

who was in danger. Two riders raced toward him in full gallop, howling and yelling like crazy. He waited calmly for them, hatless, his hair wind-blown, his nostrils flaring, his face flushed and his hands gripping his rifle. One of the riders aimed his pistol at Selim—I pulled my trigger.

Of our three attackers, only one remained, but I was unconcerned as to the result of that fight. Mirza was too expert a fighter with side-arms for the outcome to be in doubt.

A fourth uhlan remained, but when he saw from a distance what had happened, he reined in his horse so hard that the rear legs of the animal buried themselves deeply in the grass; then he began to ride away as quickly as his weary horse could gallop.

Selim shot after him, but without result, for the distance was too great.

The horse of the Prussian that Selim had shot stood with lowered heard over the lifeless body of his master, for the Prussian's hand had not let go of the reins.

Selim and I extracted the reins from that hand with difficulty, for the fingers had already stiffened; after which Selim jumped on the saddle and galloped after the two other horses. One of the horses, apparently a stupid animal, was chewing on the grass a short distance away, as if nothing had happened, while the other raced across the meadow in a gallop and declared his grief with a brief neighing.

Selim came back with the horses after a quarter of an hour; I looked around for Monsieur Vaucourt, for I did not know what had become of him.

I found him behind a cluster of rushes, lying face down on the ground, and I shook him by the shoulder.

"Monsieur Vaucourt, get up!"

"*Pardonnez moi!*" groaned Monsieur Vaucourt, thinking that a Prussian uhlan was addressing him. It did not occur to the poor fellow that a Prussian would not call out to him in French.

"Monsieur Vaucourt! It is Selim and Henryk. There are no uhlans now. It is we, your companions!"

Monsieur Vaucourt, though he did not get up, raised himself a little on his hands and looked at me with amazement, not believing his own eyes. Standing next to me with the horses was Selim.

"Yes, yes! There are no uhlans now!" Selim repeated while laughing uproariously.

Monsieur Vaucourt glanced now at us, now at the uhlans' horses, now at the bodies lying in the meadow, then he suddenly fell into such a paroxysm of joy, that we thought he had lost his senses.

"Eh bien! vous êtes donc des diables!" he cried out, unable to control himself.

"He did everything," I said, indicating Selim.

"How's that? This young man with the face of a— girl?"

"No, no!" Selim replied. "Both of us did this."

Monsieur Vaucourt laughed, danced, questioned us, then danced once again—in a word, he went crazy. Then he ran to take a look at the dead bodies. But when he stopped before the corpse of the nearest Prussian and saw a face twisted by convulsions, with red foam about the lips and compressed teeth, when he saw lifeless eyes staring up at him, the poor fellow became so weak and pale that we thought he would faint.

Selim wanted him to go through the pockets of the Prussians, but he was too frightened to do so. We only took their helmets and, mounting the horses, went off on our journey.

"I prefer a horse to that infernal thing," Selim said when we passed by the balloon, which lay on the grass and presented a sorry sight in its collapsed state.

Meanwhile darkness descended, and soon it was

nighttime. We reached some road, but we did not know if it would lead us to some village full of Prussians. We had to be very careful, for we were not out of danger yet. We were in regions occupied by the enemy and could at any moment meet up with a patrol. It was also possible that a new pursuing party was after us. Meanwhile Monsieur Vaucourt, having given free rein to his tongue, could not stop talking, and he unburdened his "boundless" and "inexpressible" gratitude so loudly that finally Mirza ordered him to be quiet.

"Why?" he asked.

"The Prussians could be nearby."

"Avec vous, je m'en fiche!" he replied with complete confidence.

His courage was now as equally "boundless" as his gratitude.

Meanwhile the forest road began to get more tortuous. Frequently, startled by some rustling, we turned to the side, halting our horses and the breath in our chests. Once a deer with her young darted across the road and, sighting us, ran in short hops to a nearby clearing, on which she began to nibble the grass calmly. In those days animals seemed to know that people were too occupied with killing each other to have time to pay attention to them. Sometimes the branch of a tree would strike our faces or catch against our clothing, sometimes a horse would snort impatiently or a tree would take on the shape of some fantastic person with open arms or hands stretched to the sky. At those times we would stop our horses, and while Monsieur Vaucourt remained behind, Selim and I, cocking our rifles, would ride up slowly to the suspicious object.

The forest rustled, the rain let up, but a wind arose instead. Along the dark heavens scattered clouds passed, now covering the moonlight, now revealing a sky covered with dim stars.

The nerves of our companion began to take the floor loudly once again. As for me, I was completely happy. The silence and the solitude, the wild surroundings, the night, the open breath of wind, the uncertainty and the danger in every minute had for me an unimaginable fascination, and I felt as if resuscitated. It had been stifling and confining behind the walls of Paris, while here I breathed freely, with the entire capacity of my lungs, like a Bedouin horseman in Arabia. There behind the walls of Paris my own thoughts and memories had gone round and round every day in a painful circle, while here my stirrup knocked against the stirrup of my fellow brother, a Tartar. Before me was a wide country— and in my hand my other brother, a rifle. And here I had freedom, forgetfulness, intoxication, death. . . .

If the safety of my companions had not prevented it, I would have raised my face to the sky and shouted out at the top of my lungs: "Hey, you noisy wilderness!"— and then listened with attentive ears to how that forest, on which the wind played as if on an organ, would answer. For a moment it seemed to me that I was back in Lithuania, somewhere in the backwoods and marshes, where at midnight the waters murmur audibly and the sharp cries of water-nymphs pierce the air, where wood dust glows with a bluish light, and a bewitched beast talks in words.

I did not, therefore, think of danger at that moment, but Mirza did. His knitted brows indicated concentration; his eyes examined every bush, every tree. The road, which was in reality one of those woodland paths that we call in our country an "auntie's lane," became rougher minute by minute.

Finally, after a ride of half an hour, Selim said:

"We have to give the horses a rest."

We turned to the side and, after riding about three hundred feet into the woods, got off our horses; then we unbridled them, and not letting go of the reins, we sat down by the trees. None of us spoke, for we were very tired. The silence was broken only by the munching of grass in our horses' teeth.

Thus we sat for quarter of an hour, when suddenly all of us sprang to our feet.

"What's that?" we whispered at the same time.

A strange sound came to us from the darkness and silent forest. It was something between the crying of a baby and the bleating of a lamb.

"That's a goat!" said Mirza.

"No, it's a nightjar," I replied.

At the same time the horses stopped chewing the grass and began to prick their ears and snort.

Most strange was the fact that this sound came to us at times from the right, at other times from the left; sometimes it reverberated close-by, then again at a distance; yet it was always weak and plaintive.

No! This was neither a goat nor a nightjar. There was something unexplainable in this, and therefore that small, plaintive voice had something horrible in it, so that it seemed supernatural. If this were the howling of wolves or the report of a rifle we would have certainly known what to have done.

Selim, though he had the courage of a lion, was superstitious to a degree, so, fixing his eyes into the darkness, he whispered:

"I don't like this at all; I like to know what I'm dealing with."

"*Mon Dieu!*" groaned Monsieur Vaucourt, whose hair stood on end.

"I see something white there," Selim whispered, indicating a dark corner of the woods.

I glanced in that direction. Mirza was mistaken. I saw nothing white, nor black, in the area he indicated.

"I'll take a look around," I said. "The devil won't grab me, after all."

I went, my rifle firmly in hand. I was also of the opinion that it is much better to know what one is dealing with. In truth, in the presence of this sound, which I heard around me and above me, I was ready to suppose that it was the souls of the departed who had occupied the trees like starlings and were now calling out or complaining.

My nerves were on edge. I gave a start at every fallen branch I broke when I stepped on it. Once it seemed to me that some voice whispered right into my ear: "Hey, *Polonais!*" But these were illusions.

I circumvented a considerable portion of the forest around the tree by which we had made our camp. The strange sound continued for so long that finally it ceased to frighten me and began to bore me.

"Hang it all!" I said to myself and returned to the tree.

By the tree I found only Monsieur Vaucourt, who, at the moment I was coming closer, was certain that the very devil was coming to take his soul away.

"Where is Mirza?" I whispered.

"He w-went to re-con-noi-ter," answered the Frenchman, his teeth chattering.

A quarter of an hour went by, then half an hour. Selim did not show up.

Now I began to be truly frightened. The danger was real. Mirza, going out too far, had probably gotten lost in this damned forest and could not find his way back to this tree.

Three quarters of an hour passed by. Selim still did not show up.

I could have, in truth, fired off a shot from the rifle or called out to indicate to him the way back, but that would have also alerted a Prussian patrol. Yet there was nothing else to do. I would not leave the tree without

Selim, even if the entire Prussian army were to surround
me. I disclosed my intention to Monsieur Vaucourt.

Monsieur Vaucourt fell on his knees before me, begging me not to do this.

"That would be the end of us!" he said.

I tried to hiss but was answered with silence; even that
sound of a lamb or a devil quieted down. So I called out
once, then twice:

"Mirza—here, here!"

Silence.

The hair on my head rose in fear for Selim's life. At
that moment that fellow was the dearest thing to me in
the whole wide world. Barely thinking, I raised the rifle
into the air and fired off a shot.

A red light flashed, then a bang reverberated. The
entire forest quieted down, as if terror-struck. Only
Monsieur Vaucourt cried out:

"God, have mercy on my soul!"

"The devil doesn't even want it," I answered, running
out of patience.

The silence, however, did not last longer than five
minutes; after which it seemed to me that I could catch
the sound of branches being crushed by the steps of
someone approaching.

It could be Selim, but maybe it was not Selim, so
Vaucourt and I concealed ourselves behind the tree.

After a moment the dark silhouette of a person could
be seen between the branches. Unfortunately, clouds hid
the moon at the same time. It became so dark that I
could barely make out the figure.

That figure, head bend out in front, advanced slowly
and carefully, stopping at every step. I noticed that the
figure held a rifle.

Fifteen feet away the black figure stopped. I strained
my eyes. It was not Selim.

Because of the darkness I was not able to see if this was

a Prussian soldier or even a soldier. I did indeed see that this person did not have a spiked helmet on his head, but Bavarians and Saxons also did not have spiked helmets, and besides, Prussians wore caps too.

Whoever this enormous fellow was, who at that moment stood fifteen feet away from me, I needed him and needed him alive, so I determined to seize him.

"Tsss!" the newcomer hissed out.

"Tsss!" I answered behind the tree.

It was a real blindman's buff, a game somewhat dangerous at that point, but interesting none the less.

The newcomer advanced two more steps. In the twinkling of an eye I threw myself on him like a tiger, and a second later I was sitting on his chest and squeezing his throat with my hands.

"Be quiet and don't move, or else you're a dead man!" I cried out.

But the stranger, evidently endowed with uncommon strength, thrashed about like crazy. I was strong also, and I held onto him as if with pincers, though barely. He wheezed and kicked his legs and almost overthrew me.

Suddenly, however, he stopped, as if a new iron strength had rooted him to the ground. I glanced up. It was my dear fellow, Selim, who now knelt on his legs and, leaning over me, placed a gleaming bayonet to his face.

"One more move, and it's over for you!" he cried out.

But the stranger had no intention of moving. Then Selim got off him, grabbed his rifle, leveled it and said to me:

"Let him go."

I did as he told me. The stranger lay still.

"Go ahead and kill me!" he said.

"Get up."

The poor fellow got up and began to speak, gasping for air with his weary lungs:

"Who are you people? What do you want of me? I've never harmed anyone. You've broken my arms and legs. If you are forest guards, take my rifle. I will pay the fine—just don't break my bones. There is a war on now. Game belongs to whoever is hungry. The German hunts the Frenchman, the wolf sheep, a cat mice; I hunt deer and rabbits. Such are the times; everyone is hunting...."

"Who are you?"

"My name is Mathieu Benoit, or old Mathieu, if you prefer."

"So, old Mathieu, calm down! We are not guards; you won't go to jail, we won't take your rifle, you won't pay a fine. The only thing you will do is show us the way."

"Yes, but you've broken my old bones," muttered Mathieu. Several pieces of gold jingled in Selim's hand.

"Buy yourself new ones, and now answer our questions."

"I'm listening."

"Are the Prussians here?"

"Yes."

"And the French?"

"The French are here also. One side kills the other. And they also burn down villages, and God looks down upon it all and is silent."

"Listen. You will lead us to the French by such a path that we won't meet up with any Prussians."

"I know many such paths."

"If we meet up with more than three Prussians, I will shoot you in the head. And so you won't feel the urge to scamper away, you will go on leash next to my horse."

"Now a dog is better than a man," grunted Mathieu.

We mounted our horses and started. Old Mathieu, who was what the French call "*un braconnier*" and what we Poles call "*wnicznik*," or, in other words, a poacher, led us by roads only he knew.

"This road," he said, indicating the path which we

had previously gone along, "would have taken you to Pont Vert where Madame Frolie has an inn. They say the woman has money. There you would find the Prussians also, who not long ago executed young Vauhart. But I know the forest like the back of my hand and will lead you well. God has given us such times that one can meet death on the road and peace in the woods. The German is in church, and Caesar is behind bars." And he added after a while: "But I'm stupid, so I don't know anything."

"To whom do you sell your game?" asked Selim.

"Sometimes to the French, sometimes to the Prussians, and if they take it from me by force, then I give it to them for free. War takes, my dear gentlemen, and it pays for merchandise—on one's back."

The old man babbled on as if nothing had happened. There was in him a mixture of stupidity and philosophy, from which one could come to this conclusion, that when giants are fighting, pygmies suffer and think that God has fallen asleep.

We questioned our guide about that particular sound which we had heard in the woods. It turned out that poachers call out to each other in this manner and that Mathieu had been in the forest with his three sons. That explained why the sound came to us from all sides.

"But it is possible," added the old man, "that the devil speaks that way also."

Then he continued:

"If you would have come across my son Jacob—he's also called 'Crooked Hand'—it wouldn't have gone so easily for you, though you are as strong as Turks."

It was perhaps two o'clock at night when the forest began to thin out, and finally we found ourselves in a ravine sided with shrubs. Mathieu told us that the forest from which we had exited was not great, but that the path we had initially taken went around it close to its borders, almost completely in a circle, so that we had gone that way in vain.

Barely had the first gleam of dawn showed itself on earth, when from a distance we heard the crowing of cocks, and soon, in the midst of the fog, which was lit up by the pale rays of dawn, we saw the roofs of houses and the church steeple of a little town occupied by the French. A loud *"Qui vive?"* of a sentinel stopped our advance. We had to wait until a patrol would arrive to change the guard. When that happened, the patrol took us with them, and in that manner we arrived at our destination.

It surprised us a little that despite our announcement that we had despatches for the dictator, the general, whose quarters were located at the mayor's residence, was not awakened immediately. We were, however, given a room, whose floor was covered with hay, and a guard was placed over us. We threw ourselves on the hay and fell into a deep sleep.

It was only on the following day, at ten o'clock, that we were called before the general, whose name I do not remember, for I have lost a portion of the notes which refer to this time period. The general, who had green eyes and a face similar to that of a fish, and who was, besides, quite fat, looked more like the perfect gourmand and loafer than a soldier.

About a dozen officers surrounded him in respectful silence. Monsieur Vaucourt spoke, and began to relate most eloquently the adventures we had encountered on our journey, occurrences barely probable, but whose truth was verified by the uhlan helmets and the horses, on which we had ridden to town.

Monsieur Vaucourt spoke the truth. To be sure, the poor fellow did not mention that I had placed the barrel of a rifle to his head to induce him to open the valve on the balloon. Besides, he always said: "we"—as in "we killed them," "we got out"—instead of saying "they."

During the entire story Selim and I stood shoulder to shoulder, leaning on our rifles. The officers glanced at us in silence, after which, when Monsieur Vaucourt finally finished his narrative, the general rose and spoke:

"Gentlemen! I present to you a valiant son of France." Here he pointed to Monsieur Vaucourt. "If all Frenchmen were like—what's his name?—our country would already be free of the enemy. This gallant man did not give heed to—what's it called?—but in a hail of bullets and—this and that—made his way to us—and that is it, gentlemen, that is it!..."

The general began to wipe his lips with a napkin, the officers smiled, the valiant son of France turned red as a beet and, confused, began to glance at us with an imploring look. Selim bit his lips, while I tried to assure the valiant son of France with my eyes that we had not the slightest intention of protesting the praise heaped upon him.

Meanwhile the general took off one of the crosses which formed on his chest a most considerable constellation, and he continued:

"Come closer, valiant son of France. I think that—what's his name?—the dictator will confirm my act, as well as this cross, which I decorate you with."

One of the officers, a tall man with a stern and unpleasant face, could not contain himself.

"General, pardon me!" he said. "It seems to me that these two gentlemen—"

But the general waved him to be silent and turned to us.

"And you, foreigners," he said, "who have just enlisted under the French flag, take a look at this hero, and perhaps one day a similar cross will glitter upon your breasts."

I was afraid that Selim would interrupt or burst out in laughter, but no: he stood quiet and cool, though one could see the entire affair both angered and amused him.

The considerate Monsieur Vaucourt, though, began to declare loudly that the cross belonged to us rather than to him. This presented the general with an enigma impossible to unravel: Was Monsieur Vaucourt more valiant or more modest? After the ceremony, Monsieur Vaucourt went on his way.

That day Mirza invited the officers to dinner, at which he threw out gold like a prince. The following day we set out to find La Rochenoire's detachment.

And that is what took place on our journey from Paris.

II

We rode to the department of Haute-Saone through a country occupied, more or less, by the French, who had little regard for the fact that Bavarian armies were operating in the south and maintaining communication with the Prussian army surrounding the capital. Danger threatened us only from French marauders, many of whom kept to the roads and who allowed themselves, here and there, to loot and steal. We were not afraid of them, however, the more so that we were three in number once again, for though "the valiant son of France," Monsieur Vaucourt, was now on the road to Bordeaux, on the second day of our journey another person joined us, a certain Jean Marx, an eighteen-year-old Alsatian boy who was not afraid of anything in the world and who, after knowing us for just one day, would have gone with us even to hell.

The country we passed through bore all the signs of being ravaged by war. We came across unworked fields and devastated villages, whose inhabitants hid themselves before us; we met groups of emaciated and hungry fellows wandering around like ghosts about the previous year's potato fields in search of rotten potatoes. The scent of war hung in the air over the entire land; almost everywhere we went we were accompanied by the stench of burning. At night the horizon would frequently turn red from the glow of a distant conflagration; during the full moon, we heard the howl of wolves from distant wildernesses. Several times we came across a field of battle which we recognized as such not by the bodies of horses and men, but by the many pieces of white paper from spent charges. In places these papers covered the ground like snow. Once we came upon an empty village in which we found skinny chickens, which ran away upon our arrival, and one old woman. This old woman, who was quite insane, sat in front of a half-dilapidated cottage talking to herself. We could barely make out from her confused answers to our questions that the villagers had fired upon a troop of uhlans a few days ago and, presuming that the village would be burned down in retaliation, were now in flight.

One night we knocked at the door of a cottage in whose window a light shone. For a long time the door remained closed, but finally it was opened by a man with a face so similar to a wolf's that we thought it was indeed a wolf who was welcoming us inside. Marx maintained that this person was a robber of dead bodies, and he advised us not to spend the night there, for, as he said, during the night one could easily get a knife under the ribs; nevertheless, because we were tired, we decided to stay. Soon, however, four similar cutthroats came in, and all began to look at us from under their brows, eyeing covetously at the same time our traveling equipment. Marx remained outside with the horses, while Mirza, without giving it much thought, seized our wolf by the throat, pressed him against the wall and, placing a pistol to his muzzle, said:

"The plague on you, you filthy animal! Throw these
rascals out the door, or else I will shoot them and you in
the head; and if something will disappear during the
night, you'll hang for it."

The cutthroats muttered sullenly. One of them even
proclaimed that he was from the mayor's office and
asked us haughtily for our passports, in answer to which
Selim grabbed a riding-whip and began to shower blows
on everyone without pity, not sparing in particular the
back of the official from the mayor's. The night passed
peacefully for us, and the following day we proceeded on
our way.

But now our journey was more difficult. We came to
a country that was almost exclusively occupied by the
Germans, among which moved sparse detachments of
volunteer riflemen, cunning and driven everywhere like
wild animals. The villages and towns were more intact
here than those along the routes on which armies met
and fought. The populace played it safe with the Germans and tolerated their superiority, but it was almost
impossible to get any kind of help or directions. We
determined, however, to reach La Rochenoire without
fail, a highly difficult task, for, on the one hand, no one
knew where La Rochenoire was keeping himself and he
changed camp from day to day; and on the other hand,
one had to get to him almost through the jaws of the
Prussians, for of all the detachments not one was more
diligently watched and scrupulously enclosed than his.

I can also say that at that time the three of us began a
real war on our own. We moved forward only at night,
guiding ourselves by the news of La Rochenoire's attacks
and battles. But we were a well-matched trio now.

Ah, what a splendid lad that Marx was with his Alsatian coolness, his comical, broken French and his indifference to everything happening around him! At times it
even seemed to me that his courage flowed from an

abundance of dulled nerves and the fact that he did not understand the danger involved. But there was another reason. Marx hated the Germans with his entire soul, and in cool temperaments hatred is generally intense. Nevertheless, he had the caution of a pointer dog and cooler blood than either of us.

III

Little of our journey was made by train, for the rail lines in the areas occupied by the French were mostly damaged, and in the face of the current defeats and disarray not much thought was given over to their repair. Furthermore, the movements of the various armies would have made such work almost impossible, everything at that time being concentrated on the fight over France.

The department of Haute-Saone, in which La Rochenoire circled, was occupied by the Germans; that is why, reaching its borders, we once again made our journey through the woods and almost exclusively during the night. Our daylight hours were spent sleeping in hop-fields or vineyards, reconnoitering and trying to figure out the best way to get to La Rochenoire. A couple of days before we reached him, we arrived at a village called La Mare. La Mare was not along our way, but Selim claimed that he had to see someone who had lived there for some time, a Monsieur La Grange, whom he knew from his days in Paris.

We approached this village very cautiously, for it was probable that a Bavarian or Prussian patrol was in it. Darkness was descending; the sun had set, and only the diffused last light of the afterglow still hung in the air. The windows in the village cottages began to light up here and there. Everything appeared to be at peace. We crawled along a hop-field like snakes. Dogs scented us, however, and began to bark. All of a sudden we saw the dark silhouettes of several human figures; they were standing by a fence and carrying on a conversation in low tones.

We immediately crouched down in the hop-field. Meanwhile the voices subsided, and one of the dark figures, leaning over the fence, examined the thickets carefully. Then, in the darkness, we heard once again a conversation in French.

"What are you looking at, friend Grousbert?"

"The dogs are barking, and there's something moving about in there."

"Eh, no! The moon is rising, so the dogs are disturbed."

Another voice added:

"Maybe it's the spirits of the dead? It is said that dogs can scent spirits."

"In the name of the Father and the Son and the Holy Ghost!"

After which, we heard sighing.

Mirza whispered to me:

"That must be a patrol."

On the road the conversation began again, but in low, secretive tones.

"The wolves are also roaming about. War increases wolves along with everything else that is bad."

"Hey, the sunset was really red today! There must have been another battle."

"Mer said that the Prussians will come here again."

"May St. Hubert protect us!"

At that point Selim got up from his hiding-place.

"Hey there!" he called out. "Where can we find La Grange?"

"Oh, oh!" cried out terrified voices. "Who's there?"

"Today we are soldiers, tomorrow God only knows! Tell us where we can find La Grange and stop asking questions."

One of the villagers said:

"I will take you to him."

We went along a wide path. It was so dark on it that we could barely make one another out. After about thirty feet we made a sharp turn to the right. We saw in the distance a small church, enclosed by a low white wall and, closer by, a great mass of trees, through which glittered lighted windows. The villager said:

"That is the Church of St. Hubert, and La Grange lives here."

We found ourselves in the midst of a park so overgrown that branches obscured its alleys and paths. The park appeared to be in a state of complete neglect. A beautiful house, shaped like a Swiss chalet, stood in the middle, but it was so profusely covered with rampant vines, or some other creepers, that its lit-up windows looked out at us as if from behind a mask.

The entrance door was open, so, not seeing or asking anyone, we went inside. In the vestibule there was no light, but the moonlight came in through the windows of the room inside, and it was so bright that we could make out everything: the table in the center, the cupboards by the walls, and the bouquets of dry ears of corn on the cupboards.

Marx knocked on the floor with his rifle. Then we heard steps; the door of the adjoining room opened, and a woman—most certainly a servant—showed up at the threshold and disappeared quickly back inside, as if frightened. Marx knocked louder.

After a while the same woman showed up, lamp in hand, while behind her was an old man with milk-white hair. Advancing toward us, this man shielded his eyes with his hand, and then asked in a slow and gentle, but very raised, voice:

"Why are you making such a racket, my friends?"

After which he cupped his ear and asked:

"Eh?"

Even if we had been making a racket, the poor old man certainly did not hear it, for he was obviously hard of hearing.

"Do you remember me?" Mirza shouted, leaning toward his ear.

The old man looked at him, collected his thoughts, pondered a while and finally said:

"Is that you, count?"

Then he said to himself, but completely aloud:

"What is he doing in these parts?"

"I want to join the army," Mirza answered.

"Welcome, welcome. What was that?"

Selim introduced Marx and me, after which the old man invited us to supper, but we had to change clothes for we looked simply awful. The servant woman conducted us to a room upstairs.

While we were changing our clothes, Mirza said:

"He's really gotten old since I last saw him and is quite senile."

"What do you want of him? He doesn't even know who he is!"

"We'll talk about it later."

Then we went downstairs.

The old man was already waiting for us at a table laid out with new tableware, and after a moment a beautiful young woman came in. She was tall and had black hair and a splendid waist. La Grange introduced her to us as his granddaughter.

I bowed rather indifferently and in silence; then I saw something which surprised me to a high degree.

Mademoiselle La Grange, seeing Mirza, became as white as a sheet, while he was no less moved.

"I see that he had his reasons for coming here," I thought.

We sat down to supper and ate in silence. In those

days, during the war, people did not waste words, and when they spoke it was in a subdued voice, as if in fear and uncertainty.

Besides, there was something between Selim and Mademoiselle La Grange. She avoided his glance, yet when he was not looking at her, she glanced at him somewhat strangely. In vain did he try to start a conversation. The silence soon became unbearably depressing, until, at the end of supper, the old man looked up to the ceiling suddenly and said, for no apparent reason:

"Monday, Tuesday, Wednesday, Thursday—yes, it is Thursday."

After supper Mirza linked his arm through La Grange's and went to talk with him to the other room. It seemed to me that he asked him about a guide, but this conversation, though it was very loud, I could not clearly make out. I sat by Mademoiselle La Grange and tried to amuse her.

At any other time this would have gone easily for me. She was quite beautiful and charming. She had dark, intelligent eyes, and beautiful hands with delicate fingers, with which she touched up her hair now and then, as if in coquetry. But this time the conversation did not go well. I was tired, and Mademoiselle La Grange was thinking of something else.

I finally asked her how long she had known Mirza.

At that point she became roused, but instead of answering me, she began to question me as to our reasons for coming to these parts. I replied that it did not matter to me where I fought, but that Mirza had insisted that it was to be in this region. Her curiosity and animation increased. Perhaps I could have drawn her out, but I was dead tired. Marx had fallen asleep on an arm-chair and was snoring, so I thought more of sleep than of all the mademoiselles in the world.

Meanwhile Mirza and the old man came out of the

other room. The old man sat beside me and, grabbing me by the knee, began to talk some nonsense, making at the same time all sorts of dramatic gestures which served to illustrate whatever he was talking about. Mirza used the opportunity to get closer to Mademoiselle La Grange. I heard as they exchanged some quick words with each other; Mirza seemed to be insistently pleading with her about something. I heard only one phrase: "I'll explain everything!" The old man made a few more gestures, after which he said:

"You will sleep in the other house. All you have to do is use the back door and there is the hop-field—right up to the forest."

Then he cupped his ear and asked:

"Eh?"

Finally we went to sleep. The second house stood deeper inside the park, about several dozen yards from the chalet. Apparently no one lived in it, for when we went inside, I was hit with the smell of emptiness and hops, which were drying below the ceiling. One of the rooms, however, was tidied up. On the floor lay three mattresses, covered with pillows and bedding. I had not seen such comfortable bed-spreads for a long time, so I immediately threw myself down on one, without thinking of taking off my clothes. Selim and Marx likewise lay down in their clothes. All of us kept our rifles by our side, just in case.

"Listen," Mirza said to me; "the time has come in which I must tell you everything...."

That was all I heard, because I fell asleep like a log at that point, and I slept for all it was worth, though not more than a couple of hours.

Around two I woke up all of a sudden.

At first I could not recollect where I was; after a moment, however, I shook the sluggishness from my

mind and glanced at the window opposite our mattresses.

A weak, rosy gleam, as if from a dying sunset, came in
through the glass.

It was not a sunset, however, but the glow of a distant
fire.

"Something's burning there," I said to myself, not
thinking of getting up from my warm bedding. "There
must be a battle going on."

And so it was.

Soon I heard the faraway sound of artillery fire.

These shots—distant, muffled, but quick and regular
like a musical scale—ceased at moments to resume again
with renewed energy.

In the silence in between I heard Marx snoring.

After a certain time it seemed to me that the shots
were getting closer; one and another artillery shot shook
the window, causing the shutters to clatter. I still did not
feel like getting up, but, just in case, I decided to wake
up Mirza.

"Selim!" I called out.

Selim did not answer.

"Selim!" I called out louder.

Only Marx answered with a snore.

Meanwhile the glow became brighter. By its red light
I glanced at Selim's bed. It was empty.

I thought that he had gone out to hear how the battle
was going, and grabbing my rifle, I went out to the
garden.

The moon shone brightly. Its rays intermingled with
the glow of the distant battle, diffusing the garden with
a mysterious half-white, half-red light. The leaves on the
trees rustled quietly and changed colors from silver to
copper; long black shadows lay on the ground. But in
the garden it was quiet. The windows of the chalet

remained dark. The people here were used to the sounds
and fiery glow of a battle.

All of this was at once both mysterious and festive. On
one side there was melancholy and the peace of the
sleeping garden, while on the other a bloody gleam, a
far-off battle, a fire and a noise similar to the sound of
an ocean.

I was so used to continual stealth since my departure
from Paris that even now, despite myself, I walked as if I
were advancing upon a Prussian outpost.

Suddenly I saw Mirza, and I stood still, as if rooted to
the ground.

On a bench, in the shadows of the thickets, sat Mademoiselle La Grange, and before her knelt Mirza, and he
was covering her hands with kisses.

The moon and the glow of the battle were lit for them.

"My one and only, my one and only!" whispered
Mirza passionately. "Do you forgive me?" he added after
a moment.

His words and kisses drowned out the approaching
shots of the artillery.

I heard one more phrase, incomplete though it was: "I
came here on purpose to—"

It became more and more ruddy in the garden. The
moonlight paled and dimmed, but the lovers seemed not
to hear nor see anything.

I thought, however, that the battle might reach La
Mare and that safety demanded that we should be on the
alert. So I retreated behind a thicket and gave a low
whistle that was our agreed-upon signal.

It was a signal that we had known for a long time, and
meant "let's go."

Almost immediately the leaves rustled, and in the next
moment Mirza stood before me, his eyes glowing and his
cheeks red, his body trembling with emotion.

"What is it?" he asked.

"They are fighting."

"That's some distance away. Don't misuse the signal, for you'll cause me to make a mistake. The signal means that danger is nearby."

"Did I interrupt you in anything?"

Mirza paused suddenly.

"Did you see everything?"

"Yes."

He became silent, and after a moment grabbed me by the shoulders.

"Very well!" he said. "Let us go to the lodging. I have to talk to you about many things. You won't fall asleep this time?"

"No."

We returned. I lay down on the mattress again, while Mirza sat on his and began to talk:

"You may think that I have acted like an egoist, but I surmised that it didn't matter to you where you fought. To me it meant everything, but not to you. So that is why I also thought that in joining your destiny with mine, I would also share with you my happiness. But this can change. I've embarked upon some dangerous things. Now I will tell you about them. If you want to, you can withdraw. There is still time. But first tell me if you would have gone to war no matter what?"

"I would have."

"Good. So I did not force you?"

"You did not."

"Now listen. In Paris, before the war, I became acquainted with Lidia La Grange and fell in love with her. She reciprocated my love. But later everything was broken off, and do you know who was the cause of this?"

"No."

"La Rochenoire."

"La Rochenoire?"

"Yes. I don't have the time to give you the details. La

Rochenoire also fell in love with her, but he was generally disliked, naked without his title and had a bad
reputation, so I prevailed easily over him. He challenged
me to a duel. We used pistols. Three times I aimed at his
skull and three times I spared his life. He doesn't know
how to shoot. I could have killed him, and I was a fool
not to have done so, since later he did not cease to seek
vengeance against me. You see, I've always loved from all
sides, and once I begin a new relationship I do not break
the old ones. Such was the case then. A year before I had
met Lidia, I made the acquaintance in the Jockey Club
of a young lieutenant in the navy with the name of
Marillac, who formed an immediate liking for me. He
was a valiant young lad, brave, honorable—in a word, a
rare and genuine knight. After several weeks he invited
me to his place and offered me his friendship, and
I—may God forgive me!—began to flirt with his pretty
wife. In our country this is considered a crime, but in
Paris this is normal. I was no better than my surroundings. To be sure, this weighed heavily on me. The husband was frequently away from home, but when he
returned, I had to feign friendship for him, which was
beyond my strength, for I was disgusted with myself.
When I met Lidia, I tried to make a break with the past,
not because my feelings for Lidia were serious—that
only happened later—but because I could not tolerate
being a hypocrite. I thought that the break would be
easy. I was wrong. Madame Marillac knew of my new
love for Lidia, and full of jealousy and revenge, she
plotted with La Rochenoire. He is not able to forgive
anything and back down from anything, that is why he
grabbed at the first opportunity to break my relations
with Lidia and revenge himself on me at the same time.
He told Lidia that I loved another. She didn't want to
believe him, she needed proof. At that point I received a
letter from Madame Marillac, asking me to come to one

last assignation. I wrote back: 'I will not come.' Then I received another letter, in which were these words: 'You know that my husband is here and you are afraid!' That was enough. I went. It was a trap. La Rochenoire was to bring Lidia and let her see my disloyalty with her own eyes. But this was not enough for him. The scoundrel, in his vengeance on me, did not hesitate to sacrifice his own conspirator, so he informed not only Lidia about the appointment but Marillac as well. He thought that Marillac would challenge and kill me, for he was the best fencer in all of France. A tragedy followed. You must have heard of it, for the entire city of Paris did not talk of anything else. I decided to let myself be killed by Marillac, but when I saw blood, my unfortunate nature was roused within me, and I pierced his chest with my sword right up to the handle. Even today I can hear how sharply it grated against his spine."

Mirza shuddered. His was pale, his eyes were animated; in his features pain was depicted and at the same time a dull, ominous stubbornness.

He covered his face with his hands and was silent. For a moment I heard the shots from the approaching battle.

"Go on," I said, "we have little time."

"What happened after that," he continued, "is easy to understand. Lidia showed me the door, and then I began to really love her. I would have taken my vengeance on La Rochenoire, but I did not know what role he had in the affair. Besides, immediately after the incident he received an order to go to Marseilles, for he was also at the time a lieutenant in the navy. Before he left, he declared himself to Lidia, who in a moment of grief and despair accepted his love. I began to lead a crazy life; I lost a lot of money. I was the leader of the Jockey Club. They took me for a hero, I took myself for a scoundrel. I suffered terribly. Besides this, I loved Lidia more than ever before and that made me even more miserable."

"How did you find out about La Rochenoire's part in the affair?"

"Leading the dissolute life I led, I met the other woman. She had fallen far, and I tried to raise her up. There was no time for that, however, for she had consumption. She died shorty thereafter, but before she died she confessed everything. I swore then that I would take revenge on La Rochenoire. And as God is my witness I would have done it, if the war had not broken out immediately after that.

"I thought," he went on, "that La Rochenoire had disappeared in the chaos of the war, and I prayed to the Christian God and my silly Mohammed to keep him safe for me. Soon his name arose from this chaos, surrounded with that ominous renown which made him one of the most notorious of partisans. And I thought: now is the time!"

"What do you intend to do?"

His hands quivering, Mirza opened the lining inside his soldier's kepi and took out of a piece of paper.

"Read this," he said, giving me the paper.

By the light of the ever-ruddier glow, I began to read, and it seemed to me that I was asleep and that everything I saw and read was just a strange dream that would vanish in the morning.

The paper which I held in my hands was, more or less, quite simply an appointment of Selim Mirza as the leader of La Rochenoire's detachment, as well as an order to hand over that La Rochenoire to a military tribunal, which would decide his fate.

I handed the paper back to Mirza in silence.

Meanwhile he came closer to me. A severe expression showed up once again on his face, giving his features a cast of true Eastern cruelty.

"I swear by this night, by that fire and by those that

are dying right now that I will have him executed without mercy."

Then, suddenly, he opened the window. One could see that he needed to get a breath of fresh air.

But I did not understand what the appointment meant, so I said:

"Explain this to me."

He paced around in silence for a moment or two. Then he spoke:

"You are surprised by the appointment and the order to hand over to a tribunal a leader who is fighting the Germans without pause. But there are reasons for this. This person thinks that now, when he stands at the head of a detachment, there is no one above him. He is an aristocrat. During battle his soldiers shout: *'Vive le roi!'*—just as if he were Louis XIV. He does not serve the Republic but Henry V. What's more, our marquis deals with people a little too unceremoniously. In Branche Verte he had the mayor executed, in Agneaux he had two villagers hung; he burned the village of Maric because they denied him provisions. When Chauze sent a courier with an order, he had the courier flogged and answered Chauze with a curse word. Just for this there is a death sentence. He wants to be a lord at the head of his own detachment. He carries on a war on his own, but this is not the way it is done. Oh, the dictator had many reasons for doing what he did!

"La Rochenoire was sentenced in absence and stripped of his command. But when it became vacant, no one wanted to take it, until I found out about it. Then I presented my qualifications, and since today's dictator knew them, as well as myself, from the Jockey Club, I became appointed without any complications. I was warned, though, that La Rochenoire, not having much to lose and having the soldiers on his side, will assuredly have whoever comes with the appointment shot."

"How is that? The government doesn't have the power to relieve him of his command?"

"The government does have the power; they could surround him with an army and crush him. But the dictator is concerned as to what the country would say. The name of La Rochenoire has become popular; he has fought about forty skirmishes already and has emerged victorious in nearly every one. So I have been ordered to proceed slowly—something which suits me, by the way. As long as he has the soldiers behind him, I will be sparing of La Rochenoire, but he is already pressing heavily on his men. He is pitiless to them. I am not suppose to show my appointment immediately, only after I win the soldiers over. If, however, La Rochenoire would give a command to have me shot, I will blow his brains out and show the appointment. But I doubt if it will come to that. La Rochenoire knows that I was on good terms with today's dictator. To have me executed would mean that he would burn all his bridges, and that he cannot wish upon himself. Anyway, we'll see. Most probably it won't go that far. The government doesn't want that. La Rochenoire doesn't know about anything. That is how things stand. Now tell me what you think."

"I think that it would have been better if you had told me everything from the start."

"I did wrong, but I was afraid that you would try to talk me out of the enterprise."

"And why did you draw me into it?"

"You have time to withdraw. You said that it didn't matter to you where you fought. Close-by is Corbeau's detachment. You can join up with it. Just in case, I made out an appointment for you there."

"Listen!" I said with animation. "You want vengeance, so get vengeance, but I don't like the path you are taking. I could understand if you had come here and simply shot

La Rochenoire in the head, but you want to, and have to, gain his confidence first and then betray it."

"I did not choose this path. Those are the instructions, which I have to follow, and I've undertaken to fulfill them because to just simply kill him means little to me. I have to humiliate him first. It makes no difference if this is pretty or not. I am a Tartar. I want vengeance." And in truth at that moment he looked like a Tartar. "To think what he did to me! To think that Lidia is his fiancée!..."

And he began to wring his hands so hard that the finger-joints cracked loudly.

After a while he said:

"So are you going with me or not?"

"I am going with you. If the affair will be settled at once, I am ready to help you, but if it will take time, then I don't want to play a game."

"You won't have to. Very well. I thank you."

He shook my hand.

"Anyway," he said, "we won't enter his camp at the same time, so as not to awaken suspicion. I have to go there first. Then you and Marx will show up. We will pretend that we do not know each other. If things don't go well, that will protect the both of you from his vengeance."

I did not want to agree to this, but Mirza said that he would not allow the innocent Marx to be drawn into the enterprise. I gave in.

"When will you go?" I asked.

"As soon as daylight arrives. You will stay here for a couple of days."

Then he grasped my hand again.

"Be kind to Lidia. I love her, I love her very much. Have compassion on me at least in this. She deserves your friendship more than I do. She has suffered a lot because she has never stopped loving me.... Now I've told you everything."

And embracing me about the neck, he placed his head on my chest. Then he rose up suddenly and said:

"I am going."

"Where?"

"To take leave of her. The poor thing is still waiting for me."

He took his rifle and went out. I remained alone with the sleeping Marx. The sounds of battle did not lessen; on the contrary, they became clearer and clearer. Only the glow began to pale, for dawn was beginning. The window turned white. The black contours of the branches beyond the window became more and more distinct. I rested on my hands and began to reflect. I did not reflect on what had happened. In my nature a certain indifference existed, which allowed me to accept with stone-like indifference a realized fact as inevitable, as a Turkish "kismet." There was in this a type of passiveness, which, nevertheless, served frequently in those days as a principle and a source of consolation. Life did not seem to me to be worth one *sou*. In those days I was a skeptic; I had lived so long on the inside that I was exhausted to the core. That is why I sought sensations from which came the smell of gun-powder—dazzling, dangerous sensations, and I did this because they tore me away from looking into the void within myself and from brooding upon matters impossible to unravel. So I only thought of Mirza, of his rich faith in life and in himself, of the exuberance that seethed in him and overflowed to the outside. He fought, loved, sought revenge, and to the bottom of his soul he was certain that it was all worth the trouble. On his soul not one shadow of doubt fell. Not one drop of Hamlet's blood flowed in him. Such people are people of action. There exuded from him hot life, by which even I warmed my numbed soul.

And now at this moment he was bidding his beautiful
lady good-bye, and in his kisses he forgot about the
entire world. Unfortunately, I in his place would have
felt that I was kissing lips that would, sooner or later,
have to be pale with death.

The day was getting brighter. Night was vanishing. In
La Mare the cocks began to crow, passing their tune from
one to the other. I went over to the open window, so as
to look at the horizon, when I suddenly saw the faint
ring of a lantern's light advancing from the shadows, and
I heard the hurrying clatter of those wooden shoes that
French villagers wear.

In a moment a small boy with shaggy hair ran up right
to our lodgings. He raised his lantern and, seeing me
standing by the window, called out in a breathless voice:

"You are not asleep?"

"What is it?"

"The Prussians are entering the village."

"Put out the lantern and scoot," I said in a low voice.

I woke up Marx, and then I went out of the hall and
whistled the signal again.

Mirza came up immediately.

"Here I am!" he called out.

"The Germans are in La Mare!"

We went straight into the hop-field, which stretched
all the way to the forest. There was no need of us going
too far. The Germans could not have known anything
about us, so we sat calmly among the leaves and began
to listen to the sounds coming from La Mare. The battle
had ended; the glow had expired. At first it was quiet and
peaceful in La Mare, but then we heard a distant uproar,
which began to get closer and louder. Soon we could
make out the hoof-beats and neighing of horses, the
blare of brass trumpets, the snarl of drums. Then we
heard the thunder of war songs. The cavalry sang *"Wacht
am Rhein!"* and their voices travelled far in the silence

among the dew. Inexpressible power and gallantry reverberated from these voices; one felt that these were the
voices of triumph, that these were Cimbrian regiments,
exhausted, still covered with blood and the dust of battle, intoxicated with joy, and that they were celebrating
a new victory with that song.

Meanwhile the first rosy rays of the morning must
have fallen like an aureole on their tall standards. We
listened in silence. The phlegmatic Marx paled from
anger and whispered through clenched teeth, in his broken language: *"C'est pien! nous ferrons!"* Mirza gave himself over completely to the moment also. This lucky
fellow forgot about everything else and lived directly,
one feeling at a time. No middle course for him, an
attitude surely worth far more than Hamlet-like reflection.

It was apparently only a passage of troops, for gradually the noise, hoof-beats and singing distanced themselves more and more, to mix with the rustle of the leaves
of the hop-field. They passed by like a noisy herd of
animals, and then only a stronger draft of wind carried
the strains of the song they were singing.

Finally everything quieted down.

"They're gone," whispered Selim.

"They're gone."

"Now I have to go. Both of you return to La Mare."

Our farewells were long and heart-felt. Finally Mirza
wiped away his tears, threw his rifle over his shoulder,
turned his kepi to the side and departed slowly, humming a song.

Then he turned around and waved us good-bye. Marx
and I returned to La Mare in silence.

IV

Three days later, in the evening, we approached La Rochenoire's camp. My heart was beating like a hammer, for I did not know if I would find Mirza alive. Along the way, I had instructed Marx on how he should behave once we got there and what he could and could not do. The brave lad, who had become attached to Selim as if to a brother, declared at first that if Selim were dead he would shoot La Rochenoire in the head like a dog.

We were guided to the camp by a peasant who was a spy for La Rochenoire, but who pretended at the same time to be a spy for the Prussians, for which he received money from them. His name was Hugon.

In order calm myself down, I began to talk to him.

"You must make a good profit?" I asked.

Hugon turned his brutish face to me and smiled. He looked like a dog baring his teeth.

"The pay is terrible," he said, "but the Good Lord sometimes gives us something more. You look around and spot a dead body; you search it; you find thalers, a watch, a ring on a finger. Otherwise, we would die of starvation."

"Ah! so you strip the dead?"

"And why not? I say a prayer over them, and if it's worth it, then two. Others don't do that. The Good Lord is compassionate. I serve the French for free! Corbeau—may the devil take him!—ordered me to be hung. It's true that I served the Prussians at the time, but La Rochenoire had me cut down. From now on, he said, you will take money from the Germans, but, he said, you will serve me. And so I serve him faithfully like a dog. I know every bush around here. I lead the Germans where he tells me, and if I sometimes go looking about a corpse, he doesn't get angry. He always calls me 'dog,' but as a lord he can do this."

We continued on in silence. After a certain while Hugon said:

"We're near the camp now!"

The camp lay in the middle of a dense forest, among trees which had been overturned by a storm. Our guide gave a hoot-signal to the outpost, which stopped us until a patrol came, and the patrol took us to the center of camp.

When we entered the camp, the sun was setting. There was not even one tent by the overturned roots of the trees or by the bushes, but everywhere there lay heaps of straw, brought by villagers. Off to the side stood about a dozen wagons, harnessed to gaunt nags. Among the wagons sat peasant drivers, nourishing themselves for the night with cheese and bits of bread. For the most part, the soldiers were lying on the straw. Some were buried so deeply in it that only their heads could be seen. Everyone looked terrible—faces emaciated and dirty, eyes bloodshot, uniforms torn. These men looked more like bandits than soldiers.

We did not get a very friendly reception. When the patrol led us through the clearing, here and there from the lairs and from under the roots peered out ruffian-like faces, and hoarse voices asked:

"Hey! Who's that?"

"Those are rascals from the boulevards."

"Here by yourself, little bird?" some ruffian called out to Marx. "Your country needs you roasted."

"You're an idiot," someone else said, looking at the hairless face of my companion, "that's not a bird, but a girl in disguise. Don't you see how she lifts her toes up when she walks?"

"The devil take you and your toes. The plague on you! If it's a girl, so much the better. Go stand in front of a speeding bullet."

"Is that so, my little goose? The fox ordered you to bow before it."

Marx made a fist at them, while I looked around for Mirza but could not find him. I thought that we would have to deal with La Rochenoire. Meanwhile we were led to a cluster of tall trees, from under which we heard pained screams. When I approached and saw what was happening, a heavy weight fell off my chest at once. The first person I saw was Mirza. Dressed in the uniform of an adjutant, he was having a private talk with a short man with curly blond hair and a regal expression on his yellow face. I surmised that this was La Rochenoire. Nearby stood a man with an athletic build and an ugly face scarred by small-pox. Instead of a military kepi, he wore a filthy white kerchief stained with dried blood. As I later learned, this person was Lieutenant Simon, the right-hand man of La Rochenoire in all things.

The patrol stopped almost right next to them in silence. Mirza passed a quick, indifferent glance at us, after which he turned away, as if he had never seen us before, and he began to shake the ashes from his cigar. La Rochenoire and Simon also did not pay attention to us at first, for they were occupied: one was talking to Mirza, while the other was monitoring the flogging of three villagers who, as the officer of the patrol informed us, had been accused of revealing under force a week ago to the Prussians where La Rochenoire's detachment was encamped. These poor fellows were shaking all over. Simon ordered them to deal with themselves in turn. Two of these three poor fellows sat on the third and flogged him to the point of raising blood, then that person got up, drank a swig of wine, and directed his attention straightaway to the next one, saying:

"Now it's your turn, friend!"

Simon supervised the operation, keeping time with his hand and repeating:

"Harder! harder!"

La Rochenoire and Mirza whispered something to each other from time to time. They seemed to be on the best of terms.

Finally the flogging was over. The officer of the patrol reported our arrival to La Rochenoire. Only then did La Rochenoire's eyes fall on us momentarily. As I live, I have never seen such eyes. Their grey color practically did not reflect light. They were like the eyes of a dead person.

"Simon, take charge of these people!" he said in a dry, truly commanding voice.

Simon took out a disgustingly greasy book, wrote down our names, then handed us over to a young officer named Touvenir, saying:

"Subsection four, in place of Blain and Renard."

Touvenir pointed to a pile of straw, saying:

"Get some rest!"

That was our induction to the camp.

Several days later I woke up at night feeling a little sick. The straw, on which I lay, was damp. Right after sunset the sky had become covered with clouds and it began to drizzle, or rather a thick, biting mist had settled on the leaves of trees and from there fell in the shape of drops on our bedding. The noise these drops made upset my nerves in a strange manner. I was disheartened and despondent. It seemed to me that everything was going for the worse. From the time I arrived at camp I saw Mirza everyday, but I had not exchanged one word with him. I could not explain his relationship with La Rochenoire. From where came that friendship? Selim was his adjutant—from where that sudden and surprising appointment? I suspected some trick in all of this; I suspected that the more cunning Frenchman was playing with Mirza as a cat plays with a mouse. This worried me. Meanwhile the drops of rain fell and fell, rolling off from leaf to leaf with greater frequency. A fever took hold of me, and images swam before my eyes. At the thought that we would remain in this camp, amid continual betrayals and trickery, I was seized with despair. With what yearning I thought of the regular army, of those cavalry divisions, going to battle in the light of day and riding like the wind! And we? We had to wander around like wolves in the darkness, lying in wait in thickets and biting when least expected.

Even before I had really experienced it, I found this type of life abhorrent.

I could not fall asleep, but after a certain time I felt as if I were in a state of intoxication. For a couple of hours I listened thoughtlessly to the rustle of the leaves and the sound of some bird or devil calling out monotonously from a nearby tree: "twee-twee! twee-twee!" What kind of bird could chat away like that during the night and the rain! At times I thought that perhaps this was a supernatural being foretelling my death.

Then I began to hallucinate. The surrounding dark forest dissolved into the four walls of a room in my family's house. A lamp burned on a table, and by the table sat my father and mother and my younger siblings. Then they all disappeared, and in their place I saw two women, unknown to me, looking over some old chronicle with illustrations. I crept up behind their shoulders and glanced at one illustration. It depicted in awkward medieval woodcuts the Battle of Agincourt. Underneath I read clearly the Gothic lettering: "The Battle of Agincourt." Suddenly, for no reason, I gave a start, and the vision disappeared. Around me was the forest once again—deep and dark—while to my ears came the patter of rain drops and the heavy breathing of my companions.

To protect myself from further hallucinations I began to repeat to myself: "I am in the forest, I am serving in the army, my leader is La Rochenoire, Mirza is the adjutant, Marx is sleeping near me."

Then I felt that I was afraid, but of what I did not know. I was so afraid that I wanted to cry out for help.

Suddenly the shrill sound of a whistle woke everybody

up. I breathed out deeply. At least this was reality. The
men sprung to their feet, and fifteen minutes later we
stood in rank, our weapons by our sides. The lieutenants, their swords unsheathed, stood by their companies,
giving orders in quiet, hoarse voices. Soon La Rochenoire showed up, and the murmur which in all ranks,
but particularly in French ones, is heard even in drills,
subsided, as if the soldiers had seen death itself approaching. La Rochenoire walked in the company of
Mirza. Both men moved slowly, looking over the ranks.
The soldiers stood as stiff as boards and presented their
weapons for inspection. Here and there La Rochenoire
threw out some word, which the lieutenants caught in a
twinkling. After a while a loud command resounded,
and the ranks broke up into two groups. Half of the
detachment, under La Rochenoire and Mirza, went to
the right; the other half, which included Marx and me,
went straight ahead under Simon.

It was still nighttime. The black masses of trees and
the overturned trunks, their roots protruding upward,
depicted fantastic, apocalyptic forms. The forest was
quite simply terrifying. We walked in complete silence
and as quietly as possible. For a thinking man being a
soldier in a war has still one more terrible aspect: one
never knows what is happening to one. Some hand
moves you like a pawn, and that's that. Such was the case
with me. I saw that La Rochenoire, having taken part in
the battle which I had heard in La Mare, had been
beaten; I presumed, therefore, that we were going to
exact vengeance, but where we were going and with what
forces we would have to contend, I did not have the
slightest idea.

Soon the forest came to an end. On the night horizon
one could discern a hill and on it a windmill, and
beyond that, thirty cottages or more, toward which we
began to creep. In the window of the windmill a light

shone through, while by the windmill stood the black, motionless figure of a Prussian soldier in a pointed helmet, leaning on a rifle.

Despite the fact that we were hidden by the overgrowth and advanced as quietly as possible, the Prussian heard a noise. A loud *"Wer da?"* reverberated in the silence, and immediately thereafter a shot rang out, rending the air with a red light. At that moment we gave out a cry and rushed with the greatest speed toward the cottages, from which shots also rang out.

A battle began raging. Marx and I, as well as a dozen or so soldiers, under the personal leadership of Simon, reached the door of one of the cottages and began to ram into it with the butt-ends of our rifles, while from the roof and windows bullets whizzed by us. The door shook and finally came apart, and we charged inside. The Germans shot right into our faces, but they did not manage to do any harm. Then the fight came down to the butt-ends of rifles, bayonets, and finally to fingernails, teeth and fists. Almost at the same time the rest of our force had reached the other cottages, so that the shooting died down everywhere, to be replaced by hand-to-hand combat. In our cottage the usual warrior fierceness changed quickly to a raging frenzy. One could only hear the cracking of shattered rifles, the grinding of bayonets, the wheezing and breathlessness of the combatants, who rolled around on the ground, pulled each other by the hair and bit with their teeth. Some tall man seized Marx by the throat and fell together with him onto the floor, but Marx, strong as a bull, was on top in a second, kneeling on his chest and savagely pummeling his head against the brick floor. Another Prussian, however, began to pester him. I wanted to rush to Marx's aid, but at that moment the butt-end of a rifle hit me in the chest and I fell full length to my right, by the chimney, in which a fire was lit.

How long I lay there, I do not know. When I came to, I could not move at first. It was quiet in the cottage. The fire had gone out. With great effort I turned, face to the ground, and raised myself up a bit. The first thing I saw by the bluish fire of the expiring coals was the body of Lieutenant Simon. His mouth was open and his teeth were bared.

I fainted again.

My second awakening, however, was sweeter. I was lying on a couch, not on the ground. My eyes fell first on the sympathetic face of Mirza, leaning over me solicitously.

"Is that you?" I asked.

"It is," he replied joyfully. "You gave me quite a fright, but there is nothing wrong with you."

In truth, I felt completely well.

The blow which I received on my chest had taken the breath out of me temporarily but, otherwise, had not done me any harm. Now I breathed freely and without pain.

I did not, however, feel like getting up off the couch. I passed my eyes over my surroundings. It was the same cottage in which we had been fighting yesterday or the day before yesterday. The signs of battle were evident everywhere: the windows were smashed, the stove was half overturned, dried blood stained the walls, and the floor was strewn with fallen plaster, though not one corpse. Through the holes in the windows the sunlight came in and also the wind, which blew away the smoke in the chimney, where a fire was lit once again. The stench of burning filled the air.

"How long have I been asleep?" I asked Mirza.

"Twenty-four hours, like a rock."

"You were not wounded?"

"Just a little scratch."

Saying this, he rolled up his shirt sleeve and showed

me his white marble-like arm. A long, red scratch and the bluish traces of bite marks marred the skin.

"These Germans don't give up easily," he said.

"But we won?"

"Just barely. Few are left alive."

"You came over to help us?"

"Yes."

"Where is Marx?" I asked after a moment of silence.

"Out on patrol. Marx is a corporal already."

"Simon—was he killed?"

"Dead and buried."

"Who has replaced him?"

"I have."

I sat up on the couch.

"Tell me what this all means."

Mirza began to laugh.

"The officers are making a few faces," he said, "but my friend Rochenoire did not want to hear of anyone else replacing Simon."

"I still don't understand."

"But it is quite simple. There is talk of a cease fire. Of course this will not happen, but that is what is being said. But when an armistice does eventually come, La Rochenoire, at odds with the government, will find himself in a sorry situation."

"Why is he backing you then?"

"So that I can back him if need be. As a wealthy foreigner I had all doors in Paris open to me, and I knew many people who are now at the head of the government. What's more, everyone liked me. I was *persona grata*, so my word carries some weight today. My presence and high rank in this camp reconciles La Rochenoire with these people in some measure, it legitimizes him. If not for this, one of us would probably have been dead already. When I arrived in camp, he fixed his grey eyes on me like a wolf who looks upon a goat that has come to him asking for a night's lodging in his den. But I said that I arrived simply to fight and that since he fought the best out of everyone, I came to him. He sniffed and laughed at me as if I were a fool. He was already turning to Simon to give him an order concerning my skin, but apparently realized during that moment that executing me would mean to personally run afoul of the dictator and the other people in government. It must have come to him that in the next battle it would be easier to do away with me. And I, seeing his smile, said: 'I see it amuses you that I come here when there is talk of a truce.' That truce was the first trump card I put on the table. He became morose and began to ask me what I knew about this. I answered that if I had seen the dictator I could have said something more definite, for the dictator always honors me with confidences and his friendship.

"That was my second trump card. La Rochenoire, though he fears nothing, knows that with One-Eye there is no joking around. What would La Rochenoire do during a cease-fire? One-Eye would surely square accounts with him during that time. Besides, La Rochenoire has other calculations. An ambitious person, he believes in the restoration of the monarchy and sees his splendid role under Henry V. He has hopes of squaring accounts at that time with everyone and of rising from a naked marquis, who in Paris could not afford even a cigar, to a powerful person. Oh, yes! Should the restoration come, this person would have a great future, if not for the fact that I stand in the way of that future."

"You are playing a dangerous game."

"I know, but I am not worried. There's more. La Rochenoire knows that before Henry can come to power One-Eye will rule, and he knows that before the sun shines, the night might be eternal for him, the more so that they knew each other from the Jockey Club also and never liked each other. He needs, therefore, to secure himself for that time and figures that he has found that safety with me."

Mirza began to laugh.

"I am playing a dangerous game, but I will win it because I know all his cards, each and every one, while mine are hidden from him."

"And do you know what this game is called?"

Instead of answering me, Mirza flew into a rage.

"Intrigue!" he cried out. "Betrayal! That was his game! And the fruits of that game: the death of Marillac, the ruin and death of his wife, the tears of Lidia. And I am to hesitate now in choosing the road to vengeance? What to do? Where to go? What to do differently? If you know, then tell me, tell me! Should I shoot him in the head so that he wouldn't even know why and by whose hand he is dying? The first good Prussian soldier can do this for me. And later on? Fame will stick to his name, so that you will not be able to separate him from it. Thank you for such a vengeance! Anyway, don't moralize, for you never become involved in anything. If you were in my place you would probably give him Lidia, and bless them besides, and then look into the mirror to see if the sacrifice suits your face. I am made of different things. Those means are good for me which go straight to the heart of the matter. Anyway, I have my instructions and I must carry them out. I am a soldier."

"Do what you want, but be on guard. Unless he is blind, your presence so near La Mare will awaken his suspicions."

Selim breathed heavily for a while, but finally calmed himself down and said:

"No! everything that has happened has blindfolded this dog. After my relationship with Lidia was severed, I formed new ones, I went insane. You know my accursed nature. I love, or rather I pretend to love, ten-times over.

I needed sensations. And La Rochenoire, who knows this well, doesn't even suspect that I give Lidia any thought these days."

Then he added quickly and as if involuntarily:

"I'm surprised even at myself...."

I could not help but laugh.

"Don't wrong Lidia or me with your suspicions!" he cried out again violently. "I love her with all my heart."

"Do you think you will marry her?"

"What? Yes, of course!"

"And then you will surely return to our country. Your father, sitting with his she-wolf by the chimney, waits for your return every day."

Mirza did not say anything, but a certain shadow of tenderness fell over his face, as if in longing for his home and a quiet life in his family nest. I knew this Mirza family as if my own. All of them stormed and thundered in their youth, but, after getting it all out of their system, they returned to their nest. That was true of the grandfather and the father, and it would certainly be true for him. I thought that he would keep his word to Lidia and marry her and return home.

Our further conversation was interrupted by the entrance of an officer already known to me, Touvenir.

"An order from the commander!" he said.

Mirza threw a glance at the paper he had been handed.

"Very well," he said.

An hour later we marched over to La Rochenoire's camp.

V

During the night the detachments joined up, and the very next day in the afternoon we were again engaged in a battle, or rather we attacked a convoy transporting wounded soldiers and completely wiped it out. Then began a life of almost superhuman hardships and exertions, a life of unbelievable marches, hunger, sleepless nights, incessant pursuits, severe regulations and desperate fighting. The patience of the Prussians was thoroughly exhausted. After having defeated large armies, they could not permit one detachment, comprised of merely five hundred people, to despatch bloody slaughter right by their camps. The commanders of the Prussian mobile units made it a point of honor to exterminate these damned Frenchies, whom, moreover, they did not even consider soldiers. There was never any greater truth than what our men said at that time: "We're living right at the Prussians' doorstep." An iron circle closed about us every day, and every day it proved to be in vain. Our men became more and more savage in these continual battles, and despite the harsh discipline imposed on them, they committed on occasion atrocities not only on prisoners but on French peasants as well.

The commanders of the Prussian mobile units thought frequently that they were pursuing us; meanwhile we did not stop for a moment to lie in ambush for them, even as we were supposedly withdrawing and slipping away. Any carelessness on their part brought them a new defeat.

That splendid military talent of La Rochenoire's was never more evident than in those difficult times. His audacity knew no bounds. Yet, it must be admitted, luck was always on his side. Sometimes it appeared that he allowed himself to be surrounded intentionally, and then he would strike suddenly like lightning. Once a Prussian detachment, numbering close to eight hundred men, went forward full force in the belief that it was following our trail, but meanwhile it was we who followed the detachment, and we finally fell upon it in a swamp at night, killing a third of its number. Another time La Rochenoire had set up a situation where two Prussian detachments shot in the dark at each other for several hours, supposing that they were shooting at us. His cool blood matched his talent. Sometimes during a battle at night, I would see by the blaze of gunfire this small person standing in the midst of a hail of bullets, a cigar in his mouth, weaponless, and looking with his grey eyes upon the course of the battle with the greatest calm.

He did not spare his own people. He was pitiless and cruel to his soldiers, as well as to the peasants, at times to a high degree. But he also did not spare himself. Observing him constantly, I formed an opinion about his character. This person, who possessed the most violent, inbred passions, had been raised by Jesuits and apparently even obtained the first ordination. His upbringing had given him a certain coolness and orderliness, it toughened him, and this made his passions the more terrible. Living in Paris, he lost his faith first, and then he learned to have contempt for people. Since he was poor, hatred was soon added to that contempt. This exhibited itself in him, an aristocrat, not only in principles but in relations with people. The lofty title of marquis, which when coupled with his poverty was rather laughable, pushed him even further on the road to aristocracy. With his entire soul he yearned for Henry V because he knew that under his rule individuals such as he would be everything and would be able to trample on others, which for someone like him would have been the greatest joy. Despite his legitimistic inclinations, however, he was a sceptic not only in religious matters but also in regard to life. He not only did not love France, he felt disdain for it. He carried on war for war's sake. In the decadent atmosphere of Paris, he lost the sense of right and wrong. For him nothing mattered. This person, with his violent, inbred passions, was one of the most dangerous people in the world, the more so that he was a man of action rather than of reflection.

And it was with such a person that Mirza fought a battle of life and death. In the beginning I was almost certain that in such a battle he would fall, but I became convinced more and more that Mirza was an equally dangerous fellow. On the surface, though, there was the best harmony between the two. They fought successfully with the Prussians, and one had to admit that Mirza contributed not a little to this success, surpassing Simon in every respect.

In the end, however, after a month of playing blind-man's buff among the woods with the Germans, our situation became desperate. The mobile units surrounded us from all sides; slipping away with a detachment that numbered five hundred men, as well as finding enough provisions for it, was no longer possible. Because of this, the war-council decided that our detachment would have to split up. One half was to be under the command of Mirza, the other half under La Rochenoire. Both leaders hoped in this manner to escape from the department of Haute-Saone and also to feed their men easier. They decided, though, to maintain a close proximity to each other in case any assistance would be needed.

From that time Mirza began to act almost on his own. I have to admit that I was curious as to how he would deal with everything, for the situation was difficult. But I had confidence in him, as so far he had surpassed all my expectations. The first day after our detachment split up he had a successful skirmish with the uhlans, in which he nearly lost his own life; then he wriggled out of the Prussians' snare with such skill that it seemed to me that he outdid La Rochenoire. At times I even thought that this person was some kind of rising, and not insignificant, military star, and I know that he himself was certain of this. The soldiers soon became devoted to him, and followed him blindly into battle.

Mirza was, nevertheless, almost as severe with them as was La Rochenoire, yet, because of this, more heedful. When a soldier perpetrated something, however, and Selim looked at him with his pale face, that soldier knew that he was in trouble. The privates called him "Mademoiselle" because of his uncommonly good looks. Once, during a bivouac, I overheard one soldier say to another:

"When Mademoiselle turns white, you are looking death in the face."

"Ha!" the other answered. "Mademoiselle knows how to be both a devil and a mother, while La Roche is just a devil."

In this difficult and tiring soldierly life, in which one was always uncertain of the morrow, a comical side was not lacking on occasion. Once when we were marching through the woods a person slipped down from a tree suddenly, as if he had fallen from the sky. Halt! Who are you? He answers: Wolak. He comes from Galicia, he served in the Turkish and Italian armies, in the French Foreign Legion. He had been in Mexico and in Algeria. What does he want? To serve here. We enlisted him. It did not take even half a day. Wolak led all the soldiers by the nose. He outtalked the most talkative, gave black eyes to the strongest; to some he gave nicknames, from others he borrowed money which he could not use, and others he beat at cards. He treated everyone like a teacher treats children. Every evening he sang an extremely silly song about a steward, which managed, however, to make our soldiers laugh their brains out. The song ended with the words: "And you, Mr. Steward, hand over the key to the —" Saying the words "Mr. Steward," Wolak would point to one of the soldiers. To be appointed the steward in this manner was considered the highest honor. It even came to quarrels and fights.

"He will never make me a steward!" cried out one soldier, squeezing his kepi in anger.

"You, a steward? You, you gapping owl!" answered Wolak. "You, who came into the world three years too early! Do you know were fishes grow? Do you know the difference between a water-mill and a wind-mill? Hey, this fellow is not quite right in the head! You have a watch, no? Is it a male or a female? Hey, everyone, take a look at him!"

And before the dazed soldier could come to his senses, everyone burst out laughing; but in occurrences such as these that laughter was sometimes interrupted by Prussian bullets.

In this manner two weeks went by. Meanwhile one had to fight a war, in which the fame of La Rochenoire faded completely. One evening we were joined by about three hundred men from Emil Corbeau's detachment, and along with them about fifty cavalry. The officer in charge stated that this detachment had been crushingly defeated the day before by a Prussian mobile unit, which most probably was still following the remaining troops of the original eight hundred men. These soldiers were indeed in a sorry state. Nevertheless, Mirza, reinforced by their number, determined to put up a fight with the mobile unit, or rather, to go and ambush it on the highway. This unit counted nine hundred men, of which about two hundred were cavalry, and its commander was a young, though quite experienced, officer—Otto von Hohenstein, a particular terror of the Frenchies. The idea of defeating such a famous opponent amused Mirza, which is why, allowing only time to feed Corbeau's people, he set off in the direction of the highway.

It was night. Over the forest hung a fog so thick that one could not see anything a few feet away. We proceeded in the bushes along both sides of the road for about two hours in a silence so deep that I heard the beating of my own heart. Under penalty of death one could not say a word. Since I was already an officer, I had to watch over not only the men but especially Wolak, who kept quiet with the greatest effort. We had specific instructions: a shot from Mirza's pistol would signal the start of the attack. I heard other hearts beating strongly near me. There is nothing more unnerving, even for experienced soldiers, than waiting in ambush. After half an hour went by, we finally heard from a distance the creaking of wheels and the measured steps of Prussian foot soldiers. Then such a silence came over us that I could hear the rustling of every leaf. The steps of the Prussian troops were coming closer. Finally the advance guard, consisting of six uhlans, rode up. These people were smoking pipes. As they rode by us, one uhlan got closer to another, and we heard their voices in the darkness:

"*Bruder,* give me a light!"

"The French will give you a light!"

They passed us by, and once again there was silence. Finally the main force drew near. The cavalry rode in front, while behind it marched the foot soldiers, but not in any particular order. No doubt these people did not expect anything to happen and did not take their usual precautions. As they marched, they repeated, according to German tradition, in time with their steps and accenting sharply every syllable:

"*Fünf—Paar—lederne Strümpfe!...*"

Meanwhile death lay in wait for them on both sides of the road.

When they reached the very middle of the highway, a pistol shot rang out in the midst of the hollow silence.

It was followed immediately by a thunderous volley of rifleshots from the left side of the road. There arose an indescribable tumult in which one could hear rifle shots, cries of "In formation!" and the voice of the German commander—resonant, calm, yet at times prevailing over everything. The Prussian front was turned to the left, and at that moment branches and leaves, knocked off by its bullets, rained down upon us. The efficient German soldiers quickly got into formation. But at that moment a second salvo from the right side shook the air mightily. The Germans formed two fronts, but in the meantime Mirza blocked off both sides of the road to them. Shots fell from all sides.

The smoke made the thick, impenetrable darkness greater. Our men howled around the Germans like a pack of hungry wolves. In the darkness these poor fellows thought that they were surrounded by God knows how many troops. They shot blindly. The horses of the uhlans, befuddled, frightened, began to snort out of terror and move this way and that. The entire German force moved forward, a salvo met it, then it moved back—to be greeted by another salvo. All of a sudden a box of powder exploded. The horses went completely mad, the confusion increased. Voices could be heard: "Torches! Torches!" The German commander had gotten an unfortunate idea about lighting up the road. We saw the Prussian soldiers raising on their bayonets wisps of burning straw. The blood-red light lit up the road and nearby trees, but this was to our advantage, for now we could see where to aim. "Get the officer! get the officer!" our soldiers began to call out. Through the blaze of the burning straw we saw a tall, proud figure in a pointed helmet, with a gold-framed pince-nez on his nose, standing impudently on a wagon and issuing commands. The flames lit up this figure from head to foot. "Get the officer!" repeated our men. Bullets whirred, sparks fell from the wisps of straw and the burning stalks of corn, but the officer remained untouched. Then Mirza himself rushed over to us.

"Shoot him!" he cried out, and tearing the rifle out of Wolak's hands, he raised it to his face. The shot boomed, and the young officer staggered and fell into expiring wisps of straw.

Meanwhile the straw among the Prussians died out, and their salvos became weaker and less frequent. They still defended themselves, but without hope, while the gunfire from our side became livelier, and the animalistic cries of our men became more and more strident.

After five minutes of this, the command "Bayonets!" resounded through all the ranks. For a moment I saw Mirza again, as with lowered head and sword in hand, he moved along with the wave of lustrous blades, but suddenly a burning wisp of straw shone again in the Prussian ranks, and by it, stretched between two bayonets, a white kerchief could be seen.

"Halt, they are surrendering!" voices cried from all sides.

And so it was. The battle was over.

Half an hour later a silence, like that which previously hung in the air, filled that blood-drenched road. I had the road cleared of bodies. I myself found Otto von Hohenstein. His face was burned. I took his papers and also a portrait of his wife or fiancée, which I still have to this day. Then I went to look for Mirza. I found him sitting by himself on a root of a tree and breathing quickly. His hair was plastered with sweat, his face was blackened with smoke, his hands were trembling, but a boundless pride shone in his eyes, which he did not attempt to hide.

In the following days his pride increased. From that time, he ignored everyone's opinion, or rather he never asked for one. He became despotic with his officers; he even behaved differently toward me, the result being that our relations cooled considerably.

From then on there was no talk of La Rochenoire between us, but I knew that Mirza was gaining the upper hand and beginning to take his opponent lightly. Of course! He now stood at the head of a force twice the size of La Rochenoire's, one blindly devoted to him, so what did he have to fear?

Two days later he attacked the village Deux-Ponts, where the Prussian staff was stationed. He did not strike at night, but in the daytime. He fought a regular battle, and that battle gave him a new laurel.

He made the attack against the orders of La Rochenoire. He knew that this would cause a crisis between them, but he figured that the time had come.

News came that La Rochenoire had sustained considerable losses in a battle. When Mirza found out about this, he said to his officers:

"La Rochenoire is wasting men that I could use."

The officers exchanged silent glances.

After all, Mirza, instead of attacking Deux-Ponts, could have gone to the aid of La Rochenoire, for at that time our movements were freer. The Prussian mobile units were beaten down, while the more considerable German forces were being gathered against the regular armies.

That evening an officer flew in from La Rochenoire with the order that Mirza should march at once to headquarters to his assistance.

I remember that moment as if it were today. It occurred at the mayor's residence in Deux-Ponts. The officer stood in the doorway, holding his fingers to the peak of his kepi, while Selim sat at a table, reading the order slowly.

I watched him carefully. The hardships of war were evident on his face. He had thinned out; his face had paled. He seemed to have aged, and besides this, a tinge of severity colored his formerly sweet and youthful features. One could see that he was a person who gave orders, not obeyed them.

Suddenly he stood up and approached the officer, and

tearing up the order right before his eyes, he let the pieces fall and then trampled them with his foot.

"Tell Lord La Rochenoire that I am going to La Mare!" he said coldly.

The officer bowed and exited.

Then Mirza turned to me: "Please call all the officers here."

In several minutes I led in all my fellow officers. Mirza calmly presented his appointment to them, saying:

"You will want to read this document aloud."

One of the officers read out the order of the dictator. While it was being read, Mirza stood proud and cold.

A hollow silence fell.

"Gentlemen!" said Selim. "From a lawless detachment of bandits you are now once again soldiers of the Republic. The courage that you showed in various battles induced the lawful government to be lenient. I have the authority to punish, but I would prefer to forgive. To those of you who have not cared for my conduct since I first came to camp, I declare that I acted according to instructions and that, in the end, I don't need to explain myself to you. I will add that I will immediately have anyone shot who shows the least insubordination."

Not one protesting voice interrupted this bold speech. After a while the oldest of the officers, a man completely grey-haired, by birth an Italian, with the name of Michaelis, assumed a position as straight as an arrow, pressed his fingers to his temple and said:

"We await your orders."

"Inform the men about the change in command."

The officers went out, and soon we heard loud voices which convinced us how the change had been accepted: *"Vive la République!" "Vive Mademoiselle!"* and *"A bas La Rochenoire!"*

If La Rochenoire could have heard these shouts, he

would have repeated with kings Solomon and Gelimer: "All is vain!"

An hour later we were on our way to La Mare.

VI

We arrived there late at night. We did not find either La Grange or Lidia at home. The windows of the house were broken; silence filled the chalet and the garden. I saw what a bad impression the unexpected absence of Lidia made on Selim. He must have promised himself to take a break from fighting and to indulge in those sweet feelings of love which for a long time had not existed in his soul; meanwhile disappointment met him. Perhaps he expected some letter or sign, because he inquired solicitously about everything from the serving woman, who had nothing other to say than that the pair had left and would be back in three days. For me their departure was completely natural, but Mirza felt pained because of it more than I expected and could not hide his dismay. For him it was one of those occurrences which in and of itself do not mean anything, but which for the time being seem to be the intentional antagonism of fate. Yet his very presence in Lidia's home seemed to have a positive effect on him. His face lost its shadow of severity and was replaced by another, far softer expression. Our relationship became warmer at once. This dangerous commander of riflemen reminded me once again of the beloved student Selim.

He linked his arm through mine and took me about the entire house. For someone in love an empty house, in which the beloved person lives, has a type of mysterious charm. Sweet memories intermingle with sorrow and the echoes resounding from the deserted walls. Each one of these echoes seems to say: "She is not here!" We went to Lidia's room. In the porcelain vases, on both sides of the dresser, stood withered flowers, while on the dresser lay a comb in the shape of a crown which women wear in their hair. Mirza turned and made a pretence of looking out the window, but I saw him press the comb to his lips. He truly must have loved Lidia. Nothing else in the room betrayed her recent presence. The curtains above the bed had been taken down, while on the bed there was no bedding. One could tell that some unthinking hand had made an order here which had erased the memory of the woman who had lived in this room. The furniture, in white slip-covers, had been placed one on top of the other; the mirrors and photographs hanging on the walls had been covered with muslin. Mirza uncovered the photographs. One of them depicted Lidia as a child in a short dress. It was an old and yellowed daguerreotype. The face was still visible, but the white stockings of the child were only two white stains now, while the dark dress merged into the background. I wanted to laugh at that portrait because Lidia had not been a pretty child, and besides this, her expression on the daguerreotype was a frightened one, with lips open and eyes wide. Selim turned away from me, as if not wanting me to look at that photograph with an indifferent, and maybe even malicious, eye. I thought that it must seem to him to be something bewitching, but I thought the way I would have thought had I been in his place. Mirza was too sober and too little sentimental, however, and when he put down the portrait with reluctance, he said:

"What a caricature!"

At that point I did laugh, and he joined me. Then I left him alone with his memories and went to the officers, who were sitting in the dinning room, drinking wine and smoking pipes.

Before going to sleep, I took a patrol and went to change the guard. The night was cold and particularly dark. By the forest beyond the hop-fields, a wolf was howling as if possessed, and the ominous modulations of his voice seemed strangely mournful. In between these howls, and from the direction of the village, the voice of some peasant was heard calling out to his wife or daughter:

"Rosina! Rosina!"

I returned by way of the garden. The windows of Lidia's room were lit up. Apparently Selim was still inside.

I thought that I would catch him dreaming, but I found him leaning over a map.

"The Germans are a day's march away," he said to me. "Their forces are considerable, but the day after tomorrow I will attack them."

"Who knows whether tomorrow you will not have to deal with La Rochenoire," I replied.

He waved his hand.

"That's nothing. It is time to be done with him, though he's not worth the trouble."

"You overestimate yourself."

"The future will tell."

And saying the word "future," he looked at the map and hit it with his fist.

The entire morning of the following day was spent in issuing orders. Selim was making preparations for battle. Before then, however, "kismet" demanded that he fight the battle that I had predicted for him.

It was three o'clock, and we were having dinner, when the door opened suddenly and La Rochenoire came in.

He had made a three-day journey in thirty-six hours. He was covered in dust and looked tired. His face was calm, however, and his eyes were motionless. One could not see any trace of emotion in him. He looked more like a priest than ever before.

When he entered, his former officers sprang to attention, despite themselves.

Mirza gave him a vague look, his eyes glittered, but he remained calm. One could see that he was prepared because he nodded to the adjutant, who immediately left the room.

La Rochenoire advanced several steps. His sinister eyes rested on Mirza.

"I sent you an order yesterday," he said in a low voice.

"And I did not recognize it."

Half of La Rochenoire's face started to twitch, as it usually did during times of battle.

"I place you under arrest," he said calmly to Mirza.

Mirza shrugged his shoulders and turned away, saying: "Michaelis! take this madman away."

In one moment the adjutant showed up in the doorway at the head of four soldiers. The soldiers advanced automatically to La Rochenoire and flanked his sides.

"In the name of the Republic you are under arrest," said the adjutant.

In a twinkling of an eye, this short person contracted and his face darkened. In one moment he realized everything: the vengeance of Mirza, the path Mirza had chosen. He realized that he had fallen into a terrible trap, from which he could escape only through death.

But this was not a person who wasted words. This victor of so many battles, this terrible partisan, did not try anything at that point. His face did not show either false pride or contempt; he did not glare at Mirza; he remained impassive, as if in the feeling that anything he could have undertaken at that moment would only have been a vain struggle and beneath his dignity.

Mirza's face, on the contrary, showed an air of authority. He did not even condescend to look at La Rochenoire. For him this person was already not a rival, nor an opponent on equal footing, but a common man before the majesty of the court—a *"pauvre diable,"* with whom it was not worth to be concerned about anymore, other than according to the paragraphs of the military code.

There was something in all of this, in the sudden change of roles and conditions, in this total humiliation of such a proud person like La Rochenoire, something so tragic, that the further events of this affair pale beside this moment.

"Escort him out," said Mirza.

The measured steps of the soldiers resounded ominously. La Rochenoire was led to the building where we spent our first days at La Mare.

After he left, a hollow silence reigned in the room. A strange feeling squeezed everyone by the throat.

Men of war are generally not good Christians, they do not forgive the opponents they capture, but nevertheless I felt an intense dislike for Mirza at that moment.

La Rochenoire had come to him unarmed, while he appeared armed with calm implacableness but in greater strength, sure of his victory and his personal safety, wombed in the dignity of authority and the majesty of a judge, supported by the terrible military clauses, in full force.

In a word, on one side was everything, while on the other nothing.

I knew, besides this, that Mirza would not forgive him. The military tribunal gathered. The judges were: Michaelis, Marx and myself. Out of duty, Mirza had to preside. Touvenir fulfilled the position of secretary.

La Rochenoire was brought in. It seemed to me that in that one hour he had grown older by at least a year, but he was quiet or, rather, wonderfully indifferent.

After the charges were read, of which any single one justified a death sentence, Mirza asked him if he had anything to say in his defense, and he merely shrugged his shoulders.

Before the sentence would be passed, he was led outside again; after which we took part in the sentencing.
Mirza removed himself from the voting.

I reminded the judges that the accused had been the
victor of over forty skirmishes. It appeared to me that my
words had some effect.

Finally we voted.

La Rochenoire was sentenced to death.

It fell upon me to notify him of the sentence. I did this
with the greatest sorrow.

To my surprise he greeted me not only calmly but even
courteously. When I had fulfilled my sad mission and
was taking my leave, he said:

"I knew that you would vote against a death sentence.
If your voice would have prevailed, you would have done
me the greatest wrong."

I left and checked over the guards. Two soldiers stood
at the door, and a guard stood by the window overlooking the hop-field.

It was impossible for La Rochenoire to escape.

I returned to headquarters, but I was not destined to
sleep that night. Since the sentence was to be carried out
in front of all of La Rochenoire's soldiers, I was given
orders to bring over that part of the detachment which
had remained where La Rochenoire had left it.

This would necessitate two full days. I did not want
to go, but more than that I did not want to ask Mirza to
have someone take my place.

So I took a dozen or so soldiers from Corbeau's cavalry
and started off.

Immediately beyond La Mare the soldiers spotted
someone near the church who wanted to hide himself in
the ruins of the cemetery wall. They seized him and
brought him over to me.

I recognized our old guide, Hugon.

"What are you doing here?" I asked him rather threateningly.

Hugon was drunk or pretended to be drunk.

"I know every bush here," he muttered. "Begging your pardon, most noble sir, I am on my way to the chalet. There are many soldiers there. I was creeping through the hop-field, for I thought that Germans were coming, but meanwhile a soldier by the kiln wanted to take his bayonet—he was a fellow countryman, a fellow countryman, not a German—"

Here Huron began to weep.

"Go to sleep, you're drunk."

"That's because I'm poor, most noble sir, poor. Today a person is under a wagon, tomorrow on a wagon—or the other way around. Yesterday the soldiers feared him, and tomorrow they will shoot him."

I had a sudden suspicion.

"You saw La Rochenoire?" I asked.

"There are many soldiers there, sir. They do not allow anyone through. So I thought: I will sleep a little in the cemetery. Today one lives, tomorrow one will be buried there."

For a moment it came to me that La Rochenoire might have found some means of making contact with Hugon and had sent him to get his men. But then I laughed at that idea. Selim, after all, had twice the force, and besides, Hugon could not reach La Rochenoire's men ahead of me. So I left him there and proceeded on with my troop.

I do not know by what miracle the news of La Rochenoire's fate reached his men ahead of me. The officers and soldiers greeted me in sullen silence.

But no one showed the least disobedience. This was now a flock of lambs with which I could do anything I pleased.

I gave the order for a march, and we moved out

immediately. Around noon I gave the soldiers two hours of rest, then I pressed them again to hasten. As we passed through villages, the peasants hid themselves before us in their cottages. I wanted horses and carts to get to La Mare as quickly as possible, so I seized all the carts with horses I could. Everywhere, though, the village mayor who had been summoned before me replied:

"We don't have any."

But the touch of a revolver's cold barrel against his nose had a strange effect on stirring his patriotism: the horses and carts were found, as if they had come out from under the ground.

We neared La Mare in deep night and in complete order. I rode in front with my cavalry soldiers about half a French mile ahead of the detachment. I wanted to get to La Mare first, and besides, I had to give the watchword to the sentinels of Mirza's detachment.

Not the slightest sound reached me from the village, which was completely dark. Mirza was always very careful, even from his days with La Rochenoire, and he did not light fires in the middle of the night.

We were not far from the church. My sergeant rode up to me.

"Lieutenant," he said, "the sentinels have fallen asleep."

"Impossible," I replied. "That's an instant death sentence."

The moon shone brightly. As far as I could see, there were no pickets.

"What's going on here?" I thought, troubled.

Nevertheless, I expected to hear at any moment from the cemetery gate:

"Qui vive?"

All around there was silence.

The sergeant rode up to me again.

"Sir, something has happened here," he whispered. "The church windows are broken."

I looked by the light of the moon. Its pale rays were broken apart on the church windows, but in a few places one could see black holes. Indeed, the windows were broken.

"There must have been a battle," said the sergeant.

The cemetery gate was open, and we entered within.

Suddenly the hoof of my horse hit some hard object, which gave out a hollow echo.

I assumed it was the skull of some man, hidden in the weeds; nevertheless, I had a soldier pick the object up.

The soldier got off his horse, bent down and handed me a spiked Prussian helmet.

Now it was certain that Mirza had been engaged in a battle during my absence and had marched off afterward.

We went further into the cemetery, examining every depression in the ground.

About a hundred feet from the place where we found the spiked helmet, we came across the first corpse of a Prussian infantryman. One could tell from the state of the body that he had been lying there about a dozen hours and that the battle must have taken place yesterday.

More and more signs stuck out of the grass and weeds. In places the ground was covered like snow with fragments of paper from charges; farther on lay Prussian corpses, and beyond them French ones, and even farther both together, lying face up and face down, and frequently propped upon heads or chests. Here the battle had apparently been fought with cold steel. The rays of the moon travelled from one cluster of bodies to another. These quiet groups seemed to be asleep.

"To the chalet!" I cried out forcefully.

We bolted away like lightning and galloped onto the

road. From a distance one could see an advancing dark mass of people. It was my detachment coming up to the cemetery wall. I stopped their advance with a sign of my hand, while I galloped on with my people, all the while passing by an increasing number of dead bodies. A minute later the chalet appeared before us. The windows of one room were lit up and wide open; the door to the hallway was also open.

I rushed inside.

In the first room it was empty and dark. From the adjoining hall came a light through the cracks in the door.

I opened the door and froze.

In the middle of the room stood a low sofa without arms, and on it lay a body covered with a sheet, through which a motionless profile was outlined.

At the head of the deceased stood two holy candles. By his feet knelt a woman dressed in black, her forehead leaning against the edge of the sofa and her hands locked above her head.

When I entered, she rose. I recognized Lidia. Her face was pale, severe, sleepless, tired, impassive and aged, but not tear-stained.

"Mademoiselle Lidia!" I called out in a suppressed voice.

She went over to me on her toes, as if afraid of disturbing the deceased, and she spoke as quietly as one does before those who have departed this world.

"He is dead!"

Saying this, she leaned against my shoulder. Dry sobs shook her breast.

Only then did it come to me that the deceased might be old La Grange.

I advanced quickly toward the body and raised the cover. A chilly breath of air drifted from under the sheet.

The yellow light of the candles fell on a grey face with swollen lips, a horrible, twisted face.

It was Selim Mirza.

VII

The next morning I made several inquiries, from which I learned the following: La Rochenoire had indeed made contact with Hugon and had ordered him to notify the Prussians of Mirza's halt at La Mare. Hugon led them through the hop-field so skillfully that the sentinels gave the warning shots only when the entire detachment had been surrounded. A battle began. Mirza was killed right at the beginning, while La Rochenoire, who acted only with vengeance in mind and did not count on his own rescue, managed in the midst of the general confusion to get to the hop-field with the help of Hugon and from there make his way to the forest.

A year later, already after the war, I learned of his stay in Venice. He had inherited a considerable fortune in Breton, had married and now lived in peace and quiet.

I never found out whether his wife was Lidia La Grange.

Other Henryk Sienkiewicz Titles
from Hippocrene:

QUO VADIS?
Henryk Sienkiewicz
Stanley F. Conrad's celebrated translation of "one of the great books of our day" (*Larousse Encyclopedia*) is a dramatic saga of love, devotion and courage among ancient Romans—a satisfying page-turner. Set around the dawn of Christianity with amazing historical accuracy, *Quo Vadis?* won Sienkiewicz the Nobel Prize.
"Conrad has provided an enjoyable and readable translation."
—*Polish American Journal*
496 pages, 6 x 9
ISBN 0-7818-0100-1 $22.50hc   (5)

IN DESERT AND WILDERNESS
Henryk Sienkiewicz
Sienkiewicz's late 19th century novel, beloved by Poles, is given new life in this modern translation. This coming of age story set in Africa tells the tale of Stas and Nell, as they encounter wild beasts and warring tribes.
352 pages, 6 x 9
ISBN 0-87052-152-7 $19.95hc   (9)

THE TEUTONIC KNIGHTS
Henryk Sienkiewicz, translated by Alicia Tyszkiewicz
Newly edited and revised by Miroslaw Lipinski
This epic is recognized as Sienkiewicz's most mature work and the author, himself, considered it his greatest achievement.

"Murder, suicide, swashbuckling action, colorful characters and a touching love story animate a monumental saga."
—*Publisher's Weekly*

"...one of the most splendid achievements of Polish literature."
—*ZGODA*

786 pages, 6 x 9
ISBN 0-7818-0121-4 $24.95   (558)

POLISH LITERARY CLASSICS
FROM HIPPOCRENE

THE DOLL by *Boleslaw Prus*, (NEW ✳ reissue), 700 pages. Twenty years after its first reprint publication by Hippocrene, this edition, with a stunning new cover by Czachorski, brings back into print one of the most striking portraits of a woman in fiction.
0097   ISBN 0-7818-0158-3 $16.95 pb

PHARAOH by *Boleslaw Prus. Translated by Christopher Kasparek*, 691 pages. First published in 1896, and now recently translated, *Pharaoh* is considered one of the great novels of Polish literature, and a timeless and universal story of the struggle for power.
0008   ISBN 0-87052-152-7 $25.00 cloth

THE DARK DOMAIN by *Stefan Grabinski. A newly translated short story collection by Miroslaw Lipinski*, 192 pages. The explorations of the extreme in human behavior, where the macabre and the bizarre combine to send a chill down the reader's spine, are by a master of Polish fantastic fiction.
710   ISBN 0-7818-0211-3 $10.95 pb

TALES FROM THE SARAGOSSA MANUSCRIPT, OR TEN DAYS IN THE LIFE OF ALPHONSE VAN WORDEN by *Jan Potocki*, 192 pages. The celebrated classic of fantastic literature in the tradition of *Arabian Nights*. "A Gothic novel, quite an extraordinary piece of writing." —Czeslaw Milosz.
0717   ISBN 0-87052-936-6 $8.95 pb

THE GLASS MOUNTAIN:Twenty-Six Ancient Polish Folktales and Fables, *told by W.S. Kuniczak*. Illustrated by Pat Bargielski, 160 pages and 8 illustrations. "It is an heirloom book to pass on to children and grandchildren....A timeless book, with delightful illustrations, it will make a handsome addition to any library and will be a most treasured gift." —*Polish American Cultural Network*
0183   ISBN 0-7818-0087-0 $14.95 cloth

OLD POLISH LEGENDS, *retold by F.C. Anstruther Wood and illustrated with engravings by J. Sekalski*, 66 pages and 11 woodcut engravings. Now in its second printing, this fine collection of eleven fairy tales, with an introduction by Zygmunt Nowakowski, was first published in Scotland in World War II, when the long night of the German occupation was at its darkest.
0098   ISBN 0-7818-0180-X $10.00 cloth

PAN TADEUSZ by *Adam Mickiewicz*. Translated by Kenneth R. MacKenzie, 553 pages with Polish and English text side by side. Poland's greatest epic poem in what is its finest English translation.
0237   ISBN 0-7818-033-1 $19.95 pb

.

POLISH DICTIONARIES AND LANGUAGE BOOKS
Modern • Up-to-Date • Easy-to Use • Practical

POLISH-ENGLISH/ENGLISH-POLISH PRACTICAL DICTIONARY (Completely Revised) *by Iwo Cyprian Pogonowski*. Contains over 31,000 entries for students and travelers. Includes a phonetic guide to pronunciation in both languages, a handy glossary of the country's menu terms, a bilingual instruction on how-to-use the dictionary, and a bilingual list of abbreviations.
0450   ISBN 0-7818-0085-4 $11.95 pb

POLISH-ENGLISH/ENGLISH-POLISH CONCISE DICTIONARY (Completely Revised) *by Iwo Cyprian Pogonowski*. Contains over 91,000 completely modern, up-to-date entries in a clear, concise format.
0268   ISBN 0-7818-0133-8 $8.95 pb

POLISH-ENGLISH/ENGLISH-POLISH STANDARD DICTIONARY
0207   ISBN 0-87052-882-3 $18.95 pb

POLISH PHRASEBOOK AND DICTIONARY (New Edition) *by Iwo Cyprian Pogonowski*, 252 pages. Revised and re-typeset, this handy guide for the English speaking traveler in Poland is now more useful than ever.
0192   ISBN 0-7818-0134-0 $9.95 pb

ENGLISH CONVERSATIONS FOR POLES (New Edition) *by Iwo Cyprian Pogonowski*, 250 pages. This handbook of our bestselling dictionary author includes 3,300 practical, up-to-date entries, indexed by main entry, with useful expressions for every need. It also features a phonetic guide to pronunciation and a dictionary with over 6,500 entries.
0762   ISBN 0-87052-873-4 $9.95 pb

AMERICAN ENGLISH FOR POLES: In Four Parts, *Institute of Applied Linguistics in Warsaw and the Center for Applied Linguistics in Virginia*, 828 pages in set. The set includes a Teacher's Guide, Exercises, Dictionary, Student's Textbook: 20 integrated units with 3,500 word vocabulary.
0441   ISBN 83-214-0152-X $24.95

ENGLISH FOR POLES SELF-TAUGHT *by Irena Dobrzycka*, 496 pages. Contains 455 lessons with dictionary of over 3,600 entries.
2648   ISBN 0-88254-873-4 $19.95 cloth

MASTERING POLISH (New) *by Albert Juszczak*, 288 pages. A teach-yourself set perfect for the serious traveler, student or business executive. Imaginative, practical exercises in grammar are accompanied by cassette tapes for conversation practice. Juszczak teaches Polish at the New York University.
0381   ISBN 0-7818-0015-3 $14.95 (paperback book)
0389   ISBN 0-7818-0016-1 $12.95 (2 cassettes)
0414   ISBN 0-7818-0017-X $27.90 (paperback and cassettes)

AMERICAN PHRASEBOOK FOR POLES/ROZMOWKI AMERYKANSKIE DLA POLAKOW *by Jacek Galazka*, 142 pages. "The book meets in an extraordinary way the needs of today's world. And it is so practical; from the laundromat to a hospital visit, it anticipates the situations likely to confront the arriving Pole who does not speak the language."—*Nowy Dziennik*
0595   ISBN 0-87052-907-2 $7.95 pb

THE POLISH WAY

A Thousand-Year History of the Poles and Their Culture

Adam Zamoyski

When first published in England in 1987, *The Polish Way* was met with great acclaim:
"The most rewarding book of the year."

—*Spectator*

"Clear, calm, beautifully written, its scope is enormous, its story enthralling and its illustrations magnificent...a stunner."

—*The Times*

"Has immediately taken its place as the outstanding study in its field."

—*Times Educational Supplement*

Now available in paperback for the first time, this masterly and lavishly illustrated history of Poland from the tenth century to the present day tells of Poland's achievement as a European nation. Poland's history of progressive laws protecting personal liberty has generally gone unrecognized by historians, as has Poland's uncanny ability to maintain religious peace even during the tumultuous Reformation and Counter-Reformation. Poland's victories over the Teutonic Knights, Tatars and Turks, and effortless conquest of Moscow, won it a reputation for over a century as the most formidable military force in Europe.

INCLUDES 170 ILLUSTRATIONS, MOST OF THEM PUBLISHED HERE FOR THE FIRST TIME OUTSIDE OF POLAND.

422 pages • 170 illustrations • 0-7818-0385-3 • $24.95

POLISH CUSTOMS, TRADITIONS, AND FOLKLORE

Sophie Hodorowicz Knab

with an Introduction by Rev. Czesław Krysa

This unique reference book is arranged by month, covering the various occasions, feasts and holidays. Beginning with December, which includes Advent, St. Nicholas Day, the *Wigilia* (Christmas Eve), nativity plays, caroling as well as the New Year celebrations, and those of the shrovetide period to Ash Wednesday, Lent, the celebrations of spring, Holy Week customs, superstitions, beliefs and rituals associated with farming, Pentecost, Corpus Christi, midsummer celebrations, birth and death.

Delicate line drawings complete this rich and varied treasury of folklore.

PRAISE FOR *POLISH CUSTOMS, TRADITIONS, AND FOLKLORE:*

"There is nothing on the subject that even approaches this book in its breadth and authority. A prodigious amount of research has gone into the work, as well as sheer education and enthusiasm that keeps an author going, and searching and reading."—*Zgoda*

"This collection is a tremendous asset to understanding the ethnic behavior of a people. Highly recommended."—Florence Waszkelewicz-Clowes, *Polish American Journal*

"Eagerly awaited...comprehensive and definitive....Most [readers] will be delighted to discover the many regional variations which enrich this informative guide."—*Polish Heritage*

$19.95 • 310 pages • 12 b/w illustrations • ISBN 0-7818-0068-4

Self-Taught Audio Language Courses

Hippocrene Books is pleased to recommend Audio-Forum self-taught language courses. They match up very closely with the languages offered in Hippocrene dictionaries and offer a flexible, economical and thorough program of language learning.

Audio-Forum audio-cassette/book courses, recorded by native speakers, offer the convenience of a private tutor, enabling the learner to progress at his or her own pace. They are also ideal for brushing up on language skills that may not have been used in years. In as little as 25 minutes a day — even while driving, exercising, or doing something else — it's possible to develop a spoken fluency.

All Audio-Forum courses are fully guaranteed and may be returned within 30 days for a full refund if you're not completely satisfied.

You may order directly from Audio-Forum by calling toll-free 1-800-243-1234.

For a complete course description and catalog of 264 courses in 91 languages, contact Audio-Forum, Dept. SE5, 96 Broad St., Guilford, CT 06437. Toll-free phone 1-800-243-1234. Fax 203-453-9774.